J

Always

An American West Romanic Saga

Dedication;

For my father, who loved a western. I miss you every day

....

Always

Copyright October 2016

Forward

1879. Any place in the world, a difficult time in history. In the American west. Tough. Harsh. Dangerous. Unpredictable.

1879. American west. For a European woman. Deadly. Vulnerable. Risky.

1879. American west. For the native American. The beginning of the end of an era.

Always

Contents

CHAPTER ONE

CHAPTER TWO

CHAPTER THREE

CHAPTER FOUR

CHAPTER FIVE

CHAPTER SIX

CHAPTER SEVEN

CHAPTER EIGHT

CHAPTER NINE

CHAPTER TEN

CHAPTER ELEVEN

CHAPTER ONE

Spring

1879

The view from the dust covered window continued to

race by in rhythm with the horses. It was strange how much

the stage coach had become home to Elizabeth over the past 5 days, with the train only going as far West as Phoenix. The coach stopped twice a day for food, to change the horses and to pick up and drop off travellers and mail. Sometimes the stage had stopped overnight. The further West it went, the stranger the stop station people were when they found her travelling alone. Elizabeth recalled smiling, and not always in the best of company. But she wasn't stupid. She had her MAS Modele six shot revolver in her pocket. Her father would not be happy she had made this journey alone and a sigh slipped from her lips as she had the same thought again. The rocking motion of the coach as it headed home and the incessant dust, working its way, she thought, running her finger around the collar of her dress, into every corner of her being. Made Elizabeth, not for the first time, reconsider the rashness of her actions.

Should she really have come? Would her uncle welcome her? Should she have stayed East? It had been years and he had not written to bring her back. Always telling her how lucky she was being in the East. How things at home were the same and nothing would compare to her experience of a city life. The more he wrote about it, the more Elizabeth became concerned. The more she needed to go home. The last letter had done it for her. No mention of when she would be going back. Elizabeth frowned and again was unsure.

"That's a considerable frown for such a lovely lady."

Elizabeth turned to the older gentleman who had recently joined them, he looked kindly and someone's grandfather she expected. *"I'm sorry I do not remember your name."*

"Mr Wilson, Oklahoma mam, I was telling you earlier, I'm in trade?"

"Arr yes, Mr Wilson, you'll forgive me, it's been a long and tiring journey and it's hard to concentrate on anything."

"Quite right Ms, quite right – and a journey for not one so young and on her own, if you will forgive me for saying." Mr Wilson smiled. "But not long now I understand, we should be in Cheyanne Junction tomorrow."

"Yes indeed Mr Wilson. But I am only going as far as Brownsville. I am nearly home." Replied Elizabeth with another frown. "Does that not please you Ms?" Elizabeth gave a strained smile. "Yes and no Mr Wilson, I'm hoping my Uncle will be as happy to see me, as I will, too see him." Elizabeth placed her hands in her lap and looked up. "It's been more than 6 six years since he sent me East to live with my great Aunt, he's not *exactly expecting me."* Elizabeth told him with a knowing

understated smile

"*Oh I see Ms, well I'm sure, he will be delighted."*

Elizabeth gave another resigned smile and thought. *"I hope*

so." New York with all its attractions was not for her. The

young men calling, the balls, it was all so false. If it hadn't

been for her interest in the family business, she thought she

would have gone mad. Elizabeth preceded to close her eyes

once again, lulled by the rocking of the carriage. She hoped

her Aunt would forgive her. Sleep she thought, maybe that

will help…..

Mr Wilson smiled at the sleeping beauty, she was quite

something, young he thought with her fresh clear complexion,

a real beauty. He couldn't think when he had last seen such

colouring, not blond not red but a captivating mixture of both

and those eyes. The richest, deepest, sapphire blue that

captivated you and no mistaking. But the clincher, he recognised – was the fact that she had no idea of the effect, she was having on the other men in the coach. He joined her in closing his eyes, his last thoughts as he drifted off. That Elizabeth, would break many a heart and hoped that this county, would not break her.

Elizabeth kept her eyes closed. She'd tried but wasn't sleeping. She hoped it at least stopped any further conversation. She had said more in one sentence than she had in many days. She really wasn't up to talking about her life. They would never understand anyway she concluded. How could see explain the complexities of her life to anyone, not even her Aunt could understand it.

Over 6 years ago she thought, Ben, her uncle had told her she was going East to school to stay with her mother's sister, Clara. That she needed to be a young woman who could stand up in a man's world and the world respect her.

That she couldn't do that, running around like a native. How

she had hated that conversation. She'd shouted and argued

till she was blue in the face. She'd stopped eating – well for a

day at least, she smiled and he had not relented. It broke her

heart the day she left and the goodbyes she'd had to make.

Her friends and her great family. Leaving was the most

difficult thing she had ever had to do.

Her thoughts turned to Ben, good and kind Ben. The

older brother to her father. A man who had rejected

'respectable' life in his youth. Who had been a gun slinger

and on the wrong side of the law for most of his younger

days. A 'reckless' young man her uncle had said, luckily for

Ben, nothing serious came of it, unlike so many others, her

uncle had turned risky law breaker to law keeper before it was

too late and after the Indian attack, ……. her heart skipped a beat as it always did, when, unwillingly, it all came back to her….

Even now, after all these years, she couldn't remember it clearly. She wasn't too sure, if she ever really wanted to remember it at all. Too young. Too scared. Too nightmarish. Or all just too fast for a frightened child, she guessed. She recalled the buggy ride and her excitement on their long journey into town. How handsome her father looked all dressed up in his Eastern finery and how pretty her mama was. Dressed in green silk. Elizabeth had loved that dress. She recalled the games she'd played with several of her father's men, along the ride.

Then, out of nowhere, they came. Elizabeth remembered at first, thinking it was part of one of the games they were playing. She was gay, laughing and pointing out the men to her mama. The men were playing dress up, painted and riding fast.   Only they were not playing at all.

Her mother screamed and called her father's name. It seemed

like a hundred screaming devils at once and quickly it turned

deadly. The shooting. The smoke. The burning of

gunpowder. Her mother's fear as she clung to Elizabeth and

her own. But mostly, she wished she could block out the

screaming. She remembered it so vividly. Indian and

American alike and the moments her mother and father were

killed and the kindly ranch hand who at that point, had

picked her up and rode like hell for the nearest farmstead. He

had saved her life that day and she was thankful.

Elizabeth had partial memories of the farmer and his

wife and later, the journey home. Mainly they tell her, she

had a fever and that's why, she couldn't remember much at

all. Elizabeth didn't remember her arrival back at the Double

T Bar. Or the many days spent in bed crying, refusing to eat

or attend her parent's funeral. What she did remember, was

the first day of the rest of her life. Waking one morning, expecting the despair she had experienced every day since to hit her again. But when she opened her eyes she found Ben standing over her. A little greyer than she remembered. He'd bent down, held her close, wiped her tears and rocked her back to sleep. The next morning, she got up. She was 7 years old and orphaned.

The days following where challenging for Elizabeth. She tried to get into her old routine, but found it hard, her mama being so much of that, that everything she did reminded her of her pain. Elizabeth decided before the week was out, that she needed a new routine. Something that would not remind her of her pain. She'd gone looking for Ben.

Elizabeth looked out across the yard. The Double T, was a ranch larger than anyone else's in the area. Her father had been most proud of that. Coming from England with "*Pennies*" he'd said, and turning it into thousands and not by false means. Having worked hard and been lucky in the gold mines. He'd headed West to continue his fortune. "*Land.*" He'd always said to her while sitting on his knee. "*A man must have land.*" And land he'd got. Hundreds and thousands of acres. It had been hard earned. But her father never forgot how his own family had been treated by land owners. Thrown off and a country starving. That became the influence on how he treated his. Fairly.

Her father had been proud of his achievement. Some of the best land in the West he'd told her. Elizabeth recalled the bargain her father made to the local Indians and how important that was to him. Her father had spoken many times of the way his family had been ejected from their land in England by those with greater power. How he wanted to respect the land and the people on it. Wanted to thank them for sharing it and bring prosperity to all. They had not believed him at first. There had been skirmishes along the way with hands and Indians setting each other off. Quickly her father had wheedled those out and the Indians came to accept his words as truth.

He was a man of conscience and principal, aware of the politics and the injustice of the native people. He had seen first-hand what those with power did. He saw how Indians were treated, the forced walks. The killing of a race and he had refused to be brought into it. He bought the land the Indians were on. They were protected within his boundary. No white man could make them do anything. He had used good will to share and return what he had and they respected him for it. Elizabeth remembered recalling how ironic, that it should be Indians to have killed him. But not the same Indians, no, never the same....

Even now, she didn't know how they knew it was the right time to come to the ranch. That she was up to seeing visitors. But she guessed one of the hands had told them and they did. It was as she was talking to Ben that they or rather she, had visitors. Indian visitors. They rode across the grass land as they always did, coming from the North. At their head, was their chief, Dull Knife. He normally came alone with his warriors but this day, he came with his two sons, Red Wolf and Running Elk as well. It was unusual to see all three together in that way. Elizabeth remembered. Running Elk was a few years younger than Elizabeth, Red Wolf several years older and not normally with the warriors. But there they were and each of them, in ceremonial mourning dress she'd found out later. Elizabeth had been so touched to see them coming to her. Dull Knife was very protective of his family.

Instinctively, Elizabeth had taken Bens hand and silently walked towards the main house and porch where she had seen her father many times, address the Indians. It had felt like a dream. She let go of Bens hand and instinctively reached out to touch the bull whip her father hung on the porch post. It was mainly ornamental. A gift from his father-in-law on his marriage. But he kept it well-oiled, had often carried it and it brought him closer to her at that moment. Elizabeth noticed the manner of the ranch hands, that they were worried, edgy, scared even. They looked ill at ease. At any other time, it would have been funny seeing the hands act this way towards their friends.

Elizabeth recalled speaking to them to ease the tensions. *"We have guests, my father's friends, we will not dishonour him or them this day."* They turned to look at her. Understood her meaning and all visibly relaxed. Elizabeth smiled as she had suddenly recalled thinking that it may not have been her call to make and looked up at Ben. He smiled down at her and nodded, she'd done the right thing.

Dull Knife, came to a stop in front of her, with his sons behind him surrounded by his men. They were a magnificent sight; it took her breath away. Elizabeth looked beyond Dull Knife to his oldest son. Red Wolf, he was older than Elizabeth by several years. She had not seen him for a long time and she remembered how strangely he looked at her then. Dull Knife had learnt English from the missionaries when he was a child and spoke it well, as did his sons. They still believed in the old ways and traditions. Some western ideas had crept in over the years but they honoured the old traditions, Elizabeth knew, they had come for her.

Dull Knife had not missed a thing. He looked about him giving each man a full gaze. His eyes settled on Ben for a short time. Feeling no anger or challenge. He turned to

Elizabeth and called out *"Esa* (her father's pet name for her and the name they had used since her father's introduction) *"I and my family come today to pay homage to a great man and his family."* Some of the hands did not look convinced. Elizabeth hadn't cared. She knew these people well.

"Your father and I shared many enemies and won many battles together. It is with heavy heart that our enemies have struck down both the strength and grace of your family, and we have lost two great friends. Dull Knife, acknowledges the great debt owed to your father and the promise shared by blood brothers and our families Esa." He continued, *"as your father was father to my sons in showing them the American way, I hope you will honour me, to be father to you in our traditional ways. From this day, our tribes are united in death as they were in life, you are under my protection and we shall never forget."* An Indian cry had gone out of his men at his declaration.

Elizabeth remembered the speech so clearly. She was so moved by the emotion it stirred, not just the sorrow but also the pride. It seemed strange to see such a strong warrior as Dull Knife looking so pale and emotional. Once he had finished speaking. Elizabeth knew she would have to answer him. It was not difficult to do. She liked the grand warrior and the tribe and had spent much time with them when they visited the ranch. It would keep the peace and the good will her father had worked so hard for. Elizabeth had moved to the edge of the porch and spoke

"Dull Knife, you honour me and my parents by coming today. I am lost without them. My father loved this life, this land and both our families. He valued friendship and honesty above all and welcomed, that he shared this with you. He spoke many times of his wish, that in friendship and in blood, we were bonded to this land." Elizabeth stood quietly for a moment. Raising her head, she had look up at him. Calmly, with no fear, she

answered him. *"Thank you, I accept your protection and willingly call you father."*

The braves behind Dull Knife and his sons, rejoiced and cried out again. Dull Knife had looked at her and registered her grief and not for the first time, was overcome by the strength in her. She was her father's child. But not a child today.

"Come visit me soon daughter." he called softly as he pushed his pony forward towards her, she nodded, no words needed. Dull Knife then bowed to her in respect of her new status and grief, as his horse turned and walked away, his place was taken by his oldest son.

Red Wolf, he did not take his eyes off Elizabeth. She gazed at him. He took in that she was still a child but knew the woman she would be and it warmed him. He paused for a long time before speaking. Elizabeth stood her ground and held his gaze. "*Come soon sister, or I shall come for you.*" He told her, bowed and pushed his pony on after his father. Running Elk took his brothers place and spoke most solemnly. "*Sister, it should not be long before we play together.*" he told her, smiled then bowed, and walked his pony on.

Each of the men in Dull Knifes group of braves, took the place before Elizabeth and each who she had seen many times before, bowed and followed their Chief. They had left as quietly as they had arrived and in much dignity.

Elizabeth remembered the feeling of calmness following their visit. She realised now, she had been comforted by it and was glad. There would have been many unsaid questions in her mind, following the nature of her parent's death. Now, she is sure, their visit was as much for her comfort as theirs. For although her parents had died at the hands of Indians, she loved those of her land.

They had opened a whole new world for her and both Running Elk and Red Wolf had come to the ranch and spent time with her and her uncle both sharing an understanding of the land, making the Double T, stronger, richer and more powerful.

Twice a year, the Double T made gifts to the tribe. Horses and cattle and the offer of work to those who wanted it. It was a time of celebration and of giving thanks. Several braves were paid scouts for the herds and men. Others looked after and trained the horses, creating strong blood lines, that became much prized across the West.

After the second visit to the tribe since her parent's death, Dull Knife had told her, it was not appropriate for a

Chief's daughter to not have female company to assist her and had instructed his sisters daughter to stay with her. She was also unmarried and was to accompany Elizabeth back to the ranch. Elizabeth had accepted this without comment.

With a smile, Elizabeth recalled, that White Dove had indeed gone with her and had never left. Ben and White Dove had fell in love and he married her two years later with the permission of Dull Knife. A bond strengthening both families, but this did not come easy. Both Ben and White Dove suffered at the hands of 'civilised' people in town and by some of the hired hands. Ben sacked them of course and shortly after, at Bens request and with the agreement of Elizabeth and Dull Knife, Red Wolf part time, took a hand in the running of the ranch. 3 Years later, he ran the braves, now taking up most of the hand jobs and they answered to him.

Brownsville their local town soon came to understand its dependence on the ranch and its people. Money generated business and many did well on the Double T. Within a very short time. A greater respect for the family came about. The towns folk knew the Double T. Had the family been less than honourable, the family could have owned it Elizabeth remembered. But that's not what they wanted and within another year, Elizabeth, reluctantly with the permission of her father Dull Knife, was sent East by Ben.

It was the hardest thing she had ever done. Saying goodbye. She swallowed hard at the memory. The family had held a party. People came from all over the county and she travelled to the Indian Village to take her leave of Dull Knife and the tribe. It was the only other time, she had seen him emotional. The only one not there strangely, had been Red Wolf. He had been absent from both.

When she did see him, it was from a distance. She was riding her pony to Brownsville to catch the stage with Ben. Red Wolf was astride his pony watching and waiting for her. As they drew up in line with him he turned his pony and rode the ridge of the hills to the south of their property. He didn't ride to her but kept pace with her for a long time, until they neared the border of their land. Then just as suddenly he disappeared from sight. When he reappeared, it was directly in front of her, on the crest of the hills, horse and rider profiled against the clear blue sky.

Elizabeth recalled the image of him. Tall in the saddle facing her. He was nineteen then she recalled. It was the first time and last she saw him, not just as her friend but as a warrior. As she passed him, his horse reared and he called to her. *"No matter where you go, how long you are gone, your life is here. Never forget."* He'd told her and then, he was gone.

Soon she would have to face them all. No one knew she was coming home. In the 4 years Ben and White Dove had been married, they had not been blessed with children. As Elizabeth was leaving to go East, Ben had gone to great lengths to explain that the ranch and land was hers and hers alone, he was happy to look after it for her, but ultimately, the Double T was her responsibility. She had taken it very seriously and she still did. She needed to be home. She needed to be back on the land, it was pulling to her. She was 20 years old, tired of her life in the East and longing for her old one. It was time to go home.

Her final thoughts as she drifted into exhaustedly sleep, were recalling children's games around the village camp fires, the stories of their great battles and of their hero's....

At that precise moment Clara her Aunt, returned home early from her vacation with friends in Boston. Her surprise and dismay were unimaginable. Clara, elegant and a striking likeness to her niece, immediately went to her writing bureau in her fashionable drawing room and wrote to Ben.

'Dear Ben', Clara stopped for a moment and considered what a wonder that man has been to them, if it hadn't been for him, she may never have seen Elizabeth. She was thankful for that. She had never realised how empty her life had been until Elizabeth had arrived. Putting pen to paper she continued. 'I have just arrived home from my vacation with friends, to find Elizabeth has decided to return home without escort. The staff tell me she left 8 days ago. I am most vexed that I was not informed immediately by staff but it seems Elizabeth fooled them into thinking I was aware of her intentions and happy for her to leave. I believe she took the 2pm train and with connections should have reached Phoenix

2 days later, that would mean she would have been on the Brownsville stage with a 6 day journey ahead of her. As you receive this cable, I believe she should be either at Bleachers Point tonight and then on the road to Brownsville. Find her Ben and forgive me. Clara.' Clara called to her maid *"Mary take this to the cable office as fast as you can, and tell them to instruct someone at Brownsville to take it to the Double T immediately it arrives"*. Mary seeing the worry and concern in her mistress's eyes replied. *"Yes mam."* and hurriedly took the note. *"Thank you Mary off you go."* *"I'm real sorry mam, Ms Elizabeth was very insistent, she would not listen to reason."* *"I'm sure she was Mary, now off you go, run child."*

CHAPTER TWO.

Mr Wilson woke Elizabeth six hours later. *"My dear, we have arrived at the overnight station."* Elizabeth sedately stretched. *"Thank you Mr Wilson, most kind."* Elizabeth was helped down by Duggie the driver.

"Over there miss, evening meal and somewhere to wash, Mrs Johnson will help you."

Elizabeth thanked him and went inside. Bleachers Point was the same as each of the other 5 night stops Elizabeth had made with the stage coach. Bleak and with few amenities, it was basic but adequate. Mrs Johnson took Elizabeth to her room and said she would call her when food was served. Elizabeth thanked her and started to pour water to clean away today's dirt.

Elizabeth washed, brushed out her hair and redressed it and changed her clothes. She knew they would only be here for a couple of hours before moving on so she made the most of it. She was glad that tomorrow she would be in Brownsville, it had been far too long.

The cable arrived in haste in the bags of one of the hands, who happened to be in town on his day off. He handed it to a concerned Ben as, Elizabeth was sitting down to dinner at Bleachers Point.

Ben sprang into action, Bleachers Point was nearer the Indian Village than the Double T but they were nearer the Town. He made his mind up quickly. At the same time he called White Dove to him and several of the hands and scouts. As he spoke all listened, his concern obvious to all.

"Elizabeth has made her own way back from New York. She should be either at Bleachers Point my now or heading to Brownsville, Hicotai, you and two braves head back to the village, tell Dull Knife his daughter is alone and on her way home and I ask his assistance to watch for her at Bleachers Point." Knowing the honour placed on him, Hicotai, immediately left and rode like the devil himself.

"Joe, Jake you ride with me, we're going to Brownsville in case she makes it that far." Turning to White Dove he gave her a reassuring smile. *"Should she be found by either, let the other know."* White Dove kissed her husband and nodded. Within 5 mins, they were gone.

Duggie, the stage driver, covered in dust and brushing himself down, walked through the stage offices doorway to join the others for dinner. *"There's going to be a short hold up folks, I need to change a wheel after dinner before we change horses and move on."*

Mr Wilson frowned *"Oh dear, that means we could be here for a few more hours yet."*

Elizabeth smiled, she felt she could do with the rest. Although she was eager to get home, her back ached as well as her head and she felt she had bruises in places she didn't know existed. Mrs Johnson a friendly and comely woman, started to serve dinner. Around the table, Elizabeth noted, not for the first time since her journey started, 8 men and one woman, Elizabeth, were seated at it. Elizabeth smiled to herself. The men were all aware of the ladies' present, all minding their manners. It was heart-warming to Elizabeth. Even in the middle of know where, strangers could behave with dignity. Sadly, it was not always the case she thought.

But then, this 'lady' had not long ago been sitting in the dirt playing stones.

Dinner passed as every other meal had on the trip. Good wholesome food, heavy to fill empty bellies. Water to drink, milk if you were very lucky and the conversation limited as you had spent all day together. Elizabeth welcomed the quiet. Only Mrs Johnson asked after her and that was expected. After dinner, Elizabeth took a stroll around the station, the air was crisp and clean. The smells a welcome remembrance. The sky never failed to impress her. So clear and vast, it spoke of the unknown.

As Elizabeth was starting her stroll, Hicotai, was riding into the village. The urgency of his arrival told all, it was important. Dull Knife and Red Wolf, were discussing the days hunting. Both turned as the rider entered the village at such speed. Quickly, Hicotai, passed on Bens message. Dull

Knife looked to his son, concern in his eyes. Dull Knife

reached out and touched his arm. Red Wolf nodded, ran and

jumped on his horse and was gone. At the same time, Dull

Knife called to his braves, 8 joined Red Wolf and rode after

him, hard.

Bleachers Point was four hours from the village. They

rode like their lives depended on it and got there sooner.

Elizabeth seemed to lose all account of time on her

stroll. She had sat for a time breathing in the cool night air

and listening to the sounds around her. She loved the night.

How long had it been since she had done that? she couldn't

remember. Time was so regimented in the East. You got up

at a certain time, you had breakfast at a certain time, you

visited at a certain time, you luncheoned at a certain time, you

afternoon tea's at a certain time, you had dinner at a certain

time, you went to the theatre at a certain time. Urrgh

Elizabeth thought, she hated the conformality of it. Her stroll had taken her further than she'd expected but the sight and smell of wild flowers and the beauty of it all had overcome her. It was so good to be nearly home. Looking at the setting Sun, Elizabeth turned to walk back to Bleachers Point.

As Elizabeth walked back towards the point, she was met by Mr Wilson. *"Hello my dear, there you are, I was quite worried and they sent me to look for you."* Elizabeth smiled at the elder man. *"That was very kind of you Mr Wilson, shall we go back?"* Mr Wilson extended his arm and Elizabeth took it.

As they walked, a breeze came up and several stains of her hair came loose, Elizabeth had had trouble controlling it though-out her journey and had not noticed, but Mr Wilson gazed at her, how lovely she looked, he thought. It was with such thoughts that they rounded the Point and were walking towards the stage, when they noticed from the opposite direction there appeared to be a group of riders, coming fast.

"Visitors my dear." Mr Wilson told her rising his hand to his face to stop the last glows of the sun from getting a clear view. Within a few moments Elizabeth increased her pace, she knew by the way these visitors rode, they were not American. She instinctively removed her hand from Mr Wilson and grasped her gun in her dress coat pocket. *"They are Indians Mr Wilson and we should return quickly."*

Mr Wilson had to almost run to keep up. Elizabeth kept her eyes on the approaching riders. Something looked oddly familiar. It nagged at her as the riders advanced towards them. Then almost at once, it hit her. Elizabeth stopped. Stood perfectly still in open ground before the stage post. Mr Wilson unaware she had continued on. The Indians slowed their ride at the same time and walked their horses in slowly. They were not here for war and wanted no trouble with the people here. They scanned the people before them in a natural predatory way. They were instinctive predators. Hunting. Red Wolf spoke to his braves and they halted 20 yards from the house and he rode slowly on. From the moment, he could see her, Red Wolf knew who she was.

His eyes never left her face. He urged his pony to walk around the stage coach where the wheel had been forgotten by the driver by their arrival. Passed the house and those now standing outside it and stopped directly in front of Elizabeth and looked at her.

For what seemed to those watching, an eternity passed between the two of them.

Elizabeth knew the rider and part of her had expected him. Red Wolf had grown into a full-blooded brave. Nearly 7 years had turned the boy into a man. She had forgotten just how magnificent the Tribe were. He sat proudly on his mount, who was impatiently stomping at the ground and it was impossible not to be stirred by his presence. After all this time. Was he really here she asked herself. Part of her would hardly recognise him but the other part, would always have known him. He was certainly unlike any young man back East. Elizabeth surprised by how much that recognition warmed her. It was as if – he had been waiting for her. Could that be possible. He had certainly grown in the time she had been gone. No more the late teenage male she'd left behind. Before her was the man. A man who was aware of who he was. Who dominated those around him. He was… glorious to behold.

He seemed bigger. Stronger. More muscular. The hair longer. He was a sight to behold in his leggings and vest astride his Indian pony. Red Wolf should have spoken to her, greeted her in the traditional manner and called her sister, but he could not. He was having serious trouble breathing. To see her after all this time. His dreams come to life. Her presence warming him. Reminding him of how much he had waited for her. He ached just looking at her. She looked fragile compared to him but he knew different. She was strong and brave. He was not surprised she had just turned up. It was typical of her. Headstrong. Beautiful. His. He told himself. Red Wolf didn't trust himself to speak, he pushed his pony on, until it almost touched her. Elizabeth reached out and touched the pony's face, her eyes never leaving Red Wolfs.

They stood in silence. Finally, he extended his arm down to her. It was clear he intended to take her. Without hesitation, Elizabeth clasped his forearm with her own and he raised her, swiftly and easily, to sit in front of him. At the same time, there was screaming from Mrs Johnson for someone to do something. Mr Wilson was protesting loudly and several of the other men were moving their hands to their guns. The braves moved in closer. Quickly Elizabeth needed to explain, before someone got hurt.

"Gentleman, please, Mrs Johnson calm yourself, there is no cause for concern. I am with family, they have come to take me home. Please take my belonging on to Brownsville, I expect I will have family there too." "Family?" Called Mr Wilson. *"My dear..... their Indians."* Red Wolf shot him a look of contempt. This was not lost on Elizabeth, who gave a kindly smile. *"Mr Wilson, I thank you for your concern, I have not lost my wits or senses, I am indeed with my family."* *"Mam, are you the Trelawney Indian Princess?"* Duggie the driver asked her. Red Wolf had stiffened in response to that question. Elizabeth had never heard it said quite like that before. She wondered what that was about. *"Believe me gentleman when I tell you, they would give their lives willingly to ensure my safety."* And with that, Red Wolf enclosed her with his other arm possessively

and walked his horse slowly passed each of them. Almost daring them to stop him as he turned and rode out, followed by his braves.

Mrs Johnson was heard to pass out.

For over an hour they rode in silence. Stopping to rest and water the horses. Elizabeth, was helped down my Red Wolf, and sat under a tree watching the men work. She had always been fascinated by their work with horses. They had such a greater understanding of the animal. Elizabeth closed her eyes and listened to the sounds of water and men. She was home. Before long and for the first time in days, without a care, she was asleep.

It was as if the silence had woken her. She sat up with a start. For a second she thought she had dreamt it all. Then from the darkness she saw his face. Her hair had come loose of the pins holding it. It hung in heavy long ringlets down and around her shoulders. Wisps clinging to her face and neck and blowing in the breeze. Red Wolf had been watching her sleep. *"Sorry."* She spoke, pushing the hair from her face. *"I had not meant to sleep."* As she got up, she tried to do something with her hair and realised it was useless. The men had moved with her, repacking the ponies and making ready to ride. Red Wolf once again when ready looked down at her and extended his arm. She looked up at him. He had still not spoken to her. She knew he would speak when ready.

For only a moment, she hesitated and looked at him and wondered why he had not spoken to her and as quickly, accepted it. She took his arm and without question, he seated her before him. As the braves had started to move off, she had expected Red Wolf to follow. Instead, he brought both hands up in front of her face. Elizabeth was perfectly still, as he touched the cheeks of her face with his finger tips and traced them back to the nape of her neck. Elizabeth felt electric, alive. She held her breath. He secured her hair with a piece of raw hide. Then dropped his hands onto his thighs either side of hers. Elizabeth naturally rested against him as she had many many times before. It was then, Elizabeth felt she had truly come home. They rode for the village.

Red Wolf had sent one of the braves to the Double T to let White Dove know of her safety, and one to the village while she slept, they arrived at the village just after dawn.

Word had spread fast when they were first spotted. The village was alive with excitement. Running Elk, was waiting at the village edge, running alongside their pony and called out to her. *"Esa, welcome home sister, father is waiting for you."* Elizabeth reached down and grasped his hand. *"Running Elk, how big you are brother, you are nearly as tall as Red Wolf and you are a warrior I see."* Running Elk held a large grin.

"Yes, I had my proving last Spring and I am to be married in the Autumn." Elizabeth stared. *"Married?"* Cried Elizabeth. Had she been gone so long? *"Congratulations. I look forward to meeting your bride."* *"Thank you sister, I must go and find my betrothed so you can meet her."* *"I look forward to it."* Elizabeth called after him as he ran to the valley.

Elizabeth was reminded how long she had been gone. *"Have I been gone for so long? So much has changed. So much I have missed."* she murmured. Red Wolf heard her and tightened his hold. She held on to him. It had been too long. Many of the younger ones had heard of their honorary daughter but never seen her. By the time Elizabeth arrived, the raw hide was having little effect on her hair.

She looked like a vision to them, a queen in her Eastern finery, as described by the visiting monks who had taught them European history and languages. The children stared at her as she rode by. Elizabeth understood and smiled at their

fascination, understanding their wonder. It lit up her face

with her laughter and joy. Red Wolf could not miss the effect

Esa was having. It was exactly how he had felt. Seeing her at

the stage post after so many years.

Elizabeth looked lovingly at the village and

remembered the good times she had with them. The main

lodge was where she expected to see it. Tepees surrounding

it. Craftwork around the homes. Fires cooking meals. She

recognised several of the young men and women, her old play

mates and they called to her and she openly returned their

greetings. She took it all in. The people looked happy. It was

as she remembered it. The river beyond and pastures. It

warmed and comforted her. Elizabeth looked ahead. Their

horse came to a stop in front of Dull Knife. Red Wolf

continued to hold her and looked squarely at Dull Knife.

What passed between them remained unsaid. Elizabeth

turned slightly in the saddle and looked at him. Just inches from his face. *"We are home."* She told him. He released her and helped her down.

Dull Knife opened his arms for his honorary daughter. *"We have waited a long time for your return child, welcome and join us for the coming night and day."* Elizabeth walked into his embrace. *"Thank you honorary father, I am now home."* She told him. Letting her go. Elizabeth turned and joined the tribe in celebration. Rejoicing at the return of one lost to them for so long.

As Elizabeth was singing with the other young women of the tribe, renewing friendships. Ben was on his way back to the Double T. He'd been at Brownsville when the stage came in. Very quickly it was obvious that Elizabeth had caused a stir and been met by members of Dull Knifes tribe. Ben found it amusing how shocked many on the coach were.

Gaining Elizabeth's things. They made their excuses and left. Stopping at the mail office to let Clara know, Elizabeth had arrived safely.

Having been alerted by the brave sent by Red Wolf. White Dove had made all preparations to go to the village. By the time Ben had reached the Double T, White Dove had made all the necessary arrangements for a trip home. She had been waiting for her husband.

Ben rode into the house grounds and White Dove was waiting. *"Husband, we are ready for the journey."* Ben never ceased to be amazed by her abilities and beauty. Ben got down from his horse and greeted his wife. As he did so, a brave removed his mount and others were replaced. Ben gave a few instructions to several hands, and noticed not for the first time, the surliness of two of them. *"Jake, you're in charge*

I'll be back tomorrow." Jake the old boy of the place, who had been with Elizabeth's father nodded.

"It will be good to see her Ben." Jake told him. *"Yes it will Jake but I could also kill her for just turning up."* Jake smiled. *"I bet, but would you have let her come, if she'd asked?"* Ben looked thoughtful for a moment and with that, he mounted his horse, waited for White Dove to get set on the buggy and the party set out. Jake's words hit him. Ben used the time on the journey to take stock. He had been shocked by hearing that Elizabeth had left New York alone. He knew she was head strong and how much she had wanted to return home. He had missed her. But he had to admit, her returning scared him. He had hoped that over time, Elizabeth would have met the man to become her husband and brought him back with her. If she ever came back at all. After all he thought, what was there here for her? Where would she find an eligible man here. One worthy of running the Double T, worthy of her?

Who would want her for herself. Not for what she could give him. Ben had seen so many men in the last years come from the civil war looking for a quick buck. Elizabeth would be a target. Ben had a moment of despair and fear for her future and as quickly he pushed it aside. That wouldn't be happening. He would make sure of it.

Elizabeth had spent the last 3 hours catching up with her childhood friends. Many of them to her surprise, were already married. Two had children of their own and she had joined them down by the river playing with the children. Part of her ached at seeing their simple joy. She wanted this too when the time was right. Leaving them with many hugs between them, Elizabeth took a walk. She loved the cool breeze off the water and the calming sensation it brought her. Not realising she had been heading in any particular direction, Elizabeth found herself at her favourite spot. An open plateau. Surrounded by tall grasses and trees, wild flowers and small ripples of water in the background. Elizabeth mused, when coming here as a child, it had always seemed perfect. Elizabeth stopped and sat down amongst the grasses. It was so peaceful. She breathed deeply. The tall grasses moving in the breeze around her. Elizabeth felt herself sway in time with them. At one with the nature all around her. Closing her eyes, she listened to the world come alive.

It seemed she had only been there moments when she had the strangest feeling she was no longer alone. She did not open her eyes, but smiled. She had caught the scent of him. Strange how her senses had come flooding back in this place. She would not acknowledge him. This was her place not his. Only when excited voices reached her did she open her eyes and look straight into his. He rose in one swift movement and looked down at her. Held out his hand and waited for her to take it. At that moment there was nothing more Elizabeth wanted than to take his hand and go wherever he wanted to go. To do so, Elizabeth instinctively understood, would be to acknowledge something she wasn't ready to do. Instead, she raised herself, turned from him and walked back to the village and the commotion, she was the cause of.

Ben and White Dove were being greeted by Dull Knife. All three turned towards them as they arrived. It was clear from their faces that they had not been expected together. Elizabeth again wondered why they would be a surprised. They were after all family. Ben looked at Elizabeth and his breath caught in his throat. She was beautiful. She had grown into a beauty. How accomplished she looked. Even in her bedraggled state. She looked …polished and all woman. Concerned hit him like a lightning bolt. Ben looked back to Red Wolf and his obvious possessiveness. He looked to be claiming ownership. Ben frowned.

Dull Knife was also concerned but for his son. His stance told his son of his concern. White Dove, came forward and greeted Esa. She gave thanks for her safe return and hugged her. Red Wolf looked at the men before him. His emotions high. They were worried for her. Red Wolf got angry. They were questioning his right. His own father not showing proper respect and his body language suggested mistrust. Red Wolf moved in front of Elizabeth in an obvious challenging stance. It was his right to protect her.

In one swift movement, Elizabeth moved from behind Red Wolf and touched his arm. He turned to face her, the depth of her eyes left him wanting. There passed a look of acknowledgement and knowing. This was not the time or place. He had nothing to prove here and they both knew it. He should withdraw. Red Wolf looked as if he wanted to argue with her but didn't. Elizabeth faced her uncle. *"I am sorry uncle, forgive me. I hope I haven't been too much trouble."*

She said as she walked towards him and hugged him close. Ben sighed and indulged her. *"No child, I'm happy to see you safe and well. Next time, let an old man know?"* Elizabeth laughed and hugged him back. *"You are not an old man. I will. I am sorry. But so very glad to be home."* Dull Knife turned to the tribe and called out. *"We have prepared a meal, join us."* With much celebration the meal was served.

Elizabeth knew she would have some explaining to do but not now. She was just happy to be with her family and enjoy being home. There would be time later for explanations, and they would have to come. She had missed this so much. New York had much to offer and she had enjoyed her time there, but Elizabeth had felt she was treading water. Biding her time. Her life was here and she had always known it to be. By mid-night, goodbyes were in motion. Elizabeth had seen White Dove talking with Red Wolf earlier. There had been a heated exchange. And he had left them. It seemed that nearly all in the tribe had come out to say goodbye. All, that is, except Red Wolf.

Running Elk and his behoved stayed the longest and were the last to leave. Elizabeth liked her very much and knew she would make her brother very happy. As he turned to go, Running Elk turned back to Elizabeth, spoke quietly to her alone. Taking her hand. *"Esa, you are truly my adopted sister and Red Wolf is my brother. I love you both. It is important to me that you both find happiness. He will not come to say goodbye. I do not think he could."* Running Elk let go of her hand and Elizabeth caught his arm as he turned from her. *"I would never hurt you or your family and I will apologise to Red Wolf if I have offended him."* Running Elk smiled sadly at her. *"The last thing you have done, is offend him Esa. I will see you soon."* And with a squeeze of her hand, he left her.

Elizabeth boarded the buggy and joined White Dove. She was confused by Running Elks conversation with her. For the life of her, she could not think what he was talking about. Surely Red Wolf had not come to say goodbye simply because she had broken protocol in some way and had offended him or he was simply on an errand and unable to do so. When she saw him next, she would make it right she told herself. With every mile nearer to the Double T. Elizabeth recalled memories precious to her. Almost every bend in the road, every rocky outcrop or land mark had one. In her excitement Elizabeth talked to White Dove about everything, the one thing she couldn't bring herself to talk about, was Red Wolf.

CHAPTER THREE

They entered under the sign of the Double T. Her
father had put this up with Jake. Elizabeth asked White Dove
to stop. Elizabeth gazed at the view and land. Her father
would have been happy she had returned. He had wanted
her here. Not in the East. She turned to White Dove. *"Its ok,
we can go now."* White Dove caressed her hand and they
moved off. It would still be another 2 hours before they
reached the house. Ben had sent riders ahead. By the time the
buggy party arrived, the bunk house was empty. All the
hands old and new were waiting to greet them. Some out of
friendship for the young girl that liked to play with horses
and chase the dog. Others out of curiosity for the daughter
who owned it all. Jake came to help Elizabeth down and held
her close, after all, he had once saved her life. *"Hi honey, we
sure have missed you, unt that right Ben?"* Smiling at her. "Sure
have, I think I've told her that 3 times today already."

Elizabeth reacquainted herself with several long-time staff. They had been like family and several new ones. When being introduced Elizabeth felt the indifference of two apparent new hands. The older one clearly leading the younger. Who ignored White Dove, and her instructions? This upset Elizabeth. Ben had to tell them again. White Dove withdrew herself and went inside. Elizabeth had the odd feeling it was not the first time this had happened. Elizabeth looked around her. It was much as she remembered. The house in a colonial style on two floors with over hanging roofs and terraces. A large swing in the front right corner. Native stone on the window surrounds and doors. All fitted with shutters in case of a raid. Her father had put those in she recalled. But they have never had cause to use them. Elizabeth turned and faced the outbuildings that had housed house staff and on the other side, at a slight distance down the road, the bunk house. The area had several corrals housing horses. And next to them the barns. A small garden on both sides at the front of the house steps, was just as she remembered it and well looked after. They had roses all the way from England in them. Another memory from her mother and father. Elizabeth smiled. It was good to be home. Elizabeth excused herself ran up the steps and went inside to join White Dove.

Elizabeth found her sitting in one of the great arm chairs by the large open fire that was used in winter. Elizabeth stopped in the large hall with the central staircase. It was beautiful and way over the top for the mid-west. Her father had had it made for her mother who missed such things from back East. It opened onto an upper floor with a gallery corridor that led to the bedrooms. All six of them. The sitting room was to her right through large double doors. The dining room through similar doors to the left. The kitchen beyond that. Behind the stairs held the house office and bathroom.

White Dove had taken up some needlecraft. Elizabeth went to her and knelt before her putting her hands over hers. *"Cousin, this is your home as much as Bens or mine, you must be happy in it. If you are ever not, you must ask me to help and I will."* White Dove hugged her. *"I know this, sometimes I forget."*

"My honorary father once told me, we should never forget and he was right as he has been many times." Smiled Elizabeth. She rose from her knees. *"If you will forgive me, it's been a long day, I will retire, say goodnight to Ben for me. I'll see you both this evening."* White Dove smiled at her. *"Your room is ready for you."* And with a nod and a hug Elizabeth left her. She climbed the stairs and found her way to her old room. The lamp had already been lit. It was just exactly as she had left it. A few grown-up edges. Some adult things had been added but it still had all her childish things. Elizabeth smiled. Her child's bed had been removed and a much larger one with a canopy stood in its place. Elizabeth moved around the room. Inspecting the old with the new and was very pleased. *"Do*

you like it?" Elizabeth turned to see Ben in the doorway. *"Ben, thank you - someone has worked hard on it."* Ben walked in. *"All White Dove honey she wanted it right for you. She has been planning this day for some time."* Elizabeth ran her hands along the lace curtains. *"Thank her for me, won't you Ben."* Ben crossed the room to hug her and gave her a squeeze. *"I will, get some sleep and we'll talk tomorrow."* He let go of her and turned to walk out. *"Ben? Are you really glad to see me?"* Elizabeth nibbled her lip. *"Esa, really I am very glad, sleep well."* He smiled *"We'll talk tomorrow."* He turned and closed the door behind him.

Elizabeth, walked around the room again. Enjoying the moment. She had a genuine feeling of pleasure at being back in her old room. She couldn't help herself but to grin widely and swing her arms wide and twirl. She ended up falling on the bed in a fit of giggles. Slowly her breathing gradually returned to normal and she lay perfectly still as she had as a child and listened to the sounds of the house. The staff coming and going, the animals being led back and forth and the comforting sounds of family throughout the house.

Elizabeth listened for some time and gradually felt herself slipping into sleep overcome with the events of the last few days. *"If I do not go to bed now."* She said aloud, and promptly rose to change for bed. Elizabeth's valise had been put in her room. She went to it and emptied its contents. *"Not so much to choose from."* Thought Elizabeth. But then the rest of her belongings would have to come later. She had not worn nightwear for 7 nights and she suddenly longed for the freedom it offered. Quickly and silently, Elizabeth undid her travelling jacket and pulled her blouse from the constraints of her skirt. She unbuttoned the blouse and removed it. At the same time, she removed her travelling skirt and tugged at her chemise. She removed the corsetry and under slip and put her nightgown over her head and was finished. Elizabeth could not remember doing it so quickly before. After a quick wash in the wash stand and brushing of her hair. Elizabeth almost fell into bed. Sleep came immediately.

Elizabeth woke to find it still night-time. Restless. The lack of sleep over the last week had finally caught up with her. The room was silent and dark, the only glow in the room coming from the moon in her open window and the soft breeze blowing the curtains. Elizabeth got out of bed and went to the window. She hadn't remembered opening it but guessed that White Dove had come in and done it. Sitting in the middle of the window seat, Elizabeth raised her knees up under her chin, wrapping her nightdress over them and hugging them close as she used to do as a child. Looking out over the land.

Even in darkness only illuminated by the moon, it was breath taking. Elizabeth thought of her parents. How much they would have loved this. Her fully grown. Home and in

her old room. She sat there gazing out for – she didn't know

how long, but as the breeze came in, she suddenly realised she

had been silently weeping. The tears were cool on her face.

Elizabeth wiped them away with her hand and suddenly felt

cold. All her pent up emotions hit her at once. She was

suddenly uncontrollable. Weeping and wiping and

shuddering all at the same time. Silently, from behind her, a

blanket encompassed her shoulders and held her close within

its embrace. Elizabeth remained motionless, still weeping,

she didn't have to look to see who it was. Her weeping was

comforted by his presence and she now knew what had

awoken her. His presence calmed her. Made her feel whole.

Elizabeth felt him move to sit behind her. Sighed deeply and

looked up again over the horizon. *"This is my home, our land,*

and I have missed them very much." She told him. The embrace

tightened slightly, pulling her back into his embrace. His

arms encompassing her. His head fell forward resting on her

shoulder. They sat as one. Elizabeth gazing out over the horizon.

She wasn't sure how long they sat together in the night. She must have fallen asleep. Elizabeth woke in her bed and wondered for a moment, if she had dreamed it all. The house stirred to life and there was a tap on her door. *"Esa, are you ready for some breakfast?"* The door opened and White Dove entered with a tray. *"White Dove, no, you're not to wait on me, I'll come down and join you and we can eat together."* White Dove smiled and nodded and withdrew. Elizabeth quickly rose and did her toilette. She was surprised to see that a package had been left for her. It contained all the ranch day wear she needed. Good sturdy trousers, some shirts and a pair of leather boots and a good hat. She wondered how Ben had known her size. Elizabeth raced downstairs and found White Dove in the kitchen with several house staff. *"Good morning."* She called out as she entered the room. *"Morning Ms."* They returned in chorus. White Dove, came forward and embraced her. *"Let me introduce you, and you can have your breakfast."* Elizabeth remembered some of them very well. She embraced Anna and others she knew she would like very much. White Dove made a point of telling the staff that they must take their instruction from Elizabeth now she was here. Elizabeth was horrified. *"White Dove no, you run this house and unless you would rather not, it is still yours to do with as you wish."* White Dove smiled. *"I would like that very much."* "Good let's have breakfast." she linked arms with White Dove and headed for the dining room. It was empty. *"Where is everyone?"* She asked. *"Esa, they and I had breakfast several hours ago."*

"Oh heck." Elizabeth said and smiled at the slang. It had been awhile since she had used it. *"I forgot how early the day starts here. All that East timing I guess. Tomorrow I want to be up with the hands, please call me till I get used to it?"* "Of

course, now eat". Anna came to the table with an enormous plate of ham and eggs. Elizabeth's favourite, she instantly got up and hugged White Dove. *"Thank you for everything."* With a huge grin she tucked in as the coffee arrived. When Elizabeth felt, she could not eat another bite, she helped take plates back to the kitchen and went outside. Elizabeth stood in the kitchen doorway and looked out over the yard. Several hands said hello to her and she returned their greeting. Elizabeth decided to take stock. It had been a while since she had walked the grounds of her home and she felt a need to bond with the land. Elizabeth walked into the barn and called to Joe who was tacking a horse. *"Hi Joe, could you saddle me a horse, I'd do it myself only I'm not sure which to take."* Joe turned to her smiling widely. *"Good morning miss. It nice to see you up and around. Sadly, we lost your pony a few years back. She had a happy life in the south paddock. Ben wouldn't sell her you know."* Elizabeth smiled back. *"Yes I know he wrote and told me, she was a beauty."* You can take 'Star' here, she's an easy ride." Elizabeth smiled she rode as well as any man, but didn't wish to upset him. She had kept up her riding while in the East. She had continued to ride like a man when possible to her aunt annoyance.

"That would be great thank you. I'm heading out South." Elizabeth took the Reins and headed out of the barn. She mounted, checked her rifle and took a slow canter, heading to the land boundary. Elizabeth rode and walked Star for 3 hours, stopping when something of interest caught her eye. She had reached the boundary fence with no problem and turned East. Elizabeth continued until she felt dinner should be soon. She then turned Star and headed North/West back towards the house. She stopped once to water Star and made good time. By the time she rode back into the house yard, she had been gone 7 hours. And, there was major panic on.

White Dove had been trying to get two of the hands to ride out after Elizabeth for the past half an hour. But they had ignored her. The older one becoming bullish, verbally abusive and aggressive. White Dove had not given up. She was standing near the barn and persisted as the older hand tried to sham her. Elizabeth rode in, they could not see her, but Elizabeth could clearly see the older hand manhandling White Dove. Elizabeth came to a stop at the porch, without dismounting, she reached up and took her father's whip and walked the horse across the yard. As she rounded the corner, the two hands saw her and the older one let go of White Dove. Elizabeth cut her horse in between them. With her eyes never leaving their faces, she called to White Dove. *"Are you alright cousin?"* Elizabeth from the corner of her eye saw White Dove rub her arm. Elizabeth fumed. *"Yes I am well Esa."* Elizabeth spoke coldly to the men. *"Your fired, get your stuff and get out."* The older of the two hands started to laugh. *"Yeah right and who's gonna make us?"* Elizabeth looked straight at them. *"I will."* This time they both laughed, the younger one nervously unsure of his loyalties. Elizabeth deliberately dropped the lead end on the bullwhip to the ground, and spoke.

"Gentleman, we can do this the easy way or the hard way, but you ARE leaving and now." Both stopped laughing and started to become very edgy. Then, it all happened very quickly. The atmosphere became strained, the older one went to touch his gun and Elizabeth let go with the ball whip. The first strike hit the older one across the face, opening up his face, the down stroke caught the younger one, the second caught the older one across his back and took the gun from his hand, the third rendered the younger one on the floor holding his arm. Both had backed off. At the same time, Red Wolf having seen the exchanged came riding into the yard.

"Get out, now and don't set foot on our land again." Elizabeth cracked the whip again. Slowly and deliberately she recoiled it. Both hands got up and went to their horses. As

the older one mounted, he snarled over his shoulder *"Indian lover."* He spat at her. The younger to his credit, looked shame faced but followed his brother. *"You'll regret this, I'll make sure you do."* The older one told her. They both rode out. Elizabeth got down off Star and went to White Dove. *"Are you sure you're ok?"* *"Yes Esa, I am well."* *"Wait till I tell Ben, he should have fired those guys. That wasn't the first time was it?"* White Dove looked worried. *"No Esa, please do not tell him."* Elizabeth frowned and held White Dove's hand. *"Where's Jake and Joe? And Ben should know."* *"I sent Jake and Joe to look for you and I know Ben, he will take this badly."* White Dove replied. *"Please don't, it's over, it will only distress him."*

"Alright as you wish." Elizabeth shock her head. *"Let's get you inside."* Elizabeth turned to Red Wolf, inclined her head, she hadn't seen him all day and continued to walk with White Dove to the house. Instinctively knowing Red Wolf and what he had seen, Elizabeth called to him as she walked

away towards the house. *"Do not harm them it will only start trouble. I want them off our land."* He gazed at her back, not surprised at her knowing. Gathering up his reins he rode after the brothers, as he had always intended to do. Hands, riders, Ben and the scouts started to drift back into the ranch yard over the next couple of hours. From a hard day's work. Elizabeth quickly explained she was ok and that no one should have been worried. She also felt the need to stress she had told Joe she was heading South. Both Joe and Jake came back in shortly after. They were relieved to see her. Ben had an indulgent smile for his niece. White Dove, Elizabeth and the house staff, prepared dinner for 25. Everyone at the Double T ate the same meal. A mixture of Native American, Mexican and American/Irish food. It was hot, favour sum and filling. Dinner for the hands was kept hot in the outdoor kitchen next to the main house. The stove kept it hot and they came and helped themselves. Dinner for the family was always at 7pm. Family included very one with a history with the family. A tradition started by her father. The older hands, had an open invitation. Sometimes they joined them. Sometimes they didn't. The house staff had the same invitation. Tonight, dinner at the house was a full-on affair. All wanted to come and all were welcome.

Elizabeth help to prepare the food and then retired to wash and change her clothes. So had White Dove. The men came in washed and changed and by 6.45pm all those who were having dinner were chatting and having a drink in the parlour, their grand sitting room. Elizabeth could hear the conversation while she got dressed. It was mainly about her coming home. Horses, blood lines and herd pasture. Elizabeth decided to do her hair in the East style she favoured. Put on the one spare dress she had with her. She came down the stairs and walked in to join the others. There were plenty of welcomes, smiles and hugs. She was offered a drink by Jake. At that moment Ben clinked his glass and everyone was silent. *"I want to welcome home Elizabeth, so join me in saying how lovely it is to have her home, everyone Elizabeth."* There was a chorus of glasses being raised and *"Elizabeth"* stated loudly. *"Now I believe Anna is trying to tell us dinner is ready, so let's go eat. I for one am starving."* There was laughter and joy as those present parted and headed into the dining room. Elizabeth turned and thought she was seeing things. There talking to Ben in full western clothes stood Red Wolf. His long black hair tied with the similar piece of raw hide he had used on her. Elizabeth couldn't take her eyes off him. She had never imagined seeing him like this. He was stunning. Somehow it made him seem more - real.

White Dove touched her arm and Elizabeth almost jumped. *"Esa, come and sit down, I'm sure they will join us soon."* *"Yes of course."* Elizabeth smiled at her, linked their arms and they walked to join the others already at the table.

"Before we go in, I want to apologise for yesterday with Esa. I am struggling with my emotions where she is concerned. My judgement was poor." Red Wolf told Ben. Ben nodded. *"You love her son?"* Red Wolf turned and looked at Elizabeth walking into the dining room with White Dove. *"More than my life Sir."* Ben slapped him on the shoulder. *"The ladies tend to do that to us son. Let's go eat."*

The dining room was a traditional affair. Set with Elizabeth's mothers things and built by her father. The furniture had come from back East but instead of the delicate furniture preferred there, this had been picked as much for its sturdiness, as it had for its beauty. The table was highly polished and of dark rich wood. Elizabeth loved to run her fingers over it. Underneath, there were more than a couple of spur marks, much to her mother's annoyance she recalled with a smile. Elizabeth loved this table. She ran her hand along the edge. She took her seat between Jake and Anna, with Joe. White Dove sat next to the space for Ben. A number of family, friends and staff sat between them and at the end of the table, with several of the family hands was a space she guessed for Red Wolf. The conversation was light and entertaining. A recalling of stories of times gone by. Ben and Red Wolf came in to join them. Elizabeth was made to remember many a story recalling an accident or childhood trick. She cringed and became embarrassed more times that she cared for and told them to stop more than once, but enjoyed the evening very much. Everything seemed perfect. As tradition called for, she helped serve the platters around the table. Although she was not good at it she gave it her best shot and dinner seemed to fly by, but Elizabeth was unsettled.

By the time guests retired back to the lounge for after dinner drinks, Elizabeth felt done in. It had been a long evening and after several after dinner conversions, guests started to make their way home. Elizabeth made her way across the room to Ben who was now talking to Jed Nelson, a young man not much older than Elizabeth. A nearby farm owner who lived with his sisters. Their parents sadly having died of the influenza several years ago. *"Jed, how's the family."* She asked. "Just fine Elizabeth thanks. They're glad to see you home." He told her. Elizabeth smiled. *"Please tell, Cathy and Sarah, I'll pop over and see them sometime soon."* Jed nodded. *"I will they'll enjoy catching up. They had wanted to be here but Cathy is not been feeling well of late and Sarah did not want to leave her."* *"O my, anything we can do?"* *"Thank you no. The Doc been to see her."* Elizabeth squeezed his arm. *"Please wish her better for me. Ben, forgive me."* Elizabeth continued. *"But I'm exhausted, please give my apologies, I'm going to go up."* *"ok honey, see you in the morning."* Ben said and bent to kiss her. As Elizabeth went to turn she remembered something. *"Ben tomorrow could White Dove and I go into town. Until my things arrive from New York I need some things and I'm sure we could stock up on some provisions while we're there. Maybe we could take a couple of hands to help, and we need a couple of new hands too, I could post a notice for you at the same time?"* Ben was about to answer as Red Wolf joined them.

"Ben, father has requested that Black Dog and his braves accompany Esa on any further trips." Elizabeth's draw dropped, his English was perfect and he'd never even said hello! What the hell. The cheek of the man. Elizabeth got angry. *"I don't need baby sitters."* She spat out more than she meant too. *"No honey, Dull Knife is right, you were gone for over 7 hours and anything could have happened."* *"But it didn't and I had my guy and rifle."* She moaned agitated. *"And I was just fine."* She said trying to stare down Red Wolf and failing. Conscious of Jed also standing there. *"I'm sorry, Esa, your father has offered the protection and it would be offensive to decline it."* In a huff, Elizabeth turned and called over her shoulder narrowing her eyes at Red Wolf. *"I wonder just how much father was involved in that decision."* She continued across the lounge and climbed the stairs. Both Red Wolf and Ben stared after her. Elizabeth

changed and got ready for bed. Walking over to the window she opened it. People were leaving. Laughter drifted up to her. Turning Elizabeth looked at her dresser. The pictures of her mother, father, the three of them when she was younger and Ben with White Dove sat proudly on it. She loved this room. It was spacious even with the larger bed in it. As a child, she had lots of room to play. Elizabeth loved the four-poster bed White Dove had purchased for her. It called to her. Crawling into the covers she fell asleep almost immediately and was woken by the morning sun and White Dove giving her a gentle shake. *"If we are going into town Esa, you must get up."* Elizabeth stretched and smiled, then jumped out of bed, fresh clothes had been laid out. *"White Dove, you must stop doing these things for me, it's not fair on you."* White Dove smiled. *"Yes it is, now hurry."* And White Dove left. Elizabeth washed and dressed quickly and decided to leave her hair down in the traditional Indian manner with braids to hold it back.

Elizabeth rushed down the stairs and did her toilette.

Heading into the dining room grabbing some biscuits from

the table as she went by and glass of milk, she headed out the

door. What awaited her was quite a sight. Red Wolf had

clearly waited for her on his pony to come down and show

herself. Elizabeth stood on the porch, stared at him, still

pissed at him and watched him ride out. Not fair she thought.

Standing before her, were Black Dog and his 3 braves, they

were about 10 years older than her and she remembered being

quite scared of them. Well, for all of a couple of weeks, till

one day they helped her catch a pony. They didn't say a lot,

and used the old hand signals for most of what they needed to

say, but they spoke English as good as any. Just chose not to.

And that was ok with her. She liked their silence.

In front of them, was the loveliest Indian pony she'd

ever seen. Mainly white with coloured patches and she was a

beauty. Elizabeth couldn't stop the excited squeal that came out of her mouth. She clapped and smiled even with the braves standing there. She didn't care. She acknowledged Black Dog and his men and welcomed them to her home in the traditional manner as she ran over to the pony. She raised her hand and followed the Indian way of greeting a horse. *"Hello Patches."* She whispered in his ear and he whinnied in return. Ben stood behind her. She turned. *"Mine?" "Yes."* He said. *"He's lovely, thank you."* Ben frowned. *"No Elizabeth it's not my gift, its Red Wolfs. One of his best I understand."* Elizabeth must have looked surprised. Ben continued. *"The pony is use to a saddle and it's from White Dove and me. She also mentioned, that you should carry the bullwhip from now on, so it's been greased and tempered."* Elizabeth went to him and hugged him. *"I asked Jake and Joe to go with you and while you're in town, you should go to the bank and make sure all is well and as you want it."* He told her. Elizabeth nodded then turned to White Dove. *"Let's go."* She couldn't hold back the excited grin.

Elizabeth mounted her pony with ease and the party of eight with Jake on the buckboard with White Dove, headed to Brownsville. The journey took them four hours. Elizabeth loved it. With each mile came a memory. It seemed to go too quickly and uneventfully. Spying the town in the distance. Elizabeth was reminded of how it used to look. It was a simple town supporting a large community of people spread wide throughout the area. A main single road down the centre of it. Several small side streets that went for a couple of blocks and that was it. The post station and livery was at the far end. Several shops, Saloons, Laundry and a Wash house were some of them. The Sheriff's office in the middle near the bank. The Doctor had his house at the opposite end to the livery. Next door to him was a Guest House. It was popular with travelling men and women who wanted something a bit more than the Saloon. She'd always loved coming to town.

They entered Brownsville with Elizabeth leading them in, closely followed by Black Dog, then White Dove and the buckboard with Jake and the band of braves and Joe bringing up the rear. Elizabeth had no idea just what an unusual sight she made. It was so natural for her to have a company of both Americans and Indians that even after all this time, she thought nothing of it. She wore buckskin top and canvass trousers. As they rode down the street, several people stopped and stared, for the sight of her alone, as much for the Indians. Elizabeth, all wavy golden autumn hair in all its glory. Indian style, made her a rich combination of western and native and her entourage made her look like what she was. Indian royalty, if not by birth, then by design. She stopped outside of the General Store. Bo Jenkins came out to see what all the commotion was about. Elizabeth greeted him.

"Good morning Mr Jenkins, it's been a long time. How are you?"

"Elizabeth? Is that you child." He asked. *"My goodness. All grown up now. You are a sight for sore old eyes. It is good to see*

you." Elizabeth smiled she liked Mr Jenkins very much he had been kind to her as a child. *"Thank you. Yes sir, I believe Mrs Trelawney has a huge list for you, I hope you can help?"* Mr Jenkins smiled. *"Yes of course, come in come in. Mrs Trelawney how are you today, please do come in."* *"Also Mr Jenkins, we have a spot for a couple of hands, could you put up our notice while I'm in town?"* Elizabeth asked him.

"Sure thing Elizabeth." And he went inside. White Dove made to get down. Elizabeth caught her arm. *"Are you able to shop alone?"* White Dove smiled, *"yes I have done it often."* Elizabeth smiled. *"In that case, I will go to the bank and see you back here. Jake, Joe your with White Dove."* Both men nodded to her and dismounted. White Dove smiled at her. Stepped down and went inside. Elizabeth signalled for the braves to stay with White Dove. *"Esa, Joe and I have to check at the post stop and have a few errands as well."* Jake told her. Elizabeth smiled. In the old days, a few errands tended to

lead to the Saloon. *"Ok, Jake see you both back here."* Elizabeth turned her pony and all but ran into Black Dog. Clearly he had other instructions. Elizabeth pierced her lips and stared at him. He gave the slightest nod of his head. Elizabeth realised he was doing what he'd been told. She headed down the street to the Bank. Black Dog closely behind her. She dismounted and dropped 'Patches' reins in the traditional way. Black Dog dismounted and did the same and followed her into the Bank.

Across the street from the General Store, Carl Steiner and his partner Buddy were watching all the action. Carl thought he had never seen anything so magnificent. The women was beautiful and from the way she handled herself, not just on the outside. Carl turned to the town barber who stood next to him. *"Excuse me. Do you know who that is."* *"Yep, sure do, that's the Trelawney family, they own the Double T."* Carl turned back to the bank. *"Who's the girl?"* *"That I expect is the prodigal. Ms Elizabeth Trelawney. Lovely child she was to, been away for a few years. Sure has grown. Kinda thought she'd have all those Eastern ways by now, guess not."* He said and turned away to go back inside. *"The prodigal?"* Asked Buddy not recognising the word. *"It means, their important and recently returned home."* Said Carl. *"O right, why not just say that then?"* Carl smiled. He watched one of the hands put a notice up and walked over to read it. At that moment, Elizabeth was sitting in Charlie Bells office with Black Dog hovering in the background. Elizabeth had explored all the pleasantries of her return with the Bank Manager who insisted on serving her coffee and who appeared to keep a concerned eye on Black Dog at the same time.

"Well Mr Bell, it has been a pleasure to meet you. I have come to access funds from my personal account, I know it's been a while, but I'm sure that everything is in order." Elizabeth assured him. *"And please call me Elizabeth."* *"Well of course Ms*

Trelawney whatever you need but I would like to take this opportunity to discuss the ranch accounts with you, if you wouldn't mind." Elizabeth was surprised by the tone of his statement. *"Mr Bell, my Uncle sees to all our accounts. As money is transferred to our New York holdings. He has diligently sent me copies of all our accounts and interests over the years. I intend to go over everything in time with him but not now and we both know, the ranch makes more money than we could ever spend."* *"Yes Ms Trelawney, Elizabeth, but your Uncle",* he looked over at Black Dog and swallowed hard. *"Is married to an Indian, and you are the rightful heir."* Elizabeth was finding it increasingly more difficult to hold onto her temper. *"Mr Bell, your new to me. Your predecessor was a wonderful man. So I do not know you and you do not as yet know us. However, I know this bank. My money started it and my family keeps it going. You forget yourself. I am Indian, by choice. Now if you would kindly access my personal funds as I have requested. Our business is completed, unless that is, you would like us to close our accounts?"*

Realising his mistake. *"That won't be necessary Elizabeth, it's my job to look to your interests and check we are doing right by you"*. Elizabeth nodded. *"I am grateful that you do. We have been with this bank for too many years to fall out now."* Elizabeth answered. *"I may well want to make a number of changes in time. I have been running several business interests in the East but for now, I am making no changes at present Mr Bell and should I do so, it will be with the express permission of my uncle and in consultation with my father and brothers. Now, if you could allow me my credit line, I have other business I must attend to and I must be going."* Mr Bell donned his hat and stood, arranged a letter of credit and Elizabeth got up. Shook hands and left. With Black Dog hot on her heels.

Elizabeth came out and looked around her. That man had left a bad taste in her mouth. She missed the old banker. He was a loveable man. The town had not changed much in the years she had been away. There were a few new shops since she had last been in town and then she saw the ladies clothing shop. A huge grin crossed her face. Perfect. Elizabeth picked up her reins and walked across the road. She dropped them at the post and walked into the shop. A bell rang over the door as she entered. Elizabeth couldn't believe it. It was a bit of the East here in Brownsville. She was pleasantly surprised. It had a bit of everything. Underwear, perfume, makeup, day and evening clothes. It was a little piece of heaven. *"Can I help you?"* Came the voice from the back.

"Yes I hope so, I would like nearly everything here!" The voice laughed. *"In that case, I hope you can afford it?"* *"Actually yes I can."* Elizabeth said with a smile. *"But I'll only take a little although I'm sorely tempted. Hello, I'm Elizabeth."* Elizabeth came around the counter, found the voice and held out her hand. A hand reached out from a large packing box. Shaking

it the voice called out. *"Sorry up to my head in boxes, hello, I'm Vera Corday and this is my shop." "Well hello Vera, I can see we are going to be great friends."* Elizabeth laughed looking around the shop. *"Well I do hope so."* Said Vera coming into the main part of the store. Elizabeth smiled at Vera. She was a petite lady with brown curly hair. Elizabeth rubbed her hands together. *"Show me everything you've got."* She told her with a cheeky grin. Black Dog remained outside, blocking the door.

Vera looked up after several purchases at the shadow blocking her door, Elizabeth followed her gaze. *"Bodyguard?" "Yes, my father's idea, but I actually think it was probably my brothers." "Brother? Don't tell me there's a male version of you that I haven't seen."* Elizabeth laughed. She'd never considered that Red Wolf would be a man that women would go after. She frowned. *"I'm not sure he's your type."* And explained to Vera why. Vera looked out the window at Black Dog. *"Well, I wouldn't mind if he didn't."* Elizabeth laughed out loud and

Vera joined in. It was a lovely way to spend a couple of hours. *"Could you send any new things up to the ranch for me to have a look at from time to time, and you'd be very welcome too any time. We'd be happy to have you." " I would like that very much and it's no problem at all Elizabeth, just send in a hand every now and then and I'll pack you up a parcel and maybe come with it."* Elizabeth laughed loudly. *"Vera, you are indeed a person worth knowing, can you send today's purchases over to the general store for collection as soon as possible."* They shock hands, each sure they had found a new friend.

Elizabeth and Black Dog remounted and headed back up town. As they passed the saloon, Elizabeth winced inwardly as she heard a voice she recognised. *"Indian lover, what's the matter with this town, putting up with dirt in your streets, treating them like people."* The voice staggered out of the saloon door barely able to stand up, followed by his brother. When they saw her fully, the older stopped. *"Dirty Indian whore.*" He called out. The younger looked visibly shocked. Embarrassed. Elizabeth paled, uncoiled the whip and flicked it. They stepped back. The whole of town seemed to be looking at them and had clearly heard what he had said. Much to her annoyance, Elizabeth reddened. Black Dog pushed his pony forward and screened her from behind.

"*Well now boys.*" She called out loudly, more confident than she felt. "*I see you didn't get very far now did you?*" "*We're not on your land, so you can't do nothin to us now.*" The older hand had answered her. Elizabeth took her time. Held the bullwhip handle and cracked it. Then rubbed it along her face, copying the scar on his face. "*How's the face and gun hand?*" She challenged. At the same time Sheriff Johnson walked up to Elizabeth and Jed came from the other direction. "*Elizabeth, lovely to see you, is there a problem here?*" The Sheriff asked her. Without dropping her gaze Elizabeth answered him. "*A slight difference of opinion on our land with these boys*

here yesterday, that's all Sheriff." *"Do you want to press charges?"*
Both men looked physically sick. *"I don't think that will be
necessary Sheriff, it's a personal matter."*

The older man started to stutter. *"Her press charges?"*
He shouted. *"She's mad, Sheriff she took a whip to us, look at what
she did."* The younger brother offered. People started to
snigger. Elizabeth leaned forward, and with a menacing edge
she didn't know she processed. *"You have your life, be thankful,
don't let me see you again."* Elizabeth sat back up and gathered
her reins. *"Sheriff, nice to see you. I believe Anna has a pie with
your name on it. Happy to see you anytime. Jed."* She nodded in
both their directions. *"Always a pleasure gentlemen."* And
turned her pony towards the general store, Black Dog
followed.

Elizabeth decided she'd had enough of 'town' for one
day, it has not been the success she had wished for in the end.
The hands comments hurt her more than she would like to

admit, but Vera's made up for some of that she thought. She stopped at the general store and waited on her pony. Joe handed her the purchase paperwork. Tried to relax in her saddle. Right leg over the hilt and looked over her paperwork Joe had given. White Dove was still busy. Black Dog dismounted, joined his men and was helping to load the wagon. Carl approached Elizabeth hat in hand. Black Dog, sensing him before seeing him, leapt in front of him cutting him off and stood between them. Carl stepped back. *"I'm sorry, I mean no harm to the lady."* He spoke directly to Black Dog and indicated to Elizabeth. Elizabeth was surprised by this; many locals didn't choose to talk to the Indians like men. *"I read your notice, you're looking for hands?"* Black Dog looked at Elizabeth who signalled to withdraw.

"Yes that's right Mr?" *"Steiner mam and that's my partner Benny."* Carl told her indicating Benny on the other side of the street Elizabeth looked over at Benny who took his

hat from his head. Elizabeth smiled. *"Well Mr Steiner, how do you feel about working for an Indians lover?"* Elizabeth said dryly acknowledging that he must have heard the conversation along with everyone else in town. He got points for treating Black Dog properly. *"I don't have an opinion mam, as long as we're paid and its honest, that's good enough."* Elizabeth said nothing. Just continued to look at him. *"Done the work before Mr Steiner?"* *"Yes mam."* Elizabeth considered him for a moment and made up her mind. *"The Double T is to the West, you can't miss it, if you still feel you'd like to give it a go, come tomorrow at sunrise, ask for Mr Trelawney, my Uncle or my brother Red Wolf."* *"Red Wolf mam, your brother?"* *"Yes Mr Steiner, my brother."* Carl looked at the ground, to look at her hurt. *"If you'll excuse me for saying Miss, you don't look as if you have Indian parents."* Elizabeth studied him for a moment, not sure if he was just being fresh or insulting, as he looked up, she frowned and made a decision. *"I don't by blood Mr Steiner, but by choice my chosen father is and therefore I am Indian too. If you can't respect Indians don't bother coming. If you chose to work for us, you know where to find us. Good day Mr Steiner."* Carl nodded doffing his hat and walked away.

Elizabeth turned as Mr Jenkins came out of the store, White Dove had already mounted during Elizabeth's exchanged with Carl, as had the other braves. *"Thank you Mr Jenkins, I'm sure to see you again soon." "Always a pleasure Elizabeth, you must come and see us again soon, I know Mrs Jenkins would welcome the pleasure of your company to dinner any time."* Mr Jenkins spoke aloud. Affirming her status to the town and his pleasure in serving her. Elizabeth nodded regally. She was completely unaware of the impact, her party made on the rest of them. Riding high in the saddle, Elizabeth was eager to get going. She moved off, slowly walking Patches down the centre of town. Her bullwhip in her hand. As she rode past the towns folk Elizabeth made eye contact as she went. And smiled to those she knew. Carl was still watching from the sidewalk. One after the other the rest of her party turned and rode out of town after her. For some, it was as if the lights of town, just went out.

Carl and Benny started out for the Double T. They were home for dinner. Elizabeth talked all through dinner about the trip into town. All except the run in with the brothers. After dinner, Elizabeth bought in some of the purchases she'd made earlier. She talked to Ben about the run in with the Bank Manager Mr Bell and told him she wasn't happy about his attitude. Ben laughed. *"It's your land honey."* *"No Ben, it's all our land"*. As Ben answered her, Red Wolf came into the room, in traditional dress. Hearing the tall end of the conversation. He sat down and joined his family. Ben and Red Wolf talked over the day while White Dove brought him some food. As she came back, Elizabeth got up and handed a present to White Dove and one to Ben. *"What's this Esa."* White Dove asked *"It's a gift to say thank you."* She said to both of them. White Dove opened her parcel, it contained a lovely silk night gown. She had not seen anything like it before and clearly loved it. Ben opened his to find a gold Double T tie pin. Choked he turned to her. *"Elizabeth its lovely how'd you find it?"* She smiled. *"I brought it with me, I had it made before I left."*

Elizabeth also had a gift for Red Wolf, Dull Knife and Running Elk. She hesitated for only a second then walked over to Red Wolf who had finished eating and had made his way into the sitting room. She stood before him and handed him his gift. *"Thank you for my pony, his lovely."* She said he looked up and stared. Without waiting for his response. *"I'm off to bed"* Elizabeth said. Walking to the dining room, she kissed Ben and White Dove and climbed the stairs. Elizabeth entered her room and went straight over to her dressing table, someone had been in to open her window for her. She'd closed it this morning and there was a note on her desk. It was from Ben. 'I'm giving you a gun. I know you can use one. It's a small one. It's loaded and if you need help in using it, ask before you do! It's in the right hand draw of this desk. Ben.'

Elizabeth opened the drawer and there is was. A small silver, onyx and black, ladies pistol. It was nothing like her MAS. Elizabeth left it in the open drawer and continued to get ready for bed. She wasn't sure if she really wanted another gun. Although her parents had had them and she had been taught shortly after Bens arrival, she understood why it was needed but she wasn't keen on them. Elizabeth brushed her hair out and opened her shirt pulling it from her trousers and unlaced her chemise. She always felt so free while doing this and started to unpin her hair, there was a knock and her door opened. Red Wolf came in and took several steps without looking at her or waiting for her to ask him in. A little shocked, Elizabeth stood and took a step towards him.

As she did, Red Wolf looked at her for the first time. Whatever he was going to say, was gone. He stopped. Elizabeth had more clothes on, than he had seen on her several times before, but somehow at that moment, in her room, a hunger in him was difficult to contain, and threatened to burst free. He could not help but take in the loose hair, the half-undone clothing. And what stirred him most. The obvious presence of what was very lightly and only partially concealed beneath. She could have been there waiting for him. Only he reasoned, she wasn't and he was here for another reason.

He looked down at the parcel in his hands and regained some composure and cleared his throat. *"I cannot take this."* He said handing her gift back to her. *"It means too much to you to give away."* He told her. Elizabeth looked at the gift he was holding out. It was the gift she had given him earlier. *"Is it not our custom to give something of equal value when* giving a gift? You gave me your horse. There is not much, more valuable in our ways, except a wife or daughter or son." Elizabeth answered, she shook her shoulders and smiled "And I have no sons to give you." She said it half-jokingly. He looked at her hard, and she realised her mistake. Trying to think of a way out of this, Red Wolf told her "This is the only image of you and your parents that you have." He whispered looking away from her. Elizabeth smiled, she did not have to answer him, there was no point. The house had become quiet and it felt as if they were the only two in the world. Red Wolf accepted defeat and slipped the gift inside his waistcoat. As he did so, he heard something from below the window and signalled to Elizabeth. He walked to the dresser and turned out the light, walking round the bed, he stopped in front of Elizabeth, putting his arms around her and guiding her to the wall. As they reached it, he passed to her her shirt and whispered. "Stay here." He let go of her. Walked to the open window and settled himself in the corner. Elizabeth held her breath and didn't move.

It seemed that they stood like that for an age and Elizabeth was just going to call to Red Wolf that he must have been mistaken – although that was unheard of - when she heard it too. There seemed to be some scrambling going on along the roof edge under her window. A tile came loose and someone swore. Elizabeth took a sharp intake of breath, she recognised the voice and was surprised for the second time that night. It was the older brother. He'd come back. All Elizabeth could think of, was that Red Wolf will kill him. Not once did she consider, why he was back and trying to gain entry to her room. The older brother pushed open the window and came in. Behind him was his younger brother, trying it seemed, to stop him. The older brother came towards Elizabeth's bed with a knife in his hand. He looked like he was going to stab the bed. He lunged and found it empty. At the same time Red Wolf dragged the younger brother through the window and was struggling with him. He had his back to the older brother, who took the opportunity of Red Wolf being distracted to lunge at him. He caught Red Wolf on the arm and struck again on his side. Red Wolf dropped the younger brother, who was now trying to stop his brother from the floor, by grabbing his legs. Red Wolf fell back against the wall holding his side. At that precise moment the older brother kicked off his brother and lunged again. This time he was aiming higher. Elizabeth wasn't sure how the gun came to be in her hand. She only realised it was, the moment it looked like the older brother would kill Red Wolf and she fired.

CHAPTER FOUR

At the sound of the shot all hell broke loose, staff were running in the yard below. The house came alive instantly. Elizabeth lit the lamp and rushed over to Red Wolf. She touched his side and his face, seeing if he was ok. She dropped her forehead to his. *"I thought he was going to kill you."* She said, before he could reply, the bedroom door opened and in rushed Ben, White Dove and several of the hands. The men had guns. *"What the hell's going on here."* Shouted Ben, as he took in Red Wolf being in Elizabeth's room. Elizabeth's state of undress and at the same time, the younger fired hand holding his older brother who was now very dead. *"Someone had better tell me what the hell is going on here and fast."* Elizabeth answered quietly. *"The older brother must have felt I had shamed him in town, he came looking to put the score right. Came in through the window. Red Wolf held him off but he attacked him again. I grabbed the gun to stop him killing him."* Ben turned to look at the younger brother. *"Is that what*

happened son?" He was honest in his response. *"Jack was gonna*

kill her. He just wouldn't let it go, I tried sir, but he wouldn't. I

thought that if I came along, I could stop him, but he wouldn't listen

to me. Knocked me down out there so I couldn't hold on to him. I'm

real sorry miss." He said crying and rocking his brother.

"Take em out" Ben ordered. *"You can take your brother or*

bury him here son." Ben said kindly. *"I've nowhere to go sir, Jack*

was all I had, I'd like to bury him here if that's ok." Ben nodded

and brothers were taken out. *"We'll go for the Sheriff tomorrow.*

You can explain it to him. Find him a bed for the night boys." The

hands nodded and helped the young man out. The boys

knew better than to leave him alone. Elizabeth rose from her

position. *"Ben please."* Elizabeth sounded like she was on the

verge of crying, *"Red Wolf he needs help."* White Dove rushed

forward and helped Red Wolf to the bed. *"Does he need the*

doctor? Do you?" Ben asked. *"I'm fine. Red Wolf saved me. He needs a doctor quickly."* White Dove looked at her and answered her husband. *"No Ben, its deep but it can be cleaned and stitched."* Elizabeth looked at her like she was mad, no doctor! *"But we should not move him."* Elizabeth was wringing her hands. *"White Dove, he needs a Dr please, Red Wolf can stay here, I'll go."* Elizabeth offered. *"You should go with Ben."* White Dove told her. Elizabeth looked at her like she was insane. *"Elizabeth come down with me, White Dove can do this, I need to make a report for the Sheriff. Red Wolf will be just fine."* Ben practically dragged her out of the room while Elizabeth continued to protest.

Down stairs Ben made Elizabeth sit and take a brandy. She was clearly in shock and agitated by what had happened and emotionally drained. This time Ben got the full story, and it clearly shocked him. All the while, Elizabeth kept looking up the stairs, wringing her hands, watching the staff come and go. Eventually White Dove came down, Ben went to her and kissed her. She gathered that Elizabeth had told him everything. And smiled up at the husband. *"How is he."* Elizabeth asked. *"He's a warrior and reminded me more than once. He will have stitches for a while and he shouldn't move too much for a day or two."* White Dove said the last bit directly at her husband who nodded his agreement. *"I'll send word to Dull Knife and get the Dr to stop by."* Elizabeth went to get up, and White Dove spoke gently to her. *"Esa, I love you like my sister, as I do Red Wolf a brother. Forgive me but I need to say something. You have been gone a long time. Things change. People change. What you knew as a child. Is not who or what you are as an adult. The choices and decisions we make have far reaching effects. You know how hard it has been for Ben and I. We choose not to live in that world because we would not be accepted. We are only now, because the Double T pays for the town. It would not be any easier for you and Red Wolf or your children."* Elizabeth was visible shocked by White Doves outburst. She slumped back down in the chair and stared at her, open mouthed.

Incredulously, Elizabeth shook her head. *"White Dove, I love Red Wolf but he's my brother."* White Dove nodded. *"Yes he is, but I fear, your heart and both your actions are saying something else."* Elizabeth couldn't believe what she was hearing. *"Honey use the guest quarters for the next few days."* Ben told her as he bent and kissed her. *"Ben, is that what you think, that my behaviour is questionable?"* *"I think, both you and Red Wolf need to know your own minds."* He put his arm around his wife's shoulders. *"Good night Esa."* Elizabeth looked up. They were the closest thing she had to family. *"Good night White Dove and thank you."* Elizabeth felt an overwhelmingly feeling of sadness. Elizabeth got out her chair and walked to the fire place. She banked it up and decided she couldn't face bed right now, it was the last place she wanted to be. Her mind to alive to switch off. White Dove's words going around in her head. How could she think that. Elizabeth asked herself. Shaking her head. Returning to her chair, she remembered what Running Elk had said to her on parting from the village. Was everyone going mad she thought. Elizabeth leaned back in the chair and closed her eyes. *"I can't think about all this."* Red Wolf and their children? *"My god, children?"* Had the world gone mad? She'd only just got home. It was too much to take in. Even as she said it, part of her soul came alive. Ignoring it. Elizabeth blew out a breath. *"How can Red Wolf think of her as anything other than his sister?"* She reminded herself. After all, he barely talks to her. He protects her. Watches over her, just as he did when they were children. She shook her head. They have it wrong, he had protected her and she had worried over him. We care for each other as family do, nothing more.

Elizabeth took a huge slog of her brandy. She choked a little on it. Ok that was not a good idea. It warmed her and the sensation spread throughout her body and clashed with the fire already burning within. She closed her eyes and thought about the last couple of days. Thought about Red

Wolf. Every memory she had of the Indians since her parents

died contained him and since she'd come back. He'd been

there every time she needed him. *"Doesn't make any sense."*

She said aloud. Shaking her head again. Then she thought

about the events of the night, and took another slog of brandy

and felt the familiar warming. *"Dear god, she said, he could have*

died." And at that moment it hit home. She did not want to

lose him. He was a part of her life. Just how emotionally

insecure that made her was telling. Tired of being rational

and a little merry from the brandy, Elizabeth found herself

dozing off. She awoke sometime later. The fire just embers.

The house quiet in the lamp light. Elizabeth was stiff from

sleeping awkwardly. For a second on waking she wondered

where she was. Taking in the room it all came back quickly.

Just how long had she been sitting there she thought. She

looked around her. Registered the fire had died down and the

embers just glowing. It was now the only light in the room.

Someone had come in and turned down all the lights but not woken her. Elizabeth had a blanket across her. Elizabeth removed the blanket and stretched. She ached everywhere. Getting up she crossed the room and climbed the stairs. Without thinking. She walked to her room and let herself in. Red Wolf opened his eyes as she came in. He was propped up in her bed. She had seen him naked from the waste up many times in the Indian way. But somehow in her bed. He looked …more. Gazing at him, her mouth went dry. Her breath caught in her throat. Elizabeth realised her mistake the moment she'd walked in and tried to retreat.

"Don't." He called out as she'd turned to leave he spoke to her softly. Elizabeth was unsure of what to say. *"I should let you sleep, are you in much pain?"* She couldn't help but ask. Red Wolf smiled grimly. *"The warrior says no, the man says yes."* Elizabeth broke into a spontaneous natural smile. It lit up her face and pain or no pain, Red Wolf could not

ignore his feelings for this woman. She was no longer the child he knew. *"Come sit by me."* He asked. *"Sleep comes hard, distract me and it might creep up on me."* He told her trying to keep the conversation light. Red Wolf winched as he tried to move to make room for her. *"I'm not sure that's a good idea."* Elizabeth moved instinctively nearer the bed. *"Don't, you'll make it worse, I'm so sorry, your injured because of me."* He stared at her. *"I'm alive because of you."* *"I'm not sure that's true"* she said quietly. *"If you hadn't been here?"* *"He may have killed you."* He finished. Elizabeth looked up at him. *"Please - sit by me."* Elizabeth couldn't ignore his plea and sat on the edge of the bed. She sighed. *"It's hard to believe I've only been home for 2 days."* Elizabeth said swallowing hard. *"Yes, it is."* Red Wolf answered. He lifted his hand and covered hers. There was no pressure, no squeeze, no demand or expectation, the touch was enough. Elizabeth looked at both their hands. His so large and dark. Hers small and so light in colour having lost its childhood colouring from the sun. But she knew the sun would change that now she was back. He was waiting and she knew it.

Elizabeth deliberately and slowly changed the angle of her hand and turned it over under his as she had done many times as a child. He opened his fingers and she slipped hers through. They both closed them together. *"Look at me."* He asked. Elizabeth raised her eyes and thought the brandy earlier was playing games with her stomach. The fire in her soul sprang into life. Elizabeth had to admit. He didn't look at all brotherly right now. In fact, he looked, Elizabeth couldn't quite express it and thought she was sitting all too close and looked away. *"Do I scare you Elizabeth?"* He asked her. *"Scare me, of course not, why would you ask such a thing?"* *"You look - nervous."* He said mischievously. *"For someone who hasn't said two words to me for over 2 days, you're doing a lot of talking."* She told him. Red Wolf smiled and leaned back against the head board. Elizabeth was trying to change the subject. *"Besides, I should let you get some sleep, it will be dawn soon."* Elizabeth unhooked their hands. Rose and went to the window. The morning chorus had started. She was reluctant to leave and leaned on the windowsill and sighed. And in doing so, realised she cannot stay there any longer. She turned to walk to the door. *"Esa?"* Elizabeth turned her head back towards him. *"Yes?"* Red Wolf looked at her long and hard, there was a clear hunger in his eyes. It was impossible for her to miss it. Elizabeth swallowed. Her fire continued to burn. *"You are not my sister."* He said quietly. Elizabeth stared at him. It wasn't easy for her to acknowledge what that meant. Finally, she had to be honest with herself, as well as with him. *"We share a father."* She said. *"But no, you are not my brother."* And she walked through the door and closed it behind her.

Elizabeth went to her guest room, undressed and got into bed. She slept the whole next day. When she eventually woke up it was to find it was nearly dinner time. Elizabeth quickly rose and got out of bed. She was famished. She washed and dressed quickly. Left her room and hesitated on the landing by her bedroom door. She didn't go in. But headed down to the bathroom. It had the luxury of inside plumbing for a toilet and bath.

Elizabeth headed to the kitchen, where all the activity was going on. The wonderful aroma made her feel like she was starving. *"Morning."* She called out, the staff and White Dove turned amused. *"Well good evening Esa."* White Dove answered. Elizabeth felt a bit embarrassed. *"Urr yes sorry. The journey and everything must have caught up with me, how can I help."* White Dove smiled. *"We have it all in hand, but if you wish, you could lay the table with Ellen."* Elizabeth went into the lounge and there was Ellen. Joe's daughter was laying the table. *"Hi Ellen, let me help you."* Elizabeth worked quietly alongside Ellen, only asking after her family and chatting about school. White Dove came into the lounge and called to her. *"Esa, would you take a tray to Red Wolf?"* Elizabeth wanted to say yes, but found that she could not. White Dove saw her struggle. *"Oh I just remembered, I need to take something up, so I can do it myself."* Elizabeth sighed with relief that only White Dove could see. And mouthed the words 'Thank you.'

Elizabeth turned and walked towards Ben as he came in the door along with others there for dinner. *"Well."* He said. *"About time you got up."* He told her smiling as he crossed to kiss his niece. *"How you feeling love?"* *"I'm just fine Ben, thank you."* She gave him a hug. *"I've sent a report to the Sheriff, he sent a note back to say he'll be out in a day or two. The Doctor will be out tomorrow too."* Elizabeth nodded placing her head on his shoulders as she walked with him back into the dining room. *"What happened to the younger brother Ben?"* Elizabeth asked him. *"Billy? He's ok. Good lad I think just been led wrong by his brother. I've offered him a job if that's ok with you.*

He didn't mean you any harm and I feel we could do something to help the boy. He's nothing and no one now." Elizabeth nodded. *"That's all right by me." "Good, where's White Dove?"* Elizabeth explained that she was taking a tray to Red Wolf. Ben nodded *"Well let's eat."* And dinner was served.

The conversation as expected was around the events of the previous evening. Elizabeth did not want to be drawn on the subject. Particularly the part where she had actually shot someone. Elizabeth struggled with having taken a life. She couldn't get her head around that or the fact that Red Wolf had been injured. Sensing her unease, those around the table left her alone. Although she hadn't eaten all day and been starving when she woke, Elizabeth suddenly felt she wasn't particularly hungry after all and picked at her food. So many thoughts and images of the past 3 days came to mind and not for the first time, did Elizabeth think, that maybe she could have done something differently. Those thoughts continued after dinner and into the night. Elizabeth must have drifted in and out of the conversation. She didn't notice when several family friends said good night. It was only as Ben was turning down the lights that Elizabeth realised how late it was. *"Sorry Ben, I've not been much company tonight."* *"That's ok, it's been a tough home coming girl. By the way, those two new hands you sent over from Brownsville, look like they'll work out just fine."* Elizabeth smiled. *"Oh, good I wasn't sure they'd come."* Elizabeth replied. *"Well they did and look ok".* Elizabeth nodded. *"Goodnight honey, don't stay up too long."* Ben bent to kiss her. *"I won't."* White Dove then bent down to kiss her goodnight as well. As she did she whispered squeezing her hand. *"He would like to see you."* Elizabeth looked at her and acknowledged her. No more words needed. They left her.

Elizabeth couldn't bring herself to go up just yet. All that extra sleep she guessed. Instead Elizabeth went for a walk outside. The breeze was cool and welcoming. She strolled the veranda running her hands over the bannister, then crossed the yard to the corral. Her pony came to her. *"Hay Patches."* She said and rubbed his nose and his whinnied at her. *"He likes you."* Elizabeth turned to see the new hand, sitting against some straw. She'd hadn't seen him as she'd walked passed. *"I should hope so, or my next ride could be a tough one."* Elizabeth said as she turned back to the Pony. *"How's your brother doing?"* He asked. *"Luckily he'll live."* She replied stroking and whispering to Patches. *"Billy, the boys brother, he's a good kid. I've been working with him all day. I don't think you have anything to fear from him."* He offered. Elizabeth turned and for the first time actually looked at him. For him, it was an unsettling experience. She took no prisoners, and took his measure in no time. *"I'm sorry, I forget your name."* She said apologetically. *"I'm Carl, my friends Buddy."* *"Oh yes Buddy I remember now."* And added. *"Thank you for your thoughts on Billy, my Uncle has already discussed it with me, but it's reassuring to hear it from one of the hands too."* Carl thought it unusual for an owner to care much about what a hand thought. It was nice to be thanked. *"Not a problem mam."* Carl replied. Elizabeth patted Patches once more. *"Well, goodnight Carl I hope you like it here."* She told him and headed for the house.

Carl watched her leave. Every time he saw her, she surprised him. Elizabeth entered the house to find Ben waiting for her. *"Everything alright?"* He asked. *"Yes sorry, I did not mean to keep you up."* She told him. *"You didn't."* He said. *"I thought I should came and talk about what you are going to do around here, considering everything, I think you should take an active role sooner rather than later, what do you think?"* Elizabeth smiled. *"I'd like that, could you put something together for me for tomorrow and perhaps we could take it from there."* Elizabeth answered. *"Sounds like a plan."* Ben said. *"Sleep well, you've got an early start."* *"I will and thanks Ben."* Ben turned and walked up stairs, Elizabeth watched him go and considered he was right. Elizabeth picked up the last few glasses left about and went into the kitchen. Putting the glasses on the side, she ran the tap and got a fresh glass and filled it with water. Suddenly hungry, Elizabeth went to the cold store and decided to make a sandwich. She then remembered that White Dove had said to check in with Red Wolf. And made two. She threw away the water and filled two glasses with milk. She smiled. If felt a bit like old times.

Not once did she consider that Red Wolf would be asleep and not be awake for her. She climbed the stairs and balanced the tray on the hall stand. Opened the door and peeped in. He was sitting up in bed reading a book. Another surprise. Looking like a small boy with a new toy. Elizabeth smiled. *"Hello, want some company?"* She asked. Red Wolf dropped the book and looked at her. *"I thought you weren't coming?"* *"Sorry, I got distracted and went out to Patches."* She replied. *"Yes I saw you."* Elizabeth hid her surprise. What was he doing out of bed. *"Hungry?"* She asked him and popped

her head back out the door and came back in with the tray and

a huge grin on her face. Red Wolf laughed softly. He couldn't

remember the last 'pic nic' he'd had and in bed too! Elizabeth

put the tray on her writing desk. And put the napkin around

his chin and the glass of milk on the night stand, along with

hers. Sitting on the edge of the bed, she looked at him and

suddenly laughed. *"You look more like a small child than a brave*

fearless warrior." "O Really?" He joined in. Grabbing her

waist and lifting her bodily from her sitting position across the

bed to a prone one on the other side of him in one easy

movement and held her fast. The effort clearly cost him dear

and he winced. *"What about now?"* He said. Elizabeth had

squalled with laughter and gave mock horror. As he did so.

Elizabeth was laughing so innocently that she failed to notice

the instinctive change in him, the way he looked at her, his

weight upon her. She gazed up at him and realised he was

pinning her down and had gone very quite. The child had gone. The warrior was back.

Red Wolf let go of her hands, shifted his weight and looked away from her. *"You should get up."* He said gruffly. Elizabeth lifted her right hand and drew his face back to her. *"Do I scare you warrior."* She asked mimicking him from earlier. Red Wolf stared at her. *"Yes and I scare myself. Get up."* Red Wolf rolled back and pushed himself up on his pillows. He hurt. Not just physically. Elizabeth got off the bed and walked around to the tray. Picking up one of the sandwiches she passed it to him. They ate in silence till almost finished. Elizabeth looked up. *"White Dove spoke to me yesterday and said some strange things. She also mentioned that I was not treating you like my brother."* Red Wolf nodded between bites. *"She spoke to me too. Reminded me that I should treat you like my sister."* Elizabeth looked back at her sandwich and put it down. Getting up and passed Red Wolf his milk.

He took it. *"I'm sorry."* She said walking to the window. *"This is all my fault. I don't know how this happened. Maybe I should have stayed back East. It's funny, the last couple of years all I could think about was coming home, being here and how right that made my life feel. Now, it feels like things seemed an awful lot easier back there."* She told him. Elizabeth turned from the window and looked at him. Red Wolf stared at her. She couldn't move. She felt like a dove caught in a trap. *"How would that have made things easier. If you had not come home. I would have coming looking for you. You're in my blood Esa, you always have been since the first day I saw you. I was only half alive the years you were away."* He told her.

A man had never spoken more movingly to her. Elizabeth was unsure how to respond. *"It's getting late, you should sleep. I have a date with Ben first thing in the morning. I'm to take on some of the responsibility of this place."* She told him. *"Good you need to."* Elizabeth walked to the door and opened it. *"Sleep well."* She told him as she opened the door before she could say something that would difficult to take back. Red Wolf watched her walk through it. Before she closed the door behind her Red Wolf called out. It wasn't easy to let her go. *"Esa, I need to know. What do you want to do?"* They both knew he wasn't talking about the ranch. *"I.... don't know, I just need some time."* Her words a sad reminder that nothing was settled.

Elizabeth had to be up in 5 hours and headed for the guest room. Red Wolf would be in her room for the next week. It will be nice to sleep in her own room again she thought. Surprised just how much she missed it already, although she'd only been back a few days. The down side she realised, would be that Red Wolf will be gone. Elizabeth couldn't think about that. It was too difficult to deal with and sooner or later, she would have to answer him. Elizabeth opened her door and got ready for bed. Sleep came easy and before she knew it White Dove was waking her. *"Esa, time to get up."* Elizabeth got out of bed washed, dressed and went down stairs and did her business. Ben was sitting at the table having breakfast giving instructions to the lead hands who joined him. Elizabeth greeted them and sat down. Watched and listened. It set the pattern for the next week. Elizabeth rose early. As her body clock clicked in. Got herself up, washed and dressed and downstairs for breakfast in time to listen to Ben give instructions. She followed where he sent her and in the evenings, they discussed the stock and the land and made plans for the coming day. Ranch life was hard. It was rare to have visitors and Elizabeth was glad of it. She remained away from Red Wolf. Stopping nightly at his door, or rather her door. To wish him good night and leaving quickly. She knew she was avoiding him and putting off the inevitable, but she could not help it.

On the fifth day of Red Wolfs convalesce, the Dr came back to check him. *"Well young man that wound is mending well enough. You can start getting up tomorrow"*. *"Thanks Doc that's great."* *"Not too much mind ok or you'll put the stitches and have to start again."* He told him. To Red Wolf this was great news, he could not stay in this room much longer. Next morning, to Elizabeth's surprise Red Wolf came in from the yard and joined them. *"Feeling better?"* She asked. Red Wolf looked at her and nodded and sat down. 'So', thought Elizabeth. Back to not talking. Maybe that was better. *"Elizabeth, I think it would be a good idea if you work on the West section. There's some fencing to be done there can you check it out and some herding, the horses need to come in"*. *"Red Wolf I want you to take it easy, take the South bring the horses through the West section pick up Elizabeth's and bring them all in, no heroics and don't overdo it."* Red Wolf nodded got up and left. *"Elizabeth you ok with that?"* *"Sounds fine."* She told him. Elizabeth got up pecked him on the cheek and walked out the door, while grabbing her hat and gloves. Her men were waiting for her. 'God I love this' she thought as she acknowledged Black Dog who passed her her reins. She mounted and noticed that one of the hands with her was Carl, she nodded to him and rode out.

They rode for a good couple of hours till they found the fencing that needed fixing, Elizabeth split the men in two parties, half went to round up the herd including Carl, the other half fixed the fence. Elizabeth went with the herders. It had been easier than she had expected. At first, she had worried that the men wouldn't listen to her. The Indians were her men and the hands respected her. She guessed that at the end of the day, she was the boss. The day moved quickly, the herd was nearly in when Black Dog came looking for her. *"Esa, we need go now get horses."* *"Ok how many men do we need?"* Elizabeth asked him. *"Three maybe four."* *"Pick three. I'll come with you."* Black Dog looked at her nodded and left.

Black Dog came back with three men. To her surprise one was Carl. Elizabeth gave instructions to the other hands on moving the herd down once the fencing was completed. They rode up into the high country. After a while, Carl moved up and rode beside her. They rode in silence then curiosity got the better of Elizabeth and she had ask. *"Tell me Carl, how did Black Dog happen to pick you and not another brave?"* *"I kinda volunteered mam."* He answered. *"Volunteered Carl?"* She questioned. *"Yeah, I saw what was happening and guessed we'd have to move to get the horses and it was obvious you'd sent him to sort it out. So I went up to him and said I should come along."* *"I see."* Said Elizabeth. *"And why would you do that Carl?"* *"Well the best view is right here mam."* Elizabeth turned to stare at him. *"Are you being fresh Mr Steiner?"* Carl smiled. *"Sure hope so mam."* Turning he headed back behind Black Dog. Elizabeth was both surprised and amused.

They found the horses, rounded them up, pulled in the stragglers and headed down. Elizabeth felt she'd never rode so hard, cutting in and out of the herd, herding them together in the right direction. It was half way down when the rain started. Slowly at first, fine as it often was, getting heavier the longer it remained. The Indians didn't use wet clothes and Elizabeth decided not to stop to put on hers. She noticed Carl didn't bother either. By the time they'd got the horses back, everything and everyone was soaked. Elizabeth rode in to the meeting point soaked to the skin, she was a sight. Red Wolf was waiting for her. Elizabeth indicated to the men to take the horses over. Carl came to her he was concerned. *"Mam, you'll excuse me for saying, but you need to get out of those clothes and fast." "I'm fine Carl, we need to get this job done."* Just as she said it Elizabeth made a fundamental mistake. She was more tired than she thought. Her reins were loose and lightning struck in the hills. Her pony became skittish. Carl put out his hand and held her. *"The jobs over mam, the men can push the* herds down." At that moment Red Wolf who had been watching the exchange, came up, he looked tired and strained and was clearly in some pain. *"Esa, I'm joining the herds and sending them down with Black Dog, the fencing is done, we're going home." "She needs to rest."* Carl said, Red Wolf stared at him. *"And she's wet through, she needs to dry off."* Carl told him.

Red Wolf looked at Elizabeth and registered her condition. *"Your job is the herds. Not my woman."* He told him. Carl wasn't sure he'd heard right, it didn't sound much like a sisterly thing he was hearing. But he nodded and rode over to the other hands and started to muster. *"That was rude and uncalled for."* Elizabeth complained suddenly struggling to remain in her seat. Red Wolf gave instructions to the hands and decided to ride on with Elizabeth. They would make it in half the time and she did look exhausted. But before going, he rode them over to the side of an enclave. Stopping by some sheltered rocks and with some difficulty got down off his

horse. *"Get down, take your clothes off and put on these."* He said
to her. Elizabeth just stared at him. *"Take them off?"* She
squeaked. *"Yes."* Red Wolf got a blanket and Elizabeth got
down. He put it around her and turned his back. Elizabeth
removed all her outer clothing and asked for the others. *"No,
take it all off or there's no point, I cannot warm you here in the open,
this is all we've got."* He told her. *"I can't. It wouldn't be right."*
Red Wolf gritted his teeth. *"Esa, this is your doing, now take
them off or I'll do it for you."* He was clearly angry and meant
every word.

Elizabeth was embarrassed. She knew this country.
Knew how the weather could be and she'd ignored it and
placed herself in this position. She removed the remaining
clothes from inside the blanket. Red Wolf passed her the fresh
clothes. She put them on. As he removed the blanket he
passed her the wet weather clothes and helped her put those
on too. Taking her head in his hands he held her. *"Don't ever*

136

ride in the rain without it again. It can kill you." He told her. *"Now let's get back."* He helped her mount, and in some pain remounted himself and they rode for the ranch house. By the time they arrived, Elizabeth was cold, very cold. Red Wolf helped her down and into the house. White Dove was sent to run a bath and blankets came from the store. Red Wolf rubbed Elizabeth warm. Gave her a slog of brandy and White Dove called to say the bath was ready. Red Wolf helped her into the bathroom. He started to remove her clothes. Elizabeth knew she should protest. But she was past caring. White Dove entered the bathroom, just in time. Spoke to Red Wolf and took over, he left. Elizabeth stayed in the bath for what must have been a good hour. The staff changed the water keeping it hot. They even fed her in there. By the time she was desperate to get out, the herds were in and the hands were back. Her temperature was good and White Dove agreed to let her get out and get dressed. As she was coming out the bathroom door, Elizabeth heard Carl at the front door, he was talking to Ben. *"I was just concerned sir, she was worn out and about done, I hope I didn't over step the mark." "That kind of over stepping is just fine Carl, I appreciate that kind of thinking."* Ben offered his hand and Carl took it. Carl turned to walk to the bunk house. Ben had second thoughts. *"Carl join us for dinner."* Carl turned *"Thank you sir. I'd like that."* He told him. *"Good it's at 7"*.

Elizabeth thought it was nice that Ben had asked Carl to dinner. Not many were coming tonight which was good, it had been a hard day. Elizabeth decided to take a nap before dinner, she wrapped herself up and laid down. She must have fallen asleep, White Dove woke her. *"Dinner, do you want to come down?" "Thank you, yes I'm starving." "Good"* White Dove said. *"Hurry"*. As White Dove left her, Elizabeth changed her clothes, brushed her hair and came down.

Elizabeth realised she was late. She could pick out already here were Ben, Carl and neighbours Mr and Mrs McKenna. Elizabeth hurried down the stairs. As she entered the room Carl stood. This gesture was not lost on Red Wolf who came in the front door at the same time and sat straight down. Elizabeth acknowledged Carl standing for her and smiled. *"Carl please sit down, we don't do that here."* She walked over to Ben and kissed him. *"Good evening everyone."* A chorus of good evenings followed. Elizabeth indicated that Carl should sit again and Red Wolf gave an impatient stare. Carl was sitting opposite Elizabeth. Red Wolf had his usual seat at the end of the table. Dinner was light and fun. Elizabeth had plenty to say, and was enjoying herself catching up with her neighbours. The conversation came around to the round up today. Elizabeth felt she should leave the conversation to the men and choose to say nothing. She was a little embarrassed about the way she'd came back. *"If you don't mind me saying sir, Ms Elizabeth worked real hard today. It's a lot for a lady."* Carl said. Ben was about to answer when Red Wolf beat him to it. *"It's our land. She'll need to do a lot to keep it!"* *"We all will."* Ben added to the whole table. *"This life is hard and Elizabeth has a large heritage to keep going, many people depend on it and it was her parents wish that she knows every stick and every blade of grass. In the end, she will need to know first-hand what it takes to run the Double T."* *"And both my fathers would expect nothing less."* Elizabeth said joining in. *"More importantly, I want to know, so that's settled."* Ben laughed. *"And no more ignoring the weather".* She told them. *"Rightly so."*

After dinner they naturally moved into the sitting room. It was clear that Red Wolf was eager to go. He spoke to Ben and Elizabeth. Outlining the plans for tomorrow. It was agreed that Elizabeth would ride over the North ridge and check out the watering holes. Red Wolf was going back to the village tonight see his father. Ben decided to let Elizabeth give out the mornings orders and helped her to format them. Carl had been watching the family work together. Then Red Wolf took his leave. Elizabeth touched his arm as he turned to go, what passed between them could not be heard.

Carl took a walk outside. It was a lovely evening. Red Wolf walked right passed him shortly followed by Elizabeth. She stared after him for some time. Elizabeth eventually turned and noticed that Carl was sitting behind her. *"Nice evening."* Carl said. Elizabeth smiled. *"Yes, it is isn't it.".* Elizabeth walked over and sat next to him. Carl pointed in Red Wolf direction. *"He didn't look too happy."* *"No."* She sighed. *"He's not".* *"I don't think I helped in there. Sorry if I put my foot in it."* Carl said. *"You didn't. I shouldn't worry about that, he wasn't going to be happy no matter what."* Elizabeth replied with a sigh. *"Want to talk about it?"* Carl asked. Elizabeth laughed. *"I don't think that will help and its far too complicated to even get into, but thank you, good night Carl."*

Elizabeth got up to go inside. *"You know the thing about love, is that the heart wants what the heart wants Elizabeth, you cannot change that."* He'd never used her first name before and he wasn't sure why he said it but he liked the sound of her name on his lips very much. *"And I'm not sure I'd want to."* Was all he heard her say, as she climbed the stairs back into the house. Carls heart sunk.

Red Wolf was angry. He'd checked the horses twice, trying to calm down. 'Can't she see.' He thought. 'She's a target for every roving man for miles, they would all love to have the Double T, she had to be careful who she let in.' He'd tried telling her, but it came out wrong and she'd got annoyed too. He was jealous, he knew that and couldn't help himself, Elizabeth had said as much and he'd acted stupid and stormed off. Things were getting out of control he told himself. He felt out of control. He would have to talk to Elizabeth. Now, before it's too late. Red Wolf passed Carl without an acknowledgement and went inside. Carl knew there was no point in saying anything. It wasn't his place.

Red Wolf ran up the stairs to the house. Entered and charged the stairs two at a time and entered Elizabeth's room. Elizabeth was sitting at her desk. She turned as he came in and stood to face him. *"I can't help what upsets you. I acted stupid today and I'm sorry."* She said calmly and quietly. Red Wolf's anger evaporated. She spoke on. *"This is the life we have. I cannot change that either. You've said you do not want me to leave and I don't want to. Then we must decide and now. How can we make this work?"* She asked him. Red Wolf walked towards her. *"I can't do this Elizabeth. Being around you is too difficult. I'll leave the ranch and go back to the village. Ben can manage without me it will be summer soon. I'll come back for the Harvest and we can see what happens then."* He said, but as he spoke, deep down, Red Wolf was hoping she would reject his offer and tell him to stay. Elizabeth smiled and looked at him,

"You say you can't do without me but you are going to leave me anyway." She spoke sadly. Red Wolf raised his hand and touched her face, he traced the line of her cheek with his fingertips. *"If you ask me to stay I will. If I stay, this, as it is now, would never be enough Elizabeth."* Both stood their ground knowing to give way would undo all their good intentions.

"The summers a long time." She whispered. Reaching up to touch his hand. Red Wolf smiled. *"I will always be with you."* He told her. *"This land is as much mine, as it is yours, no journey you take, will be without my knowledge or protection."* He reassured her. Dropping his hand he backed away towards her door. *"I'll speak to Ben tonight and say that I am returning to the village but I will be staying there for a while."* Without knowing it, Elizabeth was silently crying. *"Don't leave me."* She whispered to him. Red Wolf stood in the doorway with his back to her. He fought not to go to her or say the words his heart demanded. He dare not turn around. *"Never."* He

said emotionally and closed the door behind him. Elizabeth burst into tears. She could not control them. What was wrong with her. In the morning she knew he would be long gone.

The days that followed, took on a pattern of their own. Elizabeth withdrew. Became a robot. She would rise before dawn. Take her orders from Ben and move out with her men. The days were long and hard. Over the next 4 weeks into summer, Elizabeth spent more time in Black Dog and Carls company than she did with Ben and White Dove. Elizabeth just went through the motions. The joy in being home diminished. She lost weight, her body changed with the physical demands of the work she put herself through. She became more defined. Lost the puppy fat she had been carrying and the sun tanned her skin. She no longer made small talk. She lost much of her laughter and free spirit. Now, she was all business. Carl felt the change as did all of them. It had been commented on by some of the lesser hands, that it coincided with Red Wolf leaving. To those who did not understand as Carl did, it seemed like a minor family rift.

CHAPTER FIVE

Summer

1879

Carl started a system of his own. He would rise before the others. Check the horses. Seek out Ben and check the day's work. He would confirm that he would ride with Elizabeth and Ben would ask that he kept his eye on her. Carl was always happy to oblige. Carl would help pack the horses for the day. Including Elizabeth's. By the time she came down as dawn was on the horizon. Carl was sitting ready for the day ahead. Elizabeth barely noticed. Expecting things to be ready for her and they were. She didn't speak to anyone. Carried water and some biscuits with her from a bag left on the dining table and walked to her horse. The only real communication was with Patches.

The weeks rolled past. Summer came early that year just as calving had ended. Ben kept the working groups as they had been in the Spring. Carl remained with Elizabeth and her braves and they worked herding the steers and cows down for branding. Cook outs were the order of the day, as it was impossible to cover such ground and return to the ranch each night. Elizabeth and Carl got into a routine of securing a base camp and spending several days out at a time. The braves would hunt along with the day. Carl would cook and try to show Elizabeth. Much to her amusement of the braves, they knew Elizabeth could not cook. Had been poor at it as a child. Elizabeth eventually, unknowingly, found herself becoming comfortable in Carls quiet company. He knew often what she was thinking before it was said, and if he disagreed with her, he said so and she came to listen to him. Black Dog had also come to respect Carl. He would give orders and they took them without question. If they had a problem, they would discuss it with him. Elizabeth would always return home from such a trip, feeling that even if her life were in turmoil. At least it was a job she did well.

It had been 4 long, hard months since Red Wolf had left her. The only break from the routine was the occasional trip to town or Vera's visits with her new acquisitions. Elizabeth enjoyed her company and they became firm friends.

This particular morning Elizabeth had risen early. She hadn't slept well since Red Wolf had left her. Images from her dreams disturbed her. There was nothing she could put her finger on but it had prevented her from sleeping well. Elizabeth tossed restlessly. Giving up. Well before dawn. She dressed and headed down stairs. As she did so, she spoke to Anna and the house staff just arriving for breakfast preparations and went outside. Elizabeth found a spot on the porch swing and sat in darkness. The sun would be up soon. Elizabeth felt herself wake up with the new day. She felt lighter. Freer. Gazing around the yard. Elizabeth noticed

men walking around by lamplight. She noticed Carl, across

the yard, surprised to see him up so early. Tending the

horses and going about his routine. She realised he had a

commanding manner about him. She watched as he gave

orders to a couple of the ranch staff. It did not escape her

notice that Ben spoke to him and listened to what he had to

say or that Carl saw to her pony himself and spoke to Black

Dog who responded in a mutually respected way. Why was

he seeing to her pony? Either Carl didn't trust Black Dog or

the other hands with her horse, which would seem impossible

or he welcomed the chance to do this for her himself.

Elizabeth stared at him. He was a good man and although she

knew very little about him. Elizabeth felt him to be honest

and a kind man. Even Black Dog seemed to respect him.

Elizabeth frowned. He hadn't been here long. Was he trying

to take over?

Carl had the feeling he was being watched, he turned and looked straight at her. She was sitting on the porch in the glow from the house. It was obvious she had been watching him for some time. Carl was a little embarrassed to be found out, he finished up and walked over to her. *"Mam."* He said donning his hat. *"Can I get you something?"* Elizabeth stared. *"It would seem Carl, that you are doing enough for me already."* Elizabeth said with a smile. *"My pony is Black Dog's job. Will he not be annoyed with you?"* She asked. Carl cleared his throat. *"Err actually mam, I offered some time ago and he kinda left me to it."* Now it was Elizabeth's turn to be surprised. *"Really, did he now."* She asked thoughtfully. *"If you don't mind me saying, it's nice to see you up and in good spirits, it's been awhile."* Carl continued. Elizabeth looked at him and saw the twinkle in his eye, he was baiting her. *"Carl it is unwise to upset the boss."* *"Oh I know that mam, she's deadly with the bullwhip."* He teased. Elizabeth burst out laughing and slapped her thighs. For the first time in months she felt alive. At the same time the breakfast call rang out. *"Come join us."* She waved at him and he followed her in.

Ben watched as Elizabeth came in with Carls. But said nothing. Breakfast continued as it had on every other occasion. It was loud. Before leaving Carl checked with Ben for the day's activities and went outside. For the first-time Elizabeth noticed that the braves acknowledged Carl and his words and only the Foreman sort confirmation from either Ben or her. That knowledge was more unsettling to her. That would have been Red Wolf's role. The realisation annoyed Elizabeth. What was he doing. Without waiting, she mounted and rode out with her braves. Carl was not with her, he had not been ready. Too busy being the big man Elizabeth told herself. The passed in rounding up cattle and contemplating her annoyance from earlier. The last thing she wanted to do was confront her poor behaviour. Elizabeth sighed. What was wrong with her. That was rude and uncalled for. Not wanting to return to the Double T she gave instructions that they would camp out. Black Dog sent a brave on ahead to let Ben know what was going on. When the brave came back, it was dark, food was cooking and the camp laid out. With him came Carl, with enough food and water for another day. He was not happy. He dismounted and walked straight over to Elizabeth. And dropped his gear in an obvious gesture of anger and stood waiting for her to explain.

She tried to ignore him but he stood his ground. She turned and looked up at him, his annoyance very clear, as was her poor behaviour. Shamefaced she spoke to him. *"I should have waited, I apologise."* Carl stared at her and nodded, walked away and made his own bed for the night on the other side of the fire. Black Dog passed her her food. It was hot and good and the conversation was light and mainly Indian. Elizabeth loved the night sky. When it was like this, clear and bright. Some didn't like it because it would mean a cold night ahead. Elizabeth felt it was worth it for the view. You could see for miles. Black Dog arranged the braves who took turns in guarding her. Carl was not asked. And Elizabeth found slept easy.

Carl woke her with coffee the next morning, bacon. biscuits and beans. He had cooked. Elizabeth looked sleepy and childlike. Her hair had come loose of its plait and strands had stuck to her face. As Carl bent down to give her her food, he instinctively reached out and removed the strands away from her face. It was an intimacy she wasn't expecting. She looked at him, a little confused. *"Umm thank you."* She told him taking the plate. *"For the food"* She finished. Carl grinned. *"No problem mam."* And went back to dishing up for everyone. Elizabeth watched from her bedroll. Carl got on well with the braves and she was another surprise to her. He had also learnt some sign language. Elizabeth frown. What was he trying to do?. That was something else that seemed to bother her. Her annoyance flared again. Elizabeth ate briskly. Washed up and got ready for the day. As she was saddling Patches, Carl came to her. *"Elizabeth, Ben asked if we could follow the herd down the northern boundary and check for loses."* "Ok, sounds good." Elizabeth called to Black Dog and explained the orders. They mounted and started to move out.

Again Carl had used her given name. This too unsettled her. Elizabeth decided then and there that it was going to be all business from now on. She rode hard and they reached the herd early. The morning was spent checking and herding the stock and by lunch, Carl was offering biscuits and fruit to eat. Elizabeth didn't like the feeling this gave her. She signalled Black Dog. He approached and she signed for the push for home. He nodded his agreement and turned to inform the braves. Carl watched from his horse. It was clear what was happening but no one told him. At the last moment, Black Dog realised that Elizabeth was not going to talk to Carl and they would need his help. Riding over, Black

Dog signed for Carl. He nodded and turned to ride. Black

Dog not a particularly patient man rode to Elizabeth. *"Carl."*

He indicated with his chin. *"Good man." "Yes."* said Elizabeth

"We need him. You work with him or No more." Black Dog

threw out his arm in a disgusted gesture. Elizabeth felt three

years old being told off for being stupid. She felt she was but

couldn't stop it. She looked at her old friend. *"You are right. I*

apologise. My behaviour has been poor towards him. I will fix it."

Black Dog was not sure she would, but he turned and

rode out. The day passed in hard work. They reached the

ranch stockade by dinner. Elizabeth felt exhausted. She

signed to Black Dog to secure the animals and she went

straight towards the house. As she passed Carl she called out

to him. *"Good night Carl, thanks for your help today." "That's*

it?" He called after her, this time Elizabeth stopped, she was

tired and he annoyed the hell out of her with that tone. *"Mam, you've not spoken to me all day and failed to give me instruction, in fact, you ignored me for most of the day and in this business, that's dangerous."* Elizabeth stared at him. He had told her about the same as Black Dog had earlier. For a moment she felt like shouting and asking him what business was it of his. But common sense prevailed. He was right. They both were. And she knew she had once again acted badly. Exhausted, Elizabeth just let go. *"Carl, I don't mind telling you, lately I find you...."* She thought for a moment of how to say it. *"Unsettling. I am glad that you fit in well here and that you have found a place at the Double T, but the role you have taken on, seems more and more Red Wolfs. I'm finding that hard to come to terms with. Nothing personal."* She said looking at him. Carl smiled. Elizabeth couldn't believe he found this amusing. He did look handsome with mischief in that moment. Kind of adorable. *"Nothing personal mam?"* He challenged. *"That's exactly what it is."* He told her and smiled broadly now. Carl bowed his head. Turned his horse and headed for the choral whistling.

Elizabeth realised a little late, that she might have said more than she'd intended.

Elizabeth sighed, turned Patches and rode over to the house. She dismounted and Joe took her horse for her. White Dove welcomed her home. Elizabeth gave her a hug and asked about a bath. White Dove smiled. She knew Elizabeth by now and informed her that it was waiting for her. Elizabeth gave her a squeeze and headed upstairs for her things. She undressed in the bathroom and sank into the hot water and preceded to wash away the last couple of days. Not until that moment did she realise how much she ached and how much she needed the hot water to revive her did she realise how very tired she felt. She was in danger of falling asleep there and then. She finished washing and got out of the water and dried herself roughly. Wrapping her hair up. She stepped into her robe and headed for her room. It was warm night with another welcoming cool breeze from the window. Elizabeth laid down and covered herself with the bedspread. She fell instantly asleep.

She woke well past the dinner hour. They must have let her sleep. She thought. By the darkness of the room and the quietness of the house, it was late. She laid on the bed, only the moon showered light into her room. Elizabeth felt hot and threw off the bedspread. Her robe had opened in her sleep and she laid there semi naked, her robe barely covering anything. As she did so, Elizabeth thought she heard an intake of breath. Was someone in the room? She moved to cover herself and light the lamp. *"Don't."* She heard. There was no mistaking his voice. She turned to face it. Slowly she became aware of his outline. Elizabeth suddenly had the distinct feeling this was not the first time he had been in her room during the night and that knowledge both filled her with excitement and anxiety. Elizabeth was half sitting up. Both legs were clear of her robe and it was only held loosely at her waist. Her breasts were only partially covered and her arousal at his presence was evident through the light silk. Elizabeth felt embarrassed.

Elizabeth was completely unaware that she was fully illuminated by the moonlight from the window. She was naked and open to him. Her body glistened, the silk rustled and he could almost taste her scent. He dared not move. *"Will you not come to me."* She asked him innocently. *"I have missed you."* She stretched out her hand to him. He moved for the first time. *"I did not mean to wake you."* He told her. *"I should not stay."* He spoke as he neared her bed unable to stop himself. *"But you are here now, stay."* She pleaded. Not understanding the sudden need in her to hold him. He came within inches of her outstretched hand. He was reminded of how much her body had changed over the past few months. *"Will you not take my hand brother?"* She asked him. Red Wolf stood quietly for a long time and the space between them seemed like an eternity. Finally he found his voice and spoke. *"Esa, if I touch you, it would not be as your brother and I may not be able to stop."* Elizabeth held her breath.

Elizabeth realised just how desperately she wanted to touch him and have him touch her. She was so close to asking him, it scared her. She body was on fire. She was hot. Ached. She felt wet in places she did not want to think about. Her emotions crossed her face. She was struggling with her decision and it was clear on her face. He made it for her. He turned and headed for the window he had entered several hours before. Elizabeth realised he was leaving. *"No please."* She called after him as he reached the window. He turned to face her. His own emotions on edge. His need of her evident in his eyes. *"It is yes or it is no, Esa, it cannot be both."* He waited for a moment longer then left her room. As he did so, he heard her call out in despair. *"No, don't leave me. I need you."* He did not turn back, he knew he could not. She had to make the choice for herself. She had to be sure. No doubts. No questions. She needed to be determined in her decision. She would need that to fight for them. He also knew, he would not wait forever.

She woke next morning to find Red Wolf at the breakfast table. If she thought about it. It was not unexpected and there was no hint of the night before and he did not acknowledge her. Great. Back to the not talking. He was talking to Ben and White Dove. *"Good morning."* Elizabeth called to them as she came down the stairs to join them. They turned to greet her. Elizabeth came to the table kissed Ben and White Dove and joined them at the table. *"Red Wolf, has come with an invitation to visit your father, he has requested that you come to him instead of the journey here."* Ben told her. Elizabeth frowned. *"Is he not well?"* She asked Red Wolf. *"He is not as strong as he once was."* Elizabeth was shocked. Her Indian father was always in good health and a strong man.

"*Then I must go, Ben could we arrange for the summer gifts and take them with us.*" "*I cannot go Elizabeth.*" Ben answered her. "*I have stock to get to market and the trail must start soon, you will have to go. White Dove can go with you.*" He reminded her. "*Ok, the sooner the better, we can stay for the harvest.*" She said smiling aloud. "*You can stay for the weeks we are away, the boys can look after the house.*" Ben told her. "*Sounds great.*" Elizabeth said enthusiastically. "*We can make plans after breakfast.*" She rubbed her hands together. "*I'm starving let's eat.*" She smiled happily.

Throughout breakfast ideas and packing needs were discussed. Elizabeth could not help but think that she would see more of Red Wolf at the village. Senior hands came into the house for breakfast and instructions as plans were made. Carl was asked to come in. When Carl walked in he was not surprised to see Red Wolf at the table. Ben talked directly to him. "*Carl, I'm to start the trail in the next few days and Elizabeth*

163

is to go to see her father, she will be under his protection, so will not need you in that role." At this Red Wolf looked directly at him. Ben continued. "*I would welcome you staying here and keeping an eye on the place in our absence, could you do that?*" "*Yes sir, happy to do it.*" "*Good lad.*" Ben replied. White Dove remembered something. "Ben, Esa has no clan if you do not go. If Jake and the older hands are to stay, who will go with Esa, she cannot go alone, it is tradition." "Shoot." Thought Ben. "*I forgot that for a moment, its different if your father comes here Esa, but to go there you remember how it must be if you go there.*" Elizabeth nodded. White Dove looked directly at Carl, and remembered that he had spent the summer with Elizabeth and her men, they respected him and he was not one for taking her orders without question. If she could not go with the older hands as they were needed and Jake was not up to the journey. It's possible that Carl could do it. Carl became a little uncomfortable under her gaze. Ben picked up the look White Dove was firing at Carl and understood. "*Carl, change of plan,*

Elizabeth needs an escort to the Indian village, she will need someone to stay with her while there, share her space and act as her guardian. It's an honorary role. You won't need to do anything but be with her." Elizabeth jumped to her feet. *"You have got to be joking Ben. I don't need a guardian and I will not take Carl." "Esa, our options are limited and if Carl is willing to do it, I will be indebted to him."* Ben answered her. Red Wolf rose from the table. He was unsettled by the way Elizabeth protested Carls presence. They would have to spend a lot of time together in close company. He was also unhappy about the amount of time they had spent together in the last four months. Carl stood his ground as Red Wolf approached.

He looked hard at Carl, recognised competition when he saw it and turned to Esa. *"Do as your Uncle tells you."* Elizabeth got angry as he walked out and called after him. *"Who made you the boss of me? You don't tell me what to do Red Wolf." "Carl what do you say son?" "It would be an honour sir."*

Carl replied. *"Good I know she will be in good hands."* Carl nodded and left the room.

Elizabeth was shocked. What the hell had just happened? Carl. Take Carl to the Indian village? She said to herself over and over again. Had they all gone mad she thought. Elizabeth left the room and went outside. She needed some air. Everyone seemed to have work to do and were going about their business. Elizabeth remembered that White Dove would need her help and went looking for her. She knew that there would be no point in arguing now the decision had been made. Not happy. Elizabeth spent all morning working with White Dove making lists of things that would be needed on their journey. They checked the store, and went looking for the gifts of food and animals, as well as blankets and trinkets. And the gifts for the children. Medicine. Grain and Special gifts for Dull Knife. Ben worked on his men for the trail and secured the last of the animals that would be going. Over the next two days, they sent riders out and into town for the few things they still needed. Carl continued with his own routine, checking with Ben and going over what was required of him on this journey. Red Wolf stayed out of his way and worked with his braves. Things were a little tense.

It seemed as if every Indian on the ranch was going. The Harvest was always a big cause of celebration to the Indians and it had been combined with one of the gift days from the ranch. In a Christian way, it made sense. Not that that was a push for anyone, but now doubly so, that they were going to the village. Outside was already packed and ready to go. Several wagons would be going with them. Some belonging to the families returning home. Others for the goods being taken to join the celebrations. Elizabeth couldn't help but be excited. She rose early on the morning of her journey. Washed and dressed carefully. Went to the kitchen to make coffee but someone had beaten her to it. Coffee was just simmering on the stove. Carl, was about to pour one cup. He looked up and saw her.

Not for the first time was he lost for words. He swallowed hard. Elizabeth was in full Indian dress. She was breath-taking. *"Coffee?"* He managed. Elizabeth held back her surprise and answered. *"Yes thank you."* Carl poured another and handed it to her. *"Your up early mam."* Elizabeth smiled. *"It would seem I'm not the only one."* Carl half laughed and gave a bemused look. *"Yeah well, it's not every day a man gets to go live in an Indian village, I'm feeling a bit nervous I don't mind telling you."* Carls honestly was clear, no malice intended, just clear honest concern for the unexpected. It warmed Elizabeth. *"Don't worry Carl, I'll protect you."* She told him teasingly. And smiling turned and headed for the porch. Carl came with her. *"Mam, if its ok would you tell me how you came to be part of the Indian nation."* Elizabeth paused, no one else seemed about yet and Elizabeth stood and gazed out over the yard. She was quiet for a moment and then retold her story starting with her father's arrival in America.

When she was finished so was their coffee. Silently Carl took her cup from her and went inside and refilled them. As he handed it back to her, he spoke. *"Your father was an inspired man. Connecting with the Indians at a time when men were at war with them. It was good sense and business."* Carl gazed out over the land. *"He obviously knew how this land would end up and where the lines would be drawn. You know he helped the Indians as much as himself. Many are dying out there."* Elizabeth smiled sadly. *"Yes Carl, I think we all know that. My father believed that it was important that the Indians felt this was still their land. And, it is their land and we should feel honoured by them, for allowing us to share it. That we should be thankful and show that gratitude."*

"And that's why you pay tribute?" Carl asked. "Umm that and it seems fair don't you think, it was their land long before ours and we have gained much by using it." She answered. "Yeah, it does." He replied and was quiet for a time. "Do you think your father would have approved of Ben and White Dove?" Elizabeth turned to him surprised by that question, was he against it? "Do you not approve Carl?" Elizabeth answered pointedly. "It is not for me to say mam, but Ben seems a lucky man." He answered quietly. Elizabeth sighed, Carl wasn't trying to be bigoted. "I would like to think my father would have. Ben's here because my father died. Maybe if Ben had come home earlier things could have been different and I think Ben feels that sometimes, but this life is unforgiving Carl and there are no 'what if's".

Carl look thoughtful as Elizabeth continued. "My father always said, he wanted the Indians and us to be family. He felt that to preserve what we had we should be joined in land and blood. That it was the only way forward. In Ben. He has that don't you *think?"* Elizabeth smiled. Carl thought about that. He again looked out over the yard as it started to come to life. He liked this place. It called to him. As did this woman. He remained quiet for the longest time. He considered what she had told him. Then turned to face her. He answered her as he saw it. *"Yes, in a way your father has got that. But you should remember better than most, when your father made that wish Elizabeth, Ben wasn't here, only you were."* Elizabeth felt shocked. She hadn't thought about it in such a long time. Carl was right. He turned from her then and crossed to the paddocks.

Elizabeth watched him go. Had her father expected her to marry into Dull Knifes family? She asked herself. That seemed improbable, didn't it? Her father flew in the face of convention but did he think that too? and yet to say no, would make a mockery of all her father's beliefs, everything he had taught her. That 'all men are equal under their god'. Elizabeth felt torn by that. Not that the thought of being with a man scared her. She'd seen enough animal husbandry to know what it was all about. Just the thought of marrying one, anyone, Indian or not scared her. At that moment, Elizabeth knew without doubt, her father had loved her. He would have let her have her choice, whatever choice that may have been and dam the consequences. Elizabeth sat in silence, lost in her thoughts and watched the day awaken. The Indians were first up and about. White Dove continued with the packing of her wagon. There was very little left to do. Carl walked the yard and offered help where needed. Ben came out and wished her good morning, she returned his kiss. The hands came into the yard one by one, took orders and the animal round up started. 50 Steers and 25 horses were going with them. A number of chickens, rabbits and 10 milk cows. Along with all the other goods.

She had not seen Red Wolf at all. The wagons were filled with fruit and vegetables, flour, grain and seed. In others, there were tools, tools for the land, for the animals and for the people. A number of riffles and ammunition amongst them.

In no time, all was ready. Tepees were pulled down and Ben called everyone to breakfast. They all ate outside as was tradition on these days. A means of connecting with each other and saying goodbyes. Journeys in the time gone by tradition, 'long walks' as they were called by the Indians, often led to death for some. Elizabeth was thankful not to have witnessed that. When all was ready, Ben came from the house and gave his gift for Dull Knife to her. It was a magnificent silver inlaid riffle. Engraved with the Double T, along with the Indian sign for peace. Elizabeth thought it looked beautiful. *"He will love it."* She told him with a sob in her throat and hugged Ben. It would be the last time she saw him.

Elizabeth handed it to White Dove who was in the wagon and mounted Patches. White Dove took her goodbyes of her husband and they were ready to go at last. It had been agreed that they would return before the trail hands, to open the house ready for them. The Indian party would be gone 4 weeks.

CHAPTER SIX

Elizabeth walked her pony to the front and looked back over her shoulder. What a sight she thought. At the same time Carl mounted and stood a little to one side. He thought the same of her. Elizabeth sat proudly in her saddle. As she turned Red Wolf rode into the yard. If anyone had missed the connection between them. They saw it now. Red Wolf rode in and stopped before her. His horse was an exact copy of her own. Red Wolf acknowledged Ben and took his position at the head of the line. As he did so, he half turned to face Elizabeth. *"Esa."* He called out for all to hear. Elizabeth pushed her pony on, till they were level. He looked squarely at her, she was beautiful. He asked her in the traditional manner. *"Is your place with me?"* Elizabeth without hesitation answered him. *"Always."* Red Wolf gazed at this beautiful woman who stirred his heart. He nodded to her once and led them all home.

The journey to the village would take most of the day with the stock and wagons. It couldn't be rushed. They were expected to camp before night fall so as to enter the village fresh the next morning to many greetings and celebrations. The celebrations would go on all the next day and after that, for several days, followed by the harvest. Scouts were sent ahead to look for the best passage. Carl rode along the column where Black Dog and his men rode. No one had indicated that he should do so, but it seemed his place and he was accepted. When it was time for Black Dog and his men to scout, Carl went with them. He enjoyed their company, their silence, their quiet understanding of the land. They had left the column behind them by a good half hours' ride. When approaching from the west four riders were spotted crossing Double T land. The two forward scouts were closing on their position. Carl and Black Dog and the other two braves in the rear closed the gap fast. The forward scouts had stopped in the way of the four riders. As Carl got nearer he heard the voices of the men. They were talking to the Indians like meat not men. It sickened him. Carl pressed forward, he was angry by the men's contempt. They hadn't seen him, their voices got louder as they got braver, there was a sick excitement in the air.

Carl signalled to Black Dog to surround the riders. Black Dog hesitated for a moment. Took Carls measure and the braves split and circled the party. Carl went in and pulled up sharply. The riders were silenced. Carl signed for the forward braves to back off and stand. Within minutes, the riders realised their mistake, they were surrounded.

Carl stared at the men, taking them in one at a time. He didn't recognise anyone. Strangers, not a good thing. The riders were getting a little nervous, the one at the far end, started a conversation by introducing himself. Carl ignored him. Too many men were roaming the West looking for who knows what. The silence was strained. Carl looked away from the riders in disgust, quietly but forcefully he asked a question. *"Do you know how an Indian gets satisfaction when insulted?"* He looked up at the men. Staring at them in turn. In strained unison, they answered. *"No, no sir."* Carl nodded. *"You'd be lucky to survive."* Carl threw back at them. *"Now, you insulted my men here and they will want satisfaction."* Carl continued. *"They may take your life or your belongings, their choice, drop your guns."* He ordered. The four riders undid their gun belts and let them drop to the floor. Carl signalled to the forward two braves. They rounded the riders and helped themselves to their belongings. Carls eyes never left their faces.

As the braves moved back, Carl spoke to them again. *"Your on Double T land. Its owned by the Indian and Trelawney families. If you want to survive here. Be careful who you insult, or* you may end up dead. *Where you heading?"* He asked.

"Brownsville sir." The younger one answered. *"We're looking for work. Heard there's a trail about to start, was kinda hoping to find some work."* He continued. Carl nodded. *"The trail is with the Trelawney family. But you won't find work if you can't work with Indians."* The younger one looked uncomfortable. Carl indicated to Black Dog who came forward. *"Take their weapons, ride them off our land and return their guns."* And for the riders benefit he added. *"Any trouble, kill them, bury the bodies."* Black Dog grinned, the riders paled considerably. *"You can't do that. There's law here."* Carl looked at the surely one who'd spoken. *"Your right. Theirs."* Black Dog signalled for the four braves to escort the riders off Trelawney land. The party of six moved off. From their vantage point, Carl watched the riders till out of sight. Then rode back to join the others.

Their places were taken by other riders. Red Wolf asked Black Dog where the missing braves were, Black Dog recalled the story. Carl had rode past Elizabeth stopping only to ask if there was anything he could do for her, she had said no and he had returned to his position in the line. An hour from the village the group stopped to make camp.

Small groups gathered together in family units, others joined the larger group. Elizabeth went to help White Dove. Fires were lit and food prepared. Carl saw to his and Elizabeth's horses. Not sure if this was Red Wolfs job now or not. As he finished. Elizabeth asked him to join her and White Dove. Red Wolf would go where he wanted. Carl thanked her and laid out his bedroll within their circle. Everyone ate. As dinner finished, Carl was called on by Black Dog. *"Come."* He told him. Carl followed. Black Dog led him to Red Wolf and the returning four braves of their party. Carl nodded to them. Red Wolf turned and spoke to him. *"You turned those men away well today you made a good choice."* And he walked away. Both Black Dog and the two of braves slapped Carl on the back and went about their business. Carl returned to Elizabeth and White Dove. Not sure what had just happened. *"Everything alright?"* She asked as he returned. *"Yes, just fine, I'm going to turn in, good night."* Elizabeth was a bit surprised at the abruptness of his conversation. *"Goodnight Carl."* Elizabeth helped White Dove store the goods back in the wagon and arrange sleeping areas for White Dove and herself. They would sleep in the wagon tonight. Along with the other women and children. The men on the ground around them. Elizabeth hadn't realised how tired she was. As soon as she made the beds, she laid down and closed her eyes. It was the last thing she remembered. In the night, White Dove must have covered her. She awoke in the morning with her blankets over her, to the sounds of breakfast being made and the smell of coffee brewing.

Elizabeth smiled and stretched, she would see her father and Running Elk today. It gave her a sense of great joy. She got up quickly, stored the beds away and climbed down from the wagon. Carl was up and seeing to the horses. His bed roll already stowed away. Elizabeth was unsure where Red Wolf had spent the night and it only crossed her mind briefly as she helped prepare for the day. Elizabeth went to relieve herself and returned to White Dove making biscuits with the help of her kitchen staff and dishing up bacon and beans. The smell was heavenly. As Elizabeth joined them, White Dove asked her to call the people in. Breakfast was ready. They fed the whole group in one sitting. A line of food was prepared and several of the house staff, including White Dove and Elizabeth helped serve. The men came first, followed by the children and then the women ate. Only Red Wolf and Carl broke with tradition. Carl ate when Elizabeth and White Dove did. Red Wolf ate after everyone else had been served, he sat alone.

Within an hour of breakfast, all was cleared and put away, the men took the stock for watering, the milk cows were milked and the animals fed. By the time the stock returned. All were ready to continue their journey to the village. Red Wolf had not spoken to Elizabeth since the day before. She mounted her horse as before and waited for him. He rode up from the stock and stopped before her. His gaze hot as he took his fill of her. Her hair. Her clothes. The way she held herself. *"Have you had enough time Esa?"* He asked. Elizabeth looked back at him remembering two nights ago. *"Yes."* She answered. *"It is time then."* They turned and headed out, the rest including Carl, followed them.

Before reaching the village, Elizabeth sort out Carl and explained that he must be with her as they entered the village. That he must address Dull Knife when confronted with him and offer him his returning daughter. Carl nodded his understanding and asked to be prompted. Elizabeth smiled, and agreed. It was clear to her that Carl was nervous.

Elizabeth had not mentioned it but she was nervous herself. Not for seeing her father or family, but for what Red Wolf was going to do. He was clearly intending to do something. Elizabeth hoped it would not spoil their homecoming, but she had a feeling it might. Elizabeth found she became more and more apprehensive as they got closer to the village. White Dove must have felt it too. Grasping her hand she asked her. *"Esa, are you alright?"* Elizabeth smiled and said she was but found it hard to keep White Doves eyes. *"Red Wolf, he distresses you?"* White Dove continued. *"It is nothing."* Elizabeth reassured her. *"Esa, when a man distresses a woman, it is not nothing."* White Dove told her. Elizabeth smiled tightly and sighed. *"Yes, I expect your right."* *"Are you sure you know and want, what he is offering?"* White Dove asked her. Elizabeth looked ahead over the horizon. *"Is it that* obvious White Dove?" "A blind man could see it Esa." Elizabeth frowned. "I scared of what it will mean. I don't want things to change, I've just come home and got used to it all again, but, the time he was not with me was hard. I missed him. Didn't want to carry on without him. It was only in the last week or so, that I began to function outside of work." Elizabeth answered honestly. "Yes, we noticed and Red Wolf turned up just then." "You think he knew?" Elizabeth asked, White Dove smiled. "Esa, what doesn't he know?" Elizabeth burst out laughing and White Dove joined in. Laughingly Elizabeth replied. "Yes, what doesn't he know".

Red Wolf heard the laughter, turned and rode back. Elizabeth gained some composure as he approached. "Do I look so funny." He asked bemused. It had been a long time since he had seen her so happy. "No, you do not, but I am reminded that you are never far away or without knowing." Elizabeth answered him pointedly. "Is it not my job to look out *for you?"* He countered. *"As your sister?"* Elizabeth asked

teasingly. *"You know the answer to that Esa."* He spoke quietly.

Elizabeth waited before answering. *"Then, before we stand*

before our father, you should tell me, in what manner do you protect

me, for I would not wish, to be surprised on hearing my own life."

Elizabeth spoke challengingly. Red Wolf was amused. He

liked the playful Elizabeth. Clearly, White Dove had spoken

to Elizabeth and the unsaid words were no longer enough.

They were out of time and in sight of the village. He would

have to declare himself. Red Wolf had not considered actually

having to do that for her. Apart from doing so with his father.

He knew, Elizabeth did not require it for herself, but now, she

needed it to prepare. She was still uncertain and this troubled

him.

"Esa, I asked if you were ready and you said you were, I wish

to ask my father to offer bridle gifts to Ben and White Dove."

Elizabeth paled at its mention. *"Do you accept me Esa?"* They

186

were alone, the three of them, the others holding back as if knowing this was important to them all. Carl could see the tension in the three of them. An unspoken bond holding them together. At that moment, he felt he would never in all the world, be able to have such sway over her and a feeling of despair rushed over him. Elizabeth wanted this man. He was all she ever dreamed of in a husband. She had not known it coming back from New York. Or maybe she did know it was time. Either way. She was not letting him go. She knew it would not be easy. They would have many barriers to cross. People who did not accept it. But she wanted it more than anything in her life. *"I accept you, should our father agree."* Elizabeth wisely answered. For in this world, it was not her decision or his to make. It was for the tribal Chief, their King, to give in marriage, not only his eldest son but his beloved adopted daughter. *"So be it."* He answered her and rode back to his position. Secure in having spoken at last and sure of his father's approval.

They entered the village, crossing the stream that carried so many of Elizabeth's memories. They had been spotted for some time and the villagers came running out to meet and welcome them. Many called to her and White Dove and Elizabeth called back. Running Elk and Clear Water were waiting at the meeting place to greet them. *"Esa, White Dove, it's been so long, welcome home cousin."* Running Elk called to them. White Dove stopped the wagon, climbed down and went to hug her cousin. *"It's been too long, cousin."* She turned to greet Clear Water. *"I hear you are to be married this harvest. I hope my cousin knows how lucky he is."* She chided. Clear Water smiled embarrassed and proud. *"If he does not. I will remind him daily."* She smiled. White Dove laughed. *"I'm sure you will."* They both answered together.

Elizabeth couldn't stop grinning at the scene. It warmed her to see family reunited. Carl rode up beside her, aware that his duty was nearing its time. *"Mam, remember to kick me, should I forget my duty to you."* He told her. Elizabeth smiled at his jest, Carl was clearly unsure of how to react to being surrounded as he was. *"You will do just fine Carl, you're not asking for my hand or anything."* Elizabeth responded in kind. It was Carls turn to smile. *"Mam, that would easier."* They both had silly grins on their faces. The familiarity that passed between them, was noted by Dull Knife. His adopted daughter had affection for this young man and he her. This pleased him. She was of age and needed a man. She had great responsibility to her people and this land and would need a strong man to hold it and her. He came to stand before her and asked the village for silence. Red Wolf moved to join them. Dull knife looked around him and raised his arms in the formal greeting. Elizabeth was glad to see him well. Wearing the full Indian ceremonial clothing and headdress. *"It has been too long since I enjoyed the company of my adopted daughter at Harvest. You bring with you many gifts of friendship from your clan to ours. Who gives us such gifts and brings me my daughter?"* Elizabeth looked at Carl, he took the hint when he saw it. Clearly and loudly he spoke. *"I sir, bring gifts from our clan to yours and return your daughter to you."* There was riotous applause and Elizabeth got down from her horse and embraced Dull Knife.

The place erupted. The drums beat and dancing started. Dull Knife turned to his oldest son. *"Son, welcome."* Red Wolf dismounted and embraced his father. Both Elizabeth, Carl and Red Wolf joined Dull Knife as he went along the line of wagons. Dull knife seemed well pleased and not just with the goods. As he continued along the line he greeted extended family and met new additions and Elizabeth showed him the gifts for the tribe. As Dull Knife and Elizabeth walked the traditional walk. They were shadowed by Red Wolf and Carl. On several occasions, Dull Knife turned to Carl and enquired on items in the wagons, the herd and men. Carl answered honestly and in a friendly way without being overeager. Red Wolf found this strange, that his father should favour such a stranger. But knowing better than to question him. Dull Knife was a very happy man. The wagons started to move off and the families of those in them came to claim their kin and take them back to their tepees. Others were being set up where land had been cleared for them.

Dull Knife gestured to Elizabeth. "*I have a surprise for you daughter, come, and C-a-r-l? You come to. Son we will talk soon.*" The three of them left Red Wolf and walked through the village greeting many as they went. Elizabeth was wondering where they were going. Then spotted a tepee near her favourite spot. She turned to Dull Knife. "*Father, is this for me? I thought it was not right that a single woman lives alone?*" "*It is for you and your clan, including Carl and White Dove.*" Dull Knife answered. "*You are to stay with us for many weeks and you are a women and not a child no longer."* Elizabeth was both shocked and elated. *"Thank you father."* She replied with tears in her eyes. *"I leave you now, go and make your home, I will send White Dove to you."* And with that, Dull Knife hugged his daughter and left them.

As Dull Knife walked away, Carl turned to Elizabeth. *"Are we to share it mam, live together in it through the next few weeks?"* Carl asked a little bewildered. *"Yes we are Carl, but in the Indian manner. Families live, sleep, eat, sweat and die together. It bonds them. So we shall live as one with White Dove playing chaperone I fear. Not that we need one."* Elizabeth answered a little bemused by Carls shock. *"Mam, I can live outside, I do not have to intrude on your privacy."* He responded a little sheepishly. *"I'm sorry Carl, you have no choice as I do not, Dull Knife has made a decision and we have to accept it."* *"But, Mam, we are not married and we are not kin. This feels all wrong."* Carl protested as he followed her to the tepee. *"Carl, accept it.*

Anything else will not do I'm afraid come, let's see what awaits us."

Elizabeth entered the door. Inside the room was warm and airy, the flaps were held back to allow air to circulate. A small fire had been lit in the centre as was the custom. And a cooking rack placed above it. An area had been put aside for cooking utensils and makings. Blankets were scattered on the floor and hung around the walls. Bedding had been placed in four places around the outside rolled to make seating. Elizabeth found it to be both welcoming and comfortable. She turned to Carl. *"Carl would you go and get our bed rolls and the items we brought with us? I will start to make this home."* Elizabeth smiled at the confused look on Carls face and watched him leave.

Elizabeth busied herself with fetching fresh water and brushing out the living area. By the time she had finished, Carl was back. Elizabeth took her items from him and indicated where he should put his things. Elizabeth put down rugs on the floor around the fire place. Carl made himself busy on the other side of the room. He had decided it prudent to be as far away as possible. Before long, White Dove appeared at the doorway and knocked. *"Hello, may I come in?"* She asked. Elizabeth laughed and welcomed her. It was clear to her that Carl was not entirely happy about the shared accommodation and was making the best of it. White Dove smiled to herself and took her belongings and posted them between them. *"I shall be here."* She said. *"Now children we are asked to join the festivities."* And she guided them both out and across the village to the meeting area. Red Wolf had been sent to secure the stock brought to the village. His return coincided with their arrival at festival. It was in full swing as Elizabeth arrived. White Dove and Elizabeth were seated next to Dull Knife, next to Elizabeth sat Carl. Red Wolf, joined them and sat to his father's right next to Running Elk and his wife to be.

The food and drink flowed. It was followed by dancing and music and singing that went well into the night. The young men of the tribe danced to show their prowess. When the young women joined them, it was to show their fertility. Dull Knife turned to Elizabeth. *"You should be dancing with them my daughter." "Father, there is no man dancing who would wish my burden on them."* She replied smiling. Dull Knife slapped his thigh and laughed out loud. *"Child, that cannot be so."* He told her. Their banter continued for many hours. Carl sat watching them in fascination. It seemed unimaginable that such a warm loving relationship could have been forged in such a harsh beginning. When the time seemed right. Elizabeth excused herself and said goodnight. Carl rose to follow her. White Dove informed them that she would be in shortly. Within a few moments it was clear to Red Wolf, that Elizabeth was not going to retire to his father's tepee. He asked his father where she was going. From the look on his face, Red Wolf was far from happy by the answer.

He would not be allowed to join her. In response, he stood and walked away.

Elizabeth walked in the cool air towards her home for the next 4 weeks. Carl accompanied her. *"It's truly beautiful here."* *"Yes mam it is."* *"Carl, I think it is time you called me by my given name, you have only ever done so when I've annoyed you."* Elizabeth said smiling. Carl laughed, *"Yes and that was often but I bit my tongue most times."* He said returning the jest. As they reached the tepee, Elizabeth turned and informed Carl that she would go and prepare for bed and that she would not need his company. Carl understood her, and willingly allowed her to leave. He set about boiling some water to make coffee.

Elizabeth walked down to the stream and took her toilette. She was suddenly overcome by the coolness of the water and the clearness of the night that on impulse, checking she was alone, removed her clothes and walked into the water. It was shockingly cool to the skin, breath takingly refreshing. Elizabeth swam to the middle and surrendered herself to its rejuvenating powers. She wasn't sure how long she had been there but Elizabeth found the water perfect and was reluctant to leave. She swam for shore before it was too late. As she started to swim, Elizabeth realised she couldn't remember where exactly she'd left her clothes and looked for where she had entered the water. At that moment, Red Wolf walked towards her from the brush. He looked magnificent in the moon light. His hair long and straight around his shoulders. His traditional dress enhancing his beauty and strength. He came straight into the water. Elizabeth instinctively backed away from him.

"Do I scare you Elizabeth." He asked using their challenge and walked closer to her. *"Never."* She called to him laughing. *"But, I am naked and would wish for some clothes."*

She told him. *"I can see that."* He said removing his waistcoat.

"That is not helping me." She answered. *"No, but it may help me."*
He replied smiling. A little shocked Elizabeth laughed

nervously. *"Red Wolf please, my clothes."* She pleaded. *"You*

are now sleeping with a strange man in his lodge but you cannot

swim with me, come sister that is hardly fair?" He asked

teasingly. *"That was not my doing and you know it."* She

answered. Elizabeth was now about to be out of her depth. It

was futile to swim in circles and she held her ground. Red

Wolf swam within inches of her and Elizabeth held her breath.

Once again, Elizabeth found herself semi naked in the

moonlight. It was becoming a habit. With that now familiar

feeling of nervousness and excitement dwelling within her.

In modesty, she held one arm across her breasts. *"Esa?"* Was

all he said to her. All his wants and desires were evident in

the way he said her name. She looked into his eyes and this

time, she did not wait for him. Elizabeth lifted her free hand

and traced the outline of his face with her fingers. 'He'd been gone for so long' she thought. Her finger tips brushed over his cheek, down to his lips and then very lightly, caressed them. What would they feel like she wondered.

Red Wolf placed one hand on her waist to steady her and gently removed the arm covering her breasts with his other. Elizabeth took her hand from his face and rested it on his shoulder. Red Wolf looked down at her and thought he would burst. He let go of her arm and looked into her face. Elizabeth returned his look gaze for gaze. Encouraged, he held out his hand and caressed her shoulder. They had often swum naked as children. But this was different. The feeling within him different. It was male. It lusted. Lifting his hand from her waist he caressed her flesh below her swell of her breast. His thumb grazing the fullness of it. Elizabeth took a sharp intake of breath. His gaze came back to her face and they locked eyes. His fingers rounded the swell of her breast and outlined its fullness. Elizabeth sighed deeply and leaned into him just as his fingers found the nipple. Red Wolf

explored the feel of her skin under his and realised how

beautifully responsive she was. She enjoyed his touch. That

he could draw such emotion from her with just his touch was

a wonder to him. Elizabeth knew it to be wrong. Naked.

With this male. But she couldn't fight it. She wanted to be

here with him. Her breasts and lower body ached for him.

She had never experienced such pleasure; all convention went

out the window. She gave herself up to it completely.

In such cool water, Red Wolf had never been so hot.

The pleasure Elizabeth found in his touch was beyond any

experience he'd had before. She looked like an angel. Her

wet hair hanging down her back and floating on the water

behind her. He wanted to take her. Taste her. Make her his

then and there. But knew to do so would break with tradition.

His father would be displeased and he knew, he would feel he

had dishonoured her. Red Wolf felt Elizabeth would put up

little protest if he tried to take her. She seemed beyond all reason, she was lost in her emotions and the feelings he was bringing from her.

He let go of her and gently held her before him. Trying in desperation to save them both. Elizabeth rested her head on his chest and found it hard to breath. She kissed his chest and whispered. *"Don't stop, please don't stop."* She pleaded not knowing what she was pleading for. Red Wolf tried to put some distance between them, but he could not let her go. He placed his hands back on her waist and lifted her clear of the water. Elizabeth braced herself on his shoulders and threw her head back arching into his body as he lifted her. She glistened in the moon light above him. Both breasts free of the water and he held her there, looking up at the wondrous sight. He was so close to taking her. Her belly close to his face. He swallowed hard, gained a measure of composure and looked his fill at her exposed body. She was not the child he remembered. Not even the Elizabeth who had first arrived. She was all woman. Her skin so white, so clear, he had never seen anything like it, it seemed to illuminate. He could not take his eyes off her. Water and the moon reflected from her, the water running down her shoulders on to her up turned breasts dropped on to his face. He licked it from his lips and moaned with the pleasure it brought him. The cold and her own arousal had caused her breasts to swell and enlarge. Her nipples tight and hard. How he wanted her.

She was overwhelmingly seductive, vulnerable and unknowingly seducing him. Without thinking, his desires and instinct took over. He lowered her to him and bent his head. Opened his mouth and licked the water from her nipple. Elizabeth moaned aloud. Arched her back and lifted her legs around him. Red Wolf opened his mouth again and licked the water from the other. Elizabeth cried out. He caressed her nipple with his tongue and enclosed it completely with his lips. His tongue took over and explored her. Flicking across its hard centre, back and forth, circling the surrounding flesh, teasing, licking and sucking and all the while Elizabeth cried out and clung to him. Pulling him ever closer with her legs wrapped around his waist. He would take her and dam the consequences. From the river bank Running Elk could see little of what was going on but he saw the outline of his brother in the water with a female. The women cried out in pleasure and Running Elk smiled, his brother had not lost his touch. However, he was sent to get him and he would have to disturb him. *"Red Wolf."* He called, as he approached the water, there was no response, louder this time he called again. *"Red Wolf, our father calls for you."* Red Wolf lowered Elizabeth into the water and put his finger to her lips. *"Quiet don't say a word."* He whispered to her. *"I hear you."* Red Wolf called out angrily. Running Elk smiled. He was sure his interruption was not welcome. There would be time to humble his brother on this subject later. For now, he contented himself with that thought and walked back the way he came.

Red Wolf had disengaged himself from Elizabeth's body. The spell was broken. Having lowered her back into the water when he heard the call. He hoped that his brother had not seen who it was, but knew that if he had, it would be kept between them. Elizabeth was shaking and not from the cold. He spoke gently to her, *"I have to go."* She nodded *"I don't like to leave you like this but I must."* He told her. Elizabeth cleared the fog from her brain and regained her composure. She pushed away from him embarrassed and started to swim. *"I'll be fine, you must go."* And suddenly she was gone from him. Red Wolf turned and exited the water. As he did, he wondered how a man could feel so in control one moment and so desolate the next.

CHAPTER SIX

Red Wolf picked up his waistcoat and ran crossed the village to his father's lodge. The Chiefs home. His father. Red Wolf entered, honoured those present and sat cross legged on the floor. Dull Knife raised an eyebrow at Red Wolf being wet and preoccupied. *"The man Carl, I hear he is a good man, respects our ways, listens to what we have to say."* Red Wolf nodded and answered honestly. *"Yes he does father."* *"It is well done then. Esa, needs someone she can rely on and so do we."* Red Wolf was unsure what his father was getting at. He was still struggling with his emotions of earlier in Elizabeth's company and they were hard to shift. Dull Knife continued, *"Grey Owl, has come to ask, that he may speak of his daughter, Sky."* Red Wolf continued to look at his father and said nothing, taking that as acceptance, Dull Knife continued. *"He offers a good price and it would be a good match.".* It suddenly dawned on Red Wolf that his father was talking about marriage.

It had been a long time since their mother had died and Red Wolf had been sure his father would not take another woman, this was good news. *"If this pleases you father, it is good."* He answered. *"Yes it would please me. It has been too long without children in our lodge." "It is agreed then."* Dull Knife embraced Grey Owl. *"Your daughter and my son and their children will lead this tribe."* Red Wolf thought he was hearing things, he jumped to his feet. *"Father, did you not mean Sky for yourself?"* He asked. Dull Knife looked annoyed at his son. He knew better than this. *"You know well I would not take another woman after your mother." "But father I cannot take Sky."* It was out of his mouth before he realised. Not only had Red Wolf challenged his father in public, but he had dishonoured both Sky's father by his rejection and his own. Grey Owl, rose from his seat. Patted his old friend on the back and left without saying another word. Dull Knife was both humiliated and angry. *"That was poorly done, leave me, and return when you have found your senses.".* Red Wolf turned and left, this night was proving more challenging the longer it lasted. He headed to the young men's lodge, to find his brother.

As Red Wolf had started his walk across the village to his father, Carl had started to worry about Elizabeth, she had been gone a long time. He looked about him and remembered the general direction she had taken and followed. The path took him to the water's edge and he continued to walk for a short while. As he rounded a crop of bushes, he saw Elizabeth suddenly exit the water not six feet in front of him. He stopped short. Elizabeth had swum for as long as she could. She felt exhausted mentally and physically. Her mind, however much she tried not to, kept returning to what had just happened. Going over and over the experience, his touches her responses. Elizabeth was surprised by her feelings of exhilaration and embarrassed at her own bodies responses to him. And what he did to her. Did men treat their women like that? Did they give such attention to their bodies? Was that natural, she thought. Were men and women meant to bring such pleasure to each other. Did men touch you like that? Elizabeth had many questions and very few answers.

Carl couldn't miss that she was completely naked and clearly she had no thought as to being seen like it. This was no lady from the East, he thought. The Indian in her had taken over. As Elizabeth bent to retrieve her dress, a twig snapped under his foot. Elizabeth turned sharply and saw him. As she rose she brought the dress with her. Clearly, Carl had seen all there was to see, there was little point in fanning modesty now, but still, Elizabeth held the dress before her. Carl closed the gap between them. *"I was not spying on you, I was concerned, you had been gone a long time and I came looking for you. I have only just got here."* He told her worrying on her reaction to seeing him here. Carl was moved by the look of radiance about her. Once again he gently removed the hairs from her face with his fingers. His touch was light and caressing. Elizabeth was all confused, feelings she had only moments ago had with Red Wolf were rising in her again but now, with Carl. How could this be possible she thought. Carl saw her expression and took it for anxiety.

He walked around her and stood behind her. Elizabeth stood very still, her hair had never been cut heavily only trimmed. Heavy with water, its length was breath-taking and its thickness was covering her modesty, it would also prevent her from being dry. Carl raised his hands and without speaking, pulled the strands of hair from her cheeks to the nape of her neck. It was so heavy, it stuck to her body, as he prised it lose Elizabeth shivered. He brought the hair together in a twist and started to wring the water from it. Each circle of his hands, lightly touched Elizabeth's back. Round and around his hands went, the circulating motion, hypnotic.

Each touch of his skin on hers, caused her body to respond. Elizabeth closed her eyes, basked in the sensation of her head and body, gently massaged by the twisting motion. Her lips were suddenly very dry. Elizabeth swallowed hard and tried to wet them. Carl increased the circulating motion as his hands descended the length of her hair. Slowing and surely, Carl was working his way down her spine. He should have stopped and lifted her hair from the rest of her body and wrung it out, but his own desires were fighting him. His touch brushed passed her skin again and again, to the small of her back and he continued on in a downward motion. To Elizabeth, every nerve in her body seemed alive.

His hands brushed passed the swell of her cheeks twice and Elizabeth moaned in response and leaned back into him. As her body connected with his. Sanity came crashing back to him. Carl was both surprised and pleased. The thought that he had brought such feelings in Elizabeth alive, was a wonder to him. More than he could ever have imagined. He breathed deeply and eased her forward. *"You can put the dress on now."* He whispered in her ear. Elizabeth did not respond and Carl smiled. She was lost to the emotions and he was the cause. *"Elizabeth."* He said again, *"your dress."* This time, Elizabeth heard him. She had been lost her emotions riding her. But until that moment when he said her name, she had been imagining Red Wolf. What was she doing. She asked herself. Carl lifted her hair and Elizabeth raised the dress over her head and slipped it on.

Carl, walked back around her and looked in her eyes. Elizabeth looked back at him. She was suddenly very embarrassed. What had she done. *"We should get back."* Was all he said. Elizabeth nodded and walked away from him in silence. As they reached the tepee, to Elizabeth's relief, White Dove was already inside. White Dove took one look at them and realised that something had passed between them. She was happy for Elizabeth. Life would be easier for her with her own kind. But, the knowledge of Red Wolf's desire for

Elizabeth laid heavily on her. White Dove had come back to

the tepee knowing that Grey Owl had sort approval for his

daughter Sky to marry Red Wolf. To White Dove's

astonishment. Red Wolf seems to have agreed. Clearly,

something had made Red Wolf accept Sky over Elizabeth.   It

did not make sense to her and Red Wolf was going to have

some explaining to do later. She had worried on her return.

Became increasingly concerned for how Elizabeth was going

to take the news. Maybe now, it would be a good time to tell

Elizabeth. She had comfort with Carl and the news would not

be too distressful. It would be worse. If Elizabeth should

hear it from someone else.

White Dove smiled at them both. *"Come, food and coffee

is here, join me."* Elizabeth smiled and kissed her and sat down

to take the drink offered to her. Taking a sip she felt calmer.

Carl picked up his own food and coffee. Thanked her and sat on the other side of them. He needed some space from Elizabeth and it would allow the women some privacy. *"I hear good news is in the village."* She told them. *"Not only is Running Elk to be married shortly before Harvest. But Grey Owl asked that his daughter be taken as bride and she has been accepted. So there will be two weddings before winter in our family."* Elizabeth wasn't sure she'd heard right. *"Two weddings?"* She was confused, had Red Wolf spoken to his father already? That seemed unlikely as it would have to be done formally. *"Whose is the second in our family?"* She asked confused. White Dove slowly and quietly put down her coffee. Elizabeth started to look anxious. Troubled. White Dove now doubted her decision but it was too late to back out now. Gently, she reached out to take Elizabeth's hand. *"Sky is to marry Red Wolf Elizabeth."* Elizabeth looked at her and shook her head. *"No, that cannot be true. Red Wolf is to talk to our father about us."* She whispered looking for White Dove to change the words just spoken. Seeing no retraction, realisation dawned on her.

'O dear god' she thought. She started to rock back and forth, she started to weep. *"No that can't be true, I saw him earlier, we were together, he would have told me."* She cried in despair. What had she done. Elizabeth in that moment understood what it meant to her. What it meant to lose Red Wolf from her life. She started to cry uncontrollably. The pain. Grief. The feeling of loss. He was lost to her. And her rocking became more intense. Had a member of the tribe passed her at that moment, they would have thought she were in mourning. And Elizabeth was. Once declared, no marriage agreement could be changed. There would be no chance of a life with him now.

White Dove removed one of the blankets and wrapped it around her and held Elizabeth for all she was worth. Carl had moved forward unsure what was happening or what had been said. Staying close by them. Elizabeth cried and then silently sobbed for many hours. No one slept that night. In his own despair, Carl realised Elizabeth's emotional outpouring earlier in the evening, may not have been because of him after all. As dawn broke, Elizabeth became silent and withdrew into herself. She would have to live with the knowledge of Red Wolf taking someone else as his wife, his lover, be the mother of his children. For the sake of her sanity, she would have to make peace with it. For the next few days, Elizabeth barely left the tepee. It had been commented on by several of the tribe including Dull Knife. White Dove made up an excuse, saying she was not feeling well. She knew that it would not be long before Dull Knife sent the medicine man to look at her. She would have to be careful. Red Knife had cornered White Dove on hearing Elizabeth was unwell. He demanded to know what was wrong with her. He was unable to just walk in on her. White Dove stuck to her story telling him that Elizabeth did not want to see him while she was unwell.

He had looked at her strangely then, but he accepted it. Carl, put aside his own despair and had become nurse maid, mother, father and brother overnight. He saw to Elizabeth's every need. He brought water for her, he helped wash her, brought her food and made her coffee. He held her when she cried and White Dove wasn't present. He wiped her face and helped her when she felt sick. Elizabeth did not leave her bed and refused much of what he offered her, but he kept trying and never left her side. On the fourth day, Carl had made up his mind. Elizabeth needed to bath, eat and get out of the tepee. He got up early as was his routine. Saddled the horses and brought them to the tepee. He was going to make her get up. Elizabeth was still where he'd left her, in bed. He came to her and brushed the hair from her face and spoke. *"Elizabeth, you must get up, Red Wolf is coming to pay a visit, unless you wish to see him, we need to leave now."* He lied to her. Elizabeth looked at him. *"Coming here?"* She repeated. *"Yes. White Dove told them you were ill to give you time, but time has run out,*

*he wants to check up on you himself. He has sort permission and it
was granted."*

Elizabeth looked at him. Her emotions all over the
place. She would not see him. She wasn't ready. Finally,
when Carl thought he was wasting his time, Elizabeth moved.
Slowly at first, deliberately. With his help she got to her feet.
She was unsteady and a little giddy but with his help, walked
outside. She walked to Patches and petted her. Laying her
head on her next. Grasping the horses mane in one hand, in
one swift movement she mounted her horse and waited for
him. He was amazed by her. She sat so proud, you would
never know how fragile she was. He mounted his horse
behind her and drew up alongside. *"Ready?"* He asked.
Elizabeth nodded. They rode out.

Carl had packed the horses for several days. He had
intended to get Elizabeth away for a while. He had spoken of

it to White Dove and she had agreed. She would tell Dull Knife that Carl had gone hunting and took Elizabeth for company to make her feel better. White Dove had told him of the watering hole. Some 20 miles south of the village. It was good fishing and clean water. Carl headed in that direction. As Elizabeth and Carl put some distance between them and the village, White Dove was being cornered by Red Wolf.

"How is Elizabeth today?" White Dove spoke the truth this time. *"She's much better, in fact she's gone riding and hunting and will be back in a few days."* She told him. *"Gone riding with who?"* He asked. *"Carl."* Red Wolf grabbed her hand. *"Why did you not tell me she was up and able to ride. That I could see her?"* White Dove looked at her cousin. Was he so ignorant. *"Have you not done enough?"* She told him and walked away back to the tepee. White Dove was becoming more and more concerned with Red Wolfs behaviour and Elizabeth's reactions. Some distance between them was a very good idea.

White Dove sat stunned round the fire in her friend's lodge. There was great unrest. Red Wolf had rejected Grey Owls offer of his daughter. It had caused much upset within the village. It was a slight, against an elder and his family. It would not be taken kindly. White Dove struggled with the knowledge. Should she have told Elizabeth. Would it have been a kindness or a hindrance? She didn't know. She hoped that in not telling Elizabeth, she may have a chance with Carl. She felt in her heart, that maybe, it would be best for them all. Carl wanted her and Elizabeth had a clear affection for him. Given time, White Dove felt the two of them could make it work. But, not if Red Wolf got between them.

The ride to the water hole, took most of the day. It had been a good idea. Elizabeth became more animated the further they got from the village. By the time they arrived, they were both tired and Elizabeth after several comments from Carl, some not so subtle had to accept, he was right, she could do with a bath and something to eat. Carl saw to the horses and while Elizabeth went about her toilette. He found her fresh clothing from the packs, a cloth and soap, a brush and toothbrush. Elizabeth had looked at him confused. When had he thought to do all this she wondered. She smiled wanly at him thanked him and walked in the direction of the watering hole up stream. Carl put water on for coffee and made something to eat. Elizabeth took her time. She tried to cut the images in her mind of the last time she had entered water. It was not easy. But she got through it. She scrubbed herself clean. Suddenly only too aware that she had let herself down. She had let her pain determine who she was. That was not the person she was. With a stronger resolve Elizabeth returned to their camp refreshed and had put on the western clothes Carl gave her. 'When did Carl do all this', crossed her mind again. She realised her mind was clearer now than it had been for days; she was hungry and ready for dinner. Carl had laid out their things around the fire and laid their bedding under the trees. Elizabeth propped herself up against the tree by her bed and begun to brush out her hair. Carl watched her silently, he had never seen anything so lovely. With every stroke, he recalled the feel of her hair and her skin on his hands. Carls mouth became very dry. He looked away and made himself busy. He waited as long as he could then took the dinner to her. They ate in silence.

It was a beautiful clear night. Elizabeth gazed up at the stars. When they were finished, Elizabeth rose and took the makings to the river to wash. Carl couldn't believe how happy he was just to watch her and be in her company. Elizabeth returned and handed him the things. Carl stowed them away and Elizabeth made herself comfortable on her bed and looked out over the horizon and into the sky. They had not spoken. The beauty of the sky always left her speechless. She didn't feel the need to fill the space with words. The Indians had a saying, that the earth mother had thrown the stars from her breast into the sky to give birth to the universe. It was simple and beautiful.

Carl took his time and made himself busy. The camp became homelier. He had picked an area that had natural bushes on two sides with several trees and the river in front of them. He cleared away some of the dead on the floor and checked the horses, made sure they had feed and walked back to pour more coffee for them both. As he walked over to her and handed her a cup. Elizabeth looked at him and smiled. *"I haven't thanked you for your help over the last couple of days, I've been a bit useless, a complete mess and I hate that, I'm sorry if I've been a silly girl, a burden to you."* Elizabeth told him humbly. Carl wanted to talk about the night they were together, but couldn't bring himself to mention it. Part of him feared her answer, should it be what he didn't want to hear. *"It was my job mam, to look after you, Ben was very clear on that."* He smiled back. Elizabeth returned his smile. *"I don't think Ben had nurse maid in mind."* She replied sadly. *"Or could he have known what would happen or my reaction to it, I hardly know myself if I'm honest."* Elizabeth looked very vulnerable and alone. Carl sat down beside her, leaned back against the tree and drank his coffee. Elizabeth put her head on his shoulder and they sat in silence. No more words needed.

Carl got up from time to time, to pour or make more coffee and always brought some to Elizabeth. He kept the fire going and checked on the horses from time to time. Nothing else stirred that night, they both found the silence of the night comforting. Eventually, Elizabeth overcome with fatigue told him. *"I'm going to turn in Carl."* She quietly told him. He smiled at her and helped her into her bedroll. As he walked away to the other side of the fire, she called over to him. *"Carl, would you bring your bed nearer, I don't want to be alone."* Carl looked over at her. *"You sure about that Elizabeth."* He asked her. *"Yes."* She replied. Carl made to move his things nearer to her. *"No Carl, I'd like you to put them here, next to me."* She told him. Carl looked at her. Unsure. Elizabeth was

vulnerable and he didn't want to take advantage of her.

Elizabeth could see he was troubled by it. *"Please."* She urged

him. Carl nodded and moved his bed over next to hers. A

little nervous, Carl walked back to the fire and banked it up, it

wasn't cold but it gave him something to do.

Eventually, with nothing left to avoid her with, he

came back to his bedroll and settled himself on top of it,

looking at the night sky. *"I'm not sure this is proper Elizabeth."*

He told her. Elizabeth was half asleep. Sleepily she turned to

face him and simply said. *"Thank you."* Carl turned to her and

watched her sleep for a long time, then fell asleep himself.

Carl woke in the night with an ache in his right arm.

Sleepily he tried to move it and found that he couldn't. He

tried to stretch and failed. Carl breathed deeply and came

more awake. He realised he couldn't move because

something was on him and that something was Elizabeth. Somehow, their bed rolls had become entwined and Elizabeth was half laying across him. Gently, he moved her off his arm and in her sleep, Elizabeth moved closer and wrapped herself around him. Carl was unsure what to do. There was a little chill in the air and he had woken feeling the cold. He had thought to cover both of them but now he was torn between doing the right thing and not disturbing her. Carl was certainly not feeling the cold now. He wondered how he would manage to do it. Slowly, he brought his now revived arm, up over his head and around to catch the corner of the blanket, as he did so, he brought the blanket around them and held her to him. In doing so, he had managed to cover them both with the blanket. Carl smiled to himself, 'not bad' he thought, as he went back to sleep.

Elizabeth woke in the morning alone. Carl had woken up a couple of hours earlier, and found that Elizabeth wasn't wrapped around him any longer. Actually, he woke to finding he was wrapped around her. His face was in her hair and his arms around her body. Carl woke quickly, afraid of what his response would be. He focused on where he was and without moving, breathed in her scent. 'God this feels so good' he thought. To have such a woman. Silently, he unwrapped his body from Elizabeth and got up before he woke her. Covering her with the blankets. He was still unsure how she would react to his closeness and did not want to upset her. He wanted to give her space. Picking up his things, he headed to the stream to wash and fetch water for the horses. That done he took out some breakfast items. Took some for himself and left some out for Elizabeth to find when she woke. He headed back to the river. They'd fish for their dinner later. When Elizabeth woke, she found herself alone. She knew he wouldn't be far. She roused herself and made her bed and found the breakfast things he'd left for her and a pot of coffee still hot. Elizabeth poured her coffee and sat and ate. Walking over to the horses, she saw they were well cared for and rubbed Patches and Carls horse in hello. Elizabeth looked around her and saw him. Carl had caught one fish and was sitting on the bank with his rod in the water teasing for another. She crept up on him and touched his shoulder. Carl didn't have to turn around to know who it was. Elizabeth sat down next to him. *"Can I help?"* She asked. *"Sure, do you know how to fish?"* *"It's been awhile, but I think I remember."* She smiled. Carl gave her his rod while he made one up for her. He passed it to her and took his own. They sat for the rest of the morning fishing.

Carl wasn't sure you could call what Elizabeth did as fishing. From time to time he caught something and once, so did she. Elizabeth squealed with delight when her rod twitched and a fish was on the other end. Carl helped her reel it in and took it off its hook for her. Elizabeth was in peals of laughter as the fish jumped about. She clapped and laughed and enjoyed herself for the first time in days. The time passed quickly. Before they knew it, it was well passed lunch time and heading towards dinner. Elizabeth started to get hungry but didn't want to disrupt the good day they were having. Carl had too, but he'd said nothing, waiting for her to break the spell of the day. As the sun began to set, Carl realised he was going to have to call it a day. *"I think it's time for dinner."* He told her. *"How about fish?"* He asked. Lifting their booty smiling. *"Sounds perfect."* Elizabeth answered and they both got up and headed back to their camp.

Carl cleaned the fish and Elizabeth went in search of fire wood. When Carl came back with the cleaned fish, Elizabeth was making up the fire. Carl was surprised. *"I didn't know you could make a fire Elizabeth?"* *"Well don't look so surprised."* She told him. *"I was brought up on a ranch remember."* Carl smiled. *"How could I forget."* He said teasingly. He moved to the fire and began to set up a rack to put the fish on. Carl got some herbs from their saddle bags and other makings and began to cook dinner. The smell of fresh cooked fish permeated the air. She was starving. It was killing her, her mouth watering. Elizabeth made herself busy by making some fresh coffee. As she started to pour two cups, Carl turned to her. *"It's ready."* *"Thank goodness."* She replied. *"I'm starving."* Carl had made some beans and biscuits to go with the fish. He remembered he'd brought some fruit and nuts with them from the village for later and sat down to eat. Elizabeth ate the lot and asked for seconds. Carl was eager to please and smiled as he watched her enjoy the first, real meal she'd had in days.

After dinner, Elizabeth again took the dishes and went to clean them up. Carl as before made more coffee and settled back to enjoy it. The evening was warm with its usual cool breeze. The rippling movement of the water just beyond, lulling him. It seemed perfect. He closed his eyes and listened to the world move about him. Carl heard Elizabeth coming back long before he could have seen her. Her foot steps were light and she was humming. Carl smiled. She'd been hurt alright, but she was mending. It was a step in the right direction. Elizabeth put the things away and joined Carl with her coffee. *"I had a good day today."* She told him. *"So did I."* He told her. Nothing more needed to be said by either of them. They settled down and shortly Elizabeth said *'Good night.'* And got inside her bed roll. Carl laid awake for some time after and eventually gave in to sleep. Unsure after the night before. Carl moved his bed slightly to one side. *"Where're you going?"* She asked him. Elizabeth was clearly not as asleep as Carl had thought. Carl cleared his throat and looked at her. *"Last night, we became entangled in our sleep, I thought it better to move away a little."* He replied. Elizabeth continued to look back at him. *"Would that be so bad Carl?"* She asked him. Carl looked away from her. Not sure what to answer. *"Not so bad if you were my woman Elizabeth, but your not are you?"* He answered honestly.

Elizabeth swallowed hard, she was in pain and just needed to be wanted. *"I could be."* she whispered. Carl recognised her want and need and that it was her pain speaking. He'd seen it in himself many times and chose not to hear her. *"For now, while we are here, sleep by me."* She pleaded. Carl for all his good intentions, was never going to be able to say no. He moved his bed back. But gave a bit more distance. He couldn't deal with waking with her in his arms or him in hers. He laid down and let out a long breath. Elizabeth moved across to him laying on her front. *"Carl."* She asked softly. *"If I touch you, would that be ok."* Carl swallowed hard. How was he to ignore this woman. Moving his arm aside he encircled her in it. Elizabeth lay across him with her head on his chest and her arm resting on his shoulder. She was asleep in no time.

This became the pattern for their trip. They walked or fished in the morning. Rode or hunted in the afternoons. Made dinner together and Elizabeth fell asleep beside him. Carl had to reminded himself it wasn't real. The trouble was, he was in serious danger of believing it. He wanted to believe it. That they were the only two people in the world. That she belonged to him. But it wasn't true. And he knew it. The morning of the fourth day Carl woke early. Something felt wrong. Elizabeth was laying entwined with him. There was nothing sexual about it as far as they were concerned. Carl knew it was comfort she sought, but to an outsider, it would look intimate. Carl untangled himself from her. As he had each morning, covered her and made up the fire. As he did so, he realised they weren't alone. Carl felt uncomfortable and reached for his guns. He'd never left them far from his bedroll. He stood and looked about. In the clearing to the left of their camp, was Red Wolf. He was mounted and alone. He couldn't have missed their sleeping arrangements. Part of Carl had expected him. He knew he'd come looking for her sooner or later. Carl acknowledged him and approached. *"Is Elizabeth alright?"* Red Wolf asked him. *"She will be, she's better."* Carl answered. There was silence between them. *"The two of you?"* Red Wolf asked eventually. Carl looked at him. *"That is something you should ask Elizabeth."* Carl answered. Red Wolf nodded. *"Our father asks for her."* He rode off.

Carl walked back to their camp. Made breakfast and waited for Elizabeth to wake. As she did so. Carl told her she was wanted by her father. Elizabeth didn't ask who had told him. She knew. Their time together was over. The real world came crashing in. Once they had breakfasted, they packed up camp and rode for the village. Red Wolf came into camp a couple of hours before Carl and Elizabeth would. He went straight to White Dove. He found her in the company of friends and excused her. Once they were alone, Red Wolf asked her. *"Are Carl and Elizabeth together?"* He asked her. *"They were not when they left, his job is to protect her."* She answered. *"Does that include sleeping with her."* He spat in anger. White Dove just looked at him. *"You dishonour her and yourself with your jealousy."* She walked away from him. Red Wolf thought he would go mad. The thought of Elizabeth with another man. It had driven him crazy on the journey home. He would not be able to see them together. He would go to his father and ask to leave and prepare for the Harvest.

Red Wolf turned and headed for his father. Red Wolf reported that Elizabeth was better and on her way home. He asked permission to leave the village and prepare for Harvest. His father although surprised, agreed. Red Wolf made ready to leave. He was gone by the time Elizabeth rode into the village. Elizabeth went straight to her father as was expected. *"Child, you are better?"* He asked her. *"Yes thank you father."* *"I asked for your return as I wanted to discuss Running Elks wedding and the Harvest. You have a role to pay in those things and it's*

important that you are here." He spoke. *"Yes father. What would*

you like me to do?" She listened to all he told her and agreed on

how she could help him. Elizabeth thanked her father and

went about his bidding.

Red Wolf had said his goodbyes to his brother before

leaving. Running Elk understood why. White Dove wasn't

the only one concerned for them both.

Running Elk crossed paths with Elizabeth on her way

to seeing White Dove. Calling to her. *"Sister, how are you*

feeling?" Elizabeth hugged him. *"I am well brother."* *"Good, I*

am happy to hear it. My family seem to be coming and going. You

have only returned and now Red Wolf has gone to make ready for the

Harvest. He will be back in a few days." He told her. Elizabeth

expressed a real sense of relief. She wasn't ready to see him

yet. *"So."* She asked him. *"Your wedding. Father has asked me* to help. *What can I do."* She asked him and together they made their way to White Dove and all three worked on their plans for the wedding.

By the time White Dove and Elizabeth got back to the tepee, Carl had stowed away their belongings from the trip and was seeing to the horses. Black Dog had come looking for him. *"Tomorrow we hunt, you come."* He told him. Carl was glad to see him. *"Thank you, I'd like that."* He responded. Black Dog slapped him on the back and returned the way he came. Carl finished with the horses, made his way back to Elizabeth. Carl entered their home to find White Dove, Elizabeth and Running Elk in deep conversation. They acknowledged his arrival and continued with their business. Carl listened with interest. It was going to be a huge wedding. Both White Dove and Elizabeth would have lead roles in it as part of Running Elks family. Carl was rather relieved he would not be involved. He was beginning to feel that his involvement in Dull Knifes family was already enough.

As night drew in Running Elk made his excuses and left. White Dove prepared dinner with Elizabeth's help and before long, they were all sitting down to eat. Conversation was light. Mainly about the wedding and Carl felt unconnected to it. He thanked them for the food and announced that he was going for a walk. Carl strolled around the edge of the village and was gone for several hours. He felt he needed some time to understand what was going on with him and Elizabeth. Being near her only made matters worse, he found it impossible to think clearly around her. In his absence, White Dove took the opportunity to talk to Elizabeth. *"I saw Red Wolf before he left."* White Dove told her. *"He said something strange, he mentioned that he had seen you with Carl."* Elizabeth smiled. *"I think everyone knew that."* She replied innocently. *"No."* White Dove continued. *"That is not what he* meant Esa. *Red Wolf felt you were Carls woman. Have you any idea why, he would think that?"* White Dove asked her. Elizabeth went a little pale. *"I'm not sure, but I expect he saw us together and thought it was more than it was. Carl was good to me while we were away. I needed to be with someone. Needed to be close, I asked him to do that for me. No demands, no expectations, just company. I don't think I could have got through the last few days without him."* Elizabeth answered her.

White Dove looked at her niece. *"Esa, is there anything that your uncle or father should be concerned about."* Elizabeth felt like laughing, she shook her head. She'd allowed Red Wolf to lick and suckle one of her most intimate of places and stood openly naked before him, willing him, asking him, to take her, and White Dove was asking about Carl. It was truly laughable. *"No, White Dove, Carl and I are friends, he comforted me that's is all."* Elizabeth had conveniently dismissed her own naked episode with Carl and her reactions to it. White

Dove accepted her answer and dropped the subject much to Elizabeth's relief. As they finished the dinner things, White Dove announced that she was going to see friends and would be back later. Elizabeth asked her to say hello for her and wished her good night. Then Elizabeth was alone, nothing to stop her thoughts running through her mind. Everything that had happened, since she'd come home. Elizabeth recalled the moment she had first seen Red Wolf again outside the stage post. The sight of him, had taken her breath away. It had felt so right, so natural him coming for her. And it seemed she'd been waiting all her life for him, for that moment. Suddenly her tears over came her and that's how Carl found her. Slumped in a corner with tears running down her face.

Carl rushed over to her. *"Elizabeth don't."* Without knowing or asking why she was crying, it didn't matter to him, he wrapped his arms around her and held her close. It broke him to see her like this. When White Dove came back it was late. She entered the tepee quietly. Carl and Elizabeth were asleep. He was still holding her. Carl woke early as usual. Elizabeth was lying next to him. He got up quietly and went outside. White Dove was working at the fire. Black Dog approached him. *"We go hunt, come."* Carl, touched White Doves shoulder. *"She still sleeps, I don't know what upset her last night but I came back and she was crying."* He told her. White Dove looked at him. *"I will see to her today."* Carl smiled gratefully at her and he was gone.

Carl followed Black Dog across the compound to their horses. Part of him was grateful that he wouldn't have to think too much about last night or the days he had spent with Elizabeth alone. Their party was made up of Black Dogs braves and Carl. They had makings for two days they told him. Carl suddenly realised that he would be gone for a couple of days. He hoped Black Dog had told White Dove, but knew instinctively that she would know anyway.

Elizabeth woke sometime later. And realised it was late and she was alone. Wondering where everyone had gone. Elizabeth made quick work of straightening up inside. Then went out looking for everyone. White Dove was sitting by the fire talking to friends. Elizabeth said good morning to them. Some she knew very well. They left the two of them alone shortly after. It was clear that White Dove had something on her mind. *"Is there something wrong White Dove."* She asked. *"Esa, I came back last night and Carl was physically comforting you, you were asleep together."* She said gently. Elizabeth looked embarrassed. *"I did not intend for it to happen, I became distressed after you left, Carl found me crying and held me. Nothing more."* She told her. *"Nothing more as far as you are concerned Esa, maybe, but for Carl, he has feelings for you."* Elizabeth looked shocked. Carl had feelings for her? When did that happen. He had spent all their time keeping his distance. Trying to give her space. Was that why she wondered. *"Is it fair to him, if your love is elsewhere."* She asked her. *"My love?"* Elizabeth repeated. *"I have no love, White Dove, he belongs to someone else."* Before White Dove could respond, Elizabeth got up and walked away. She spent the day seeing old friends, playing with their children and talking with Running Elk, Clear Water and Dull Knife. No one mentioned Red Wolf and his rejection of Grey Owls daughter. For the villagers, it was a family thing and the family, choose to ignore it, each for different reasons.

As she made dinner White Dove let Elizabeth know it would just be the two of them for a couple of days. Black Dog having taken Carl hunting. Elizabeth was happy for him. They ate in silence and the evening passed in quiet female company. Elizabeth turned in early and found to her surprise, she missed Carl. Elizabeth didn't know what to think any more. She had a restless night. And woke early. For once, she was up before White Dove. Elizabeth walked down to the river and bathed. She came back and found White Dove up and making breakfast. *"Good morning."* Elizabeth told her and bent to kiss her. White Dove accepted her kiss and thought that it was the first time since coming to the village that Esa, had done that. *"I'm going riding today."* She told her. *"I'll be back later."* White Dove nodded to her and they ate in silence, when finished Elizabeth rose and hugged White Dove. She left her without another word and went in search of Patches.

CHAPTER SEVEN

Red Wolf had started out early that day too. He had worked his way back towards the village. He'd intended to stay out for at least a week but he wanted to see her. He had worked longer and harder than needed and had decided to make the longer round trip back. Elizabeth was setting off on Patches as Red Wolf was on his way back.

Elizabeth wasn't sure where she was going. She just wanted to get away on her own for a bit. On any other day. Black Dog would have come with her. So for once she was alone and glad of it. She headed away from the village watering hole. It was a lovely day she thought to herself pushing her pony on. Elizabeth remembered she'd rode this way as a child on many occasions. There were a number of old uninhabited Indian rock homes in this direction at Bluff cliffs. It was a ride but she was up for it. She had been fascinated as a child and it had become a play den for them. The lower rooms were used as emergency store houses and safe houses in extreme weather for the village. She had many fond memories of those days. The fun of hide and seek and exploring the unusual surroundings. Looking for discarded items left by the ancient and more recent warriors. On the spare of the moment, Elizabeth decided to head that way.

Carl was watching Black Dog track a Deer. He was amazed by their skill and envied them.

The morning passed quickly and still Elizabeth rode on. She wasn't worried about getting back late, she was on Indian ground and White Dove would understand.

Red Wolf with one of his braves was making his way across a stream. A good half days' ride and he would be back at the village. Slowly it started to rain. Red Wolf looked up to the sky and realised that it would rain and heavy for some time. A storm was coming. He needed shelter.

Elizabeth had almost arrived at the bluff cliffs when the rain started to pour. Within a few minutes, the heavens opened and thundered is arrival. Lightning struck. She pushed her pony on the last bit. Talking to him all the while. Soothing him. Pushing him on. She rode up the well-worn track that had began to run with water and pushed on again. Entering one of the lower rock rooms with Patches. Elizabeth was wet to the skin, not again she thought. She dismounted and looked around her. Luckily some old straw had been left by a previous inhabitant. Elizabeth grabbed a couple of handfuls, took Patches saddle off and wiped him down. The storm raged on and lightning struck outside the entrance. Patches reared up and Elizabeth became desperate to sooth him but found it difficult. The enclosed musty space was making him nervous. Her growing fear wasn't helping.

Lightning struck again and this time Patches slipped from her hold and bolted with Elizabeth half clinging on and running back into the rain after him. Red Wolf was approaching the rocks when the lightening started. He'd crossed over dismounted and sheltered. When the second lightning struck, he was amazed to see Patches run out from the cliffs further up, followed by Elizabeth clearly desperate to gain control of her horse and in some danger of lightening striking either of them. Just as quickly as Elizabeth's exit from her cliff space had been, Red Wolf jumped on his horse, unleashed it and rode after Patches.

Elizabeth shocked to see him riding out across the plateau after Patches, watched open mouthed as Red Wolf signalled to her to return and taking the hint, Elizabeth went back inside and waited. Bear, Red Wolfs brave came in after her. She had known him for as long as she had known the tribe. He greeted her without words as was the custom and saw to his horse. Elizabeth suddenly found herself feeling very nervous. 'This was not going as planned. The last time she had been alone with Red Wolf....' Elizabeth shut off that thinking. She couldn't handle it. It had not ended well she reminded herself. 'Just as well we are not alone.' She thought. She took comfort in Bear's presence. And sat towards the back of the opening. Red Wolf came bounding back all too quickly she thought and had her pony with him. Elizabeth was so happy to see Patches safe and well she forgot how or why he was here. Red Wolf dismounted. Spoke to Bear and unusually tied up their horses.

He didn't look at her, but picked up the straw Elizabeth had tried to use earlier and completed the job on both horses. All three sat in silence. It felt like hours but the weather started to look like it was improving. Elizabeth was relieved. She couldn't stay here with Red Wolf for much longer. Red Wolf called to Elizabeth. *"Do they know you are here?"* He asked her. Elizabeth frowned. She had told them she was going riding not where she would be. But then, this morning she hadn't known where she would go. She sighed. *"No."* Red Wolf spoke quickly to Bear. To Elizabeth's despair, Bear mounted and was gone. Red Wolf turned to face her. He'd tried to ignore her but couldn't put it off any longer and drank in the vision before him. Even wet and miserable, she took his breath away. It felt like he had been away from her for so long. He noticed Elizabeth's despair at Bear's departure. It was obvious where he had gone and why. *"Your wet."* He told her. It came out harsher than he meant. *"Is there any firewood or makings?"* He asked as he walked towards her. *"I didn't have a chance to look, I'd only just got here when Patches bolted."* Elizabeth said defensively. Trying her best to ignore him and shaking, the wet from her hair. *"There's plenty of straw in the back, I'll get some."* She offered. *"I'll look for some firewood, we've got plenty of water and some food and you need some heat."* He told her.

Elizabeth went to the back of the caves. She wasn't sure she needed any heat. She was feeling hot enough. Trying desperately not to think of what he was doing here. She came back laden and piled it up for the ponies to eat. She also found an old tin bucket and some tins and took them to the edge of the rocks to collect water. They were soon filled. She brought them back and gave the bucket to the animals. She brushed and soothed them. They were nervous but gladly drank in turn. She took it back to refill. The smaller tins were over flowing but she delayed returning to Red Wolf. The bucket was soon filled again and Elizabeth brought it back and let the ponies have their fill. When they were finished, Elizabeth tided the straw. Eventually she looked over to where Red Wolf was trying to build a fire. He must have found wood and kindling. Elizabeth kept her distance. She suddenly felt suffocated, damp and desperate for some air and walked back to the edge of the cave and stood by the entrance. Elizabeth leaned on the wall looking out at the torrent of rain. The beauty of its savagery stirred her.

She didn't hear him come up behind her, the noise of the rain was deafening. He must have called her name but she hadn't heard him. The first she realised his presence was as he touched her arm. Elizabeth jumped as if he had burnt her. Red Wolf backed away a little hurt by her reaction to his touch. *"Your wet."* He repeated. *"Come and dry off."* He told her. Elizabeth followed him to the fire. *"It seems."* He told her drolly. *"That I am continually telling you to remove your clothes."* More soberly, and looking around him he continued. *"But this time we have no other clothes. Take this blanket and slip out of your outer clothes. When did you change back into wearing western clothes?"* He asked her. Elizabeth ignored the question and wrapped the blanket around herself. She took off her pants. Hide jacket and her shirt. He took them from her and laid them over the rocks near the fire to dry. *"Are you cold?"*

He asked Elizabeth, recalling the last time she was wet and cold, she answered him nervously. *"I am fine do not worry."* She told him.

Red Wolf noticed that she did not answer his question about the clothes but decided to let it go. *"Hungry?"* He asked. *"Yes"* This was safer ground she thought. *"I'll make something to eat."* He told her. Elizabeth thought that should be my job sadly. She busied herself with wringing out her hair and rubbing it on the blanket. Elizabeth kept her silence and walked nearer the fire to shake out her hair and allow the warmth to dry it. She wrapped the blanket tightly around her. Red Wolf, as he had many times before, put together an evening meal. They sat in silence while he cooked. Elizabeth could not bring herself to speak. She sat running her hand through her hair. Red Wolf handed her the food. *"Thank you."* He would wait until they had finished he told himself, then they would talk.

Elizabeth picked at her food although hungry. *"Eat."* He told her and she did. The food was good and hot. Elizabeth suddenly realised that she hadn't eaten all day and she was starving. Red Wolf watched her discretely. He felt better seeing her tuck into her meal. He could sense her anxiety and did not want that to spoil the food or Elizabeth's chance to eat. He banked up the fire. There had been a surprising amount of wood hidden in the back of the cave. He guessed someone had been using them recently. Elizabeth was soon finished. She got up and poured some coffee. "Would you like some." She asked him. "I would yes." He told her. Elizabeth poured another and handed it to him. The cave took on a homely feel. It became warm very quickly. The glow of the fire and its warmth gave a sense of ease and the aroma of food comforting. They both sat and listened to the fire cracking. The rain beating down outside. It was surprisingly peaceful after such an extreme day.

At the same time, Carl was sheltering with Black Dog and the braves. They had come across an abandoned cabin and took shelter. Carl had lit a fire and food was cooking.

Red Wolf looked at his tin cup and spoke, he could not wait any longer. *"We need to talk."* He said quietly gazing into his coffee. Elizabeth ignored him. If she did it long enough maybe he'd stop she thought. *"Are we not going to speak?"* He asked her. Elizabeth took a moment and spoke. *"I fear I have little to say." "There is much to be said, plans to make, arrangements to be made."* He replied. Elizabeth laughed incredibly. *"Plans, arrangements? Your plans can and have been made without me."* She responded angrily. Red Wolf looked at her unsure for the moment if she were insulting him or sincere. *"Without you?"* He repeated rising to her temper. What was wrong with her he wondered. Elizabeth pierced her eyes at him. *"Decisions have already been made, have they not?"* She bristled at him. Red Wolf didn't know what to make of it. Was she rejecting him. After everything that had happened between them. Had she found love with Carl after all? Red Wolf jumped to his feet. Threw his cup to one side and in three strides. Was across the room and pulling her to her feet.

"Without you." He repeated again through gritted teeth. *"What would be the point without you?"* He shouted at her. *"You go off with Carl for a week, you spend days and nights with him, share his bed and you insult me."* He raged almost out of control. The thought of her in another man's arms, his bed, spoken aloud for the first time, pushed him to the edge. He shook her. *"Deny it."* He demanded. *"Tell me you were not in his bed."* He spoke verminously shaking her. *"Go on, deny it."* Elizabeth realised she had pushed him too far. She was in danger of losing her blanket. She tried to increase her hold on

it, while Red Wolf ranted. Elizabeth felt how close Red Wolf was to losing his control. She spoke keeping her voice level. *"I have nothing to explain and have no reason to explain to you."* She tried to remove herself from his grip. *"Oh no, we are dealing with this now."* He said wrestling with her. *"You are with another man and yet I still want you."* He spat. *"How low I am".* *"Red Wolf don't please. Your hurting me."* Elizabeth cried out. Red Wolf looked at her anguish, fear and pain and instantly, his anger evaporated. He felt shame. He'd hurt her. When even after everything she'd done. It was the last thing he ever want to do. He felt like he was gut ripped.

This woman, so much a part of him. He couldn't stand being apart from her. *"Then if I have given you no reason to explain to me, I guess this won't mean anything either."* He said calmly and quietly as he looked meaningfully into her eyes. He brought his face close to hers. Elizabeth held her breath and her anxiety got the better of her. She backed away from him, letting out her breath as she went. Red Wolf smiled at her. Hadn't she learnt that you never run from a predator. Sensing her feelings, he walked with her backwards. Lifting the long strands of her hair back from her face and wrapped them round the back of her neck. As he did so, his fingers lightly brushed her skin sending goose bumps across her flesh. Elizabeth shuddered. Too close. He was too near her she cried out in her head. Red Wolf lightly caressed her cheek. Then her neck. Elizabeth couldn't back up any more. She was at the rock face. Red Wolf smiled down at her. Nowhere to go. He exposed her flesh at her neck with his hands, his mouth went in search of it. Red Wolf felt the blood rush to his cock. He slowly released his grip on her. Elizabeth held her breath. He used his mouth to kiss his way down her neck, along her shoulder and continued down her body. Elizabeth clung to her blanket, it was the only thing keeping her modesty alive. Elizabeth was emotionally torn and mentally exhausted. She desperately wanted to stop him or put her arms around him and crush him against her but felt paralysed. 'He wasn't hers' she cried out in her head. And couldn't bring herself to do either.

Red Wolf was driven. He'd waited long enough. He needed to touch her, hold her, caress her, but after his outburst earlier he was scared to. He remembered how her skin felt under her touch, under his mouth, the taste of her, the rain, salt, her essence filling him. He became more aroused. Moving his mouth along her collarbone to the base of her throat. He sucked. Elizabeth leaned into him. Licking the spot he kissed his way and explored the crevasse between her breasts. Elizabeth held her breath. The blanket the only thing between them. She clung on and still hadn't touched him. His mouth and tongue were nibbling her hands clinging to the blanket and her skin above her camisole, caressing her. His mouth moved against the blanket backwards and forwards. Elizabeth struggled to hold on to it. It was in his way. It was holding her modesty. And she didn't want it any more. Elizabeth dropped the blanket and leaned back.

Red Wolf hesitated for the barest second. Mind made up his mouth went in search of what it wanted. As his lips found it, Red Wolf slipped his hands onto hers, his tongue licking the top of her breast. Elizabeth jerked. He raised her hands above her head and with one hand he held them there. He let his mouth search for what it wanted and with his other hand, explored what was his.

Elizabeth thought she'd lose her mind. She'd wanted to resist him but her body betrayed her. Every touch of his mouth, sent shock waves down her body. Elizabeth arched her back into him and spoke aloud. *"Oh god, Red Wolf, this is wrong. We can't do this."* Red Wolf bit her nipple and sucked it hard through her chemise. Elizabeth cried out. Panting. He tongued it soothing the bite. Elizabeth moaned. *"I. Yes. O yes. Feels so Good."* Red Wolf popped the nipple from his mouth and crushed her lips with his. His tongue in search of hers. Breaking from her and breathing hard he told her. *"This is anything but wrong."* And went back in search of her breast. Elizabeth started to believe him. Something this good couldn't be wrong. Could it? He kissed the tip of her nipple and slowly sucked it back into his mouth. This other hand stroked over her other nipple. Elizabeth was on fire. Something was building within her and she couldn't explain it. Red Wolf sucked on her breast as he squeezed and pulled on her other breast with his hand. The rhythm hypnotic. Elizabeth ached. Her body responding. Her breasts aching and swelling her nipples so hard. Her Stomach and lower her body pulsed. She wanted more. Her breathing became choppy. She was hot so hot and needed more. Suddenly Red Wolf stepped back. He hadn't let her hands go and he now looked at her. Elizabeth looked lost. Wanton. *"Have I given you reason now Elizabeth?"* He asked her. Then abruptly, let her go and stood away from her. He was as hard as iron.

Elizabeth stood there confused. A moment ago she was in ecstasy at his hands and mouth. Now she stood cold. Alone. Exposed. She didn't understand. *"You want me to explain, now?"* She asked incredulously. She stood semi naked and shaking with emotion. Red Wolf looked at her with raw hunger in his eyes. *"Do you want me Elizabeth?"* He quietly asked her earnestly. *"Do you want me for a mate, for a husband, for life?"* He demanded. *"I will not play this game no longer. Make a decision and make it now."*

Elizabeth shook her head and fell back against the rock wall. She closed her eyes and with a sigh she told him. *"We have been through all this, you are not free, father wishes you to marry Sky, it is arranged, and I have made my peace with it."* Red Wolf came back to her pushing his body against hers, leaving her with no doubt of his need of her. Grabbing the back of her neck he pulled her face to face with him. With an angry tone in his voice. *"But I have not made peace with it."* He told her desperately searching her face for some recognition. Suddenly scared she would be lost to him. Red Wolf let go of her neck and slid his hands round and under her chemise along her waist as his mouth found hers. He kissed her putting all his longing into it. A deep demanding kiss, exploring, searching, probing and tantalisingly exotic. Elizabeth felt bombarded. She had never been kissed like this. Like he could take her over. She groaned. Red Wolf gave up to his own emotions and his hands, once again, explored the body he craved. This time Elizabeth gave in to the need in her. She returned his kisses. Became more demanding, more frantic with every moment. Elizabeth hardly noticed when Red Wolf slid his hands inside the band of her cami knickers and cradled her naked buttocks into him while his body pushed and rubbed into hers. She felt him, hard and strong, there was no mistaking what he was rubbing against her. He rubbed her just right. Sending need through her.

Elizabeth had seen plenty of stallions in mating and understood what she was feeling. She suddenly felt scared. Vulnerable. Excited at the same time. He was pushing into her and causing a delicious friction. She moaned and ran her hand through his hair across the back of his head and held it to her. Red Wolf felt her tongue search for him and was barely holding on to his own control. He felt her body move with his. Meeting him as he rubbed against her. Unable to control it any longer. He bent to suckle her breast back in. 'I will have her' he told himself. 'No one will take what's mine'. Red Wolf knew he had to prepare her. He felt for all his bluster. She was pure but he had to know. His hands caressed her hips and one moved around to cup her. Elizabeth cried out and pushed at him. Her conscious rising to the top. Red Wolf bit her nipple teasingly between his teeth as his tongue lathered it. Elizabeth moaned gave up any objections overcome with need and caressed his head. Red Wolf punished her breasts with his mouth. Elizabeth started to thrash. Too much too powerful. Just out of reach. She needed something. Red Wolf felt it. She was close. Slipping his hands back round to her hips he pushed her knickers down. They fell to the floor. Elizabeth hadn't even felt it. So caught up in the moment. He ran his hands up her thighs and parted them slightly. Running his fingers up the inside of them. Red Wolf rose the hand that had been stroking her inner thigh, he slowly teased and stroked the skin between her legs. As he got higher so did his anticipation of having her. Swiftly he parted her and slipped a finger inside her and fingered her pleasure zone with his thumb. Elizabeth came undone. She screamed his name as wave after wave of release overcame her. Elizabeth was shaking. He pushed her leg free of her undergarments. And held her in place. He wasn't done.

Elizabeth still riding her release, moaned again. She caught her breath as he touched her, she felt an increasing instinctive need to feel him skin on skin and started to remove some of his clothes. Red Wolf continued to push his finger into her. He broke from kissing her breast and placed his free hand on the top if her chemise, it had only been partially open all this time. Red Wolf looked again into her eyes as he took hold of the front of it. He was breathing hard, it was clear what he was going to do, Elizabeth made no move to object and in one swift motion, he ripped it from her body and exposed her, bodily to him. He looked at her and felt completely out of his depth. He kissed her mouth hard and demanding, pumping her with his fingers and using his free hand playing with her breast, pinching her nipple, stroking her. Elizabeth called out. *"Yes O Yes."* His mouth broke free of her lips and bit down on her other breast. As he pushed two fingers into her. Elizabeth struggled under his mouth at the violation. No she thought, this cannot be. Red Wolf had expected her reaction and responded to it. Pushing and stroking her pleasure zone. Elizabeth cried out and called his name over and over again and clinging to him urging him on. Elizabeth started to ride his hand. Red Wolf tried to hold onto some reason. But the nagging feeling that he may be second hurt him and he wanted to hurt her back. Make sure, she never wanted another man but him.

His control slipped. Could not wait any longer, he removed his mouth from her nipple and crushed her lips again, searching, demanding and probing with his tongue. Elizabeth was breathless. Caressing him. Pushing into him. Rubbing herself at him.

Quickly, he began to ride his fingers back and forth inside her and caress with his thumb her most intimate of places. Elizabeth shocked at what he was doing to her but unable to control herself, her emotions rose with every stroke he took of her, she clung to him. Stopped struggling and gave herself up to the wave rising again to consume her and the emotions he was drawing from her.

She pulled her mouth from his. *"My God."* She cried out. The feeling of his invasion indescribable. *"Not God, Elizabeth, just me."* He told her and watched her, as he continued to pump his fingers inside her. He searched her face and registered the pleasure he was giving her as he plunged his fingers in deeper and deeper. Elizabeth gasped, lifted her hands to his face and with her eyes drank him in, while he pleasured her. How could a man bring her so much pleasure she thought.

Elizabeth's lips and mouth were dry, she tried to moisten them, she was so hot, unconsciously, her body pushed into his hand while he pumped her. She could feel the closeness of her emotional wave. Her body teetering on the cusp. He felt her body move under him. She stroked his face and kissed him. It wasn't enough. Elizabeth thought she would explode. She held onto him. Red Wolf kissed her again, caressed her breast and she responded eagerly. She started to open her legs to him, he felt her move, he wanted to taste her but, unsure how she would respond to him. Red Wolf removed his fingers and Elizabeth cried out at the sudden emptiness she felt. She'd been so close. He shifted his weight and replaced his fingers with his left hand and continued to ride her back and forth and whisper her name.

He looked at her. Lifted his right hand to his face and Elizabeth looked on as Red Wolf opened his mouth and sucked on both the fingers. Elizabeth gasped, he sucked them dry then kissed her demandingly. Elizabeth shocked and dazed, held back, he tasted of something forbidden. It was erotic. This time, he broke free of her and kissed his way down the centre of her body, now fully exposed to him. As he

got to his knees, he lifted her left leg over his shoulder.

Elizabeth did not stop him or protest, she was on fire. Red

Wolf lifted her slightly, removed his fingers from her body

and replaced them with his mouth. His tongue flicking in and

out of her. Elizabeth suddenly realised Red Wolf was using

his mouth and tongue on her most intimate of places. Almost

out of her mind with pleasure, she didn't think she could

stand much more. She cried out. *"Stop - you can't do that, dear*

God, you can't." She clung to the wall. Red Wolf took her

other hand and placed it at the back of his head pushing his

head in closer with every thrust of his tongue. It intensified

her pleasure and Elizabeth soon understood what he was

asking of her. It felt so good. The intense pleasure rising in

her was back. Elizabeth took over, he let her go and let his

tongue go wild. He was so close and so was she. When he

could wait no longer, he replaced his mouth with his fingers

and pumped her hard and fast and sucked on her pleasure

zone. Elizabeth cried out and arched her back clinging to his

head as the most intense emotional wave overcame her. She

crested on his tongue crying out for him. Red wolf rose from

his knees to kiss her again.

Elizabeth was spent. Her body quivering with

emotion. The man awed her. She stroked his face again and

again, responding to his kisses in return. Red Wolf yanked

open his buckskin and bent his knees and pushed himself

against her core. Elizabeth felt him again, harder than before,

stronger, bigger even and instinctively rubbed her body

against him as she caressed him.

Red Wolfs fingers continued to work their magic,

riding back and forth across her pleasure zone increasing their

pace with her caresses. Suddenly he knew it had to be now,

neither of them could wait any longer. Red Wolf lifted her

and placed her over his shaft. *"Are you sure Elizabeth?"* He asked strained. Not sure if he could stop had she told him to.

"*Yes.*" She answered, mouth dry and body wet. Before her answer was fully out of her mouth he had crushed them with his lips and lowered her onto him. Elizabeth cried out in pain under his lips, Red Wolf smiled to himself, she was his after all as he broke her barrier.

Slowly his body took over from where his fingers stopped. He pushed slowly and lightly into her, he didn't want to shock her now. She was so tight, 'god she felt good' he thought as he drove in and out, in and out, deeper and deeper, each new push bringing gasps of pleasure from her. She was his and he was taking everything she had to offer. Faster and faster he drove into her, she clung to him as her breast bounced with his pounding of her from the outside as well as the in. Elizabeth lifted her legs and held him to her. Begged him for more. Elizabeth felt that building sensation within her again. It gained pace with Red Wolf's every move.

He was riding her, fast and hard and she was eagerly driving

him on. Red Wolf held onto the wall to protect her back as his

pace became frantic. Elizabeth reached her climax and

exploded clinging to him screaming his name. Red Wolf

waited for her and wasn't finished. He slowed his pace and

let her enjoy the waves of emotion from her climax, the first of

many he hoped joined together. Smothering her in light

kisses while she regained her breath to feel what he could give

her. The slower pace of entering her and pulling out

increasing the pleasure she would gain from it, he spoke her

name over and over again. The intensity of her muscles

surrounding his cock in the aftershock of her climax undid

him. He could wait any longer. He grasped her thighs and

held her tight. Pounding into her fast and hard and climaxed

like he had never before. Within a few moments of his release,

Red Wolfs knees gave way and they fell to the floor. He held

on to her tightly and rolled her on top of him. Both exhausted, saturated in sweat and riding the wave of emotion crashing through them. *"I have always loved you."* she told him.

Red Wolf couldn't let her go, he gently laid her on the floor, stroked her and spoke her name. In time he made love to her again and later, again still. The night closed in around them. Elizabeth fell asleep in his arms. Red Wolf left her only to see to the fire. It woke her, she stretched and looked for him. She looked her fill of her naked man in the fire light. She couldn't believe how wonderful it felt to be with a man. The way he touched her, made her feel, the need he drew from her to touch him, the feel of his body on hers. The feel of him inside her. Elizabeth couldn't stop herself from grinning. She had never known it could be like this. Red Wolf caught her smiling to herself. It brought such joy to him. He walked back towards her in all his naked glory, leaned over and kissed her. Elizabeth willingly responded and he pulled open the blanket exposed her nakedness to him and marvelled in the sight of her. He reached down and caressed her breast brushing over her nipple. Elizabeth responded by placing her hand over his. *"Your going to have to stop tempting me."* He told her smiling growing hard. Elizabeth opened her legs and caressed him against her. She loved the feel of him. *"Why would I want to do that?"* She whispered. Red Wolf bent down and pulled her to him. He placed his cock at her entrance and slipped inside her. He watched her face as he entered her. He was in no doubt of the pleasure she enjoyed. And began to take her body and soul. Elizabeth rode the wave he created and cried out with joy when she could hold back no longer. Red Wolf buried himself deep within her and gave her his seed. Completely exhausted, both were soon asleep.

That's how Carl found them. Naked, alone and together.

He had searched ahead of his party to find a cave to shelter in. They had left the shelter of the cabin as the weather improved only for the heavens to open again. There was no mistaking what he saw or what had happened there. Carl had quickly been able to hold back Black Dog and the rest of the hunting party having spotted Red Wolfs and Elizabeth's ponies. They had camped in a nearby cave. Carl knew, the smoke from their fire would soon alert Red Wolf. Time would, after all, reveal all. Carl felt physically sick.

No matter how much he tried to sleep, Carl couldn't. The images of Red Wolf and Elizabeth, together haunted him. The intimacy of both wrapped around each other, left no doubt of the pleasure they had shared. Their nakedness. He acknowledged his envy at Red Wolf being the one to share her naked embrace and the pleasure she would have given him. And it tore at him.

Part of him knew this was always how it was going to be. But still, he had hoped it would have been him and not Red Wolf laying with her. He couldn't escape his emotions. She was lost to him. The realisation of that alone, threatened to break him. Carl realised, that if he were to stay at the Double T, he would have to find a way of living with this knowledge. Either that or he would have to leave. Could he see her each day knowing she was laying with another man each night. Carl wasn't sure he could do that. But to leave, he thought, leave her, that he was not ready to do. Eventually exhaustion over took him. Carl was woken by the sound of voices at sun rise. Black Dog was talking with Red Wolf and he indicated in Carls direction. Red Wolf approached Carl and bent down to him. For several moments neither man said anything. Eventually, Red Wolf looked at him *"Thank you."* Red Wolf whispered. Carl stared back. *"And I'm sorry."* Red Wolf told him as he rose and walked back to his braves. There was no point Carl telling him, he hadn't done it for him, or

Carl shouting his feelings and calling him out, they both knew

that already. The battle was over before it had begun.

CHAPTER EIGHT

The morning moved on quickly. Camp broke and both camps came together. Horses were prepared and they moved out. Elizabeth found it hard to look Carl in the eye. It made both men uneasy. The journey back to the village took most of the day and everyone kept their own company. Carl couldn't believe it had only been 48 hours earlier that he had so much. Their arrival had been expected. Bear had made it back to the village and informed Dull Knife of what had happened to Elizabeth. Dull Knife came out to meet them. The welcome was warm and inviting. White Dove was also there. And she registered the strained atmosphere between Elizabeth and Carl and the intimacy between Red Wolf and Elizabeth. She knew then, time had run out.

White Dove went to Elizabeth as she dismounted and greeted her. As she did so, Dull Knife addressed the tribe.

"Now my son and daughter are both here, I invite you all to join me in the celebration of my oldest son's marriage." Elizabeth looked visibly shocked. She turned to Red Wolf. How did Dull Knife know, she thought? *"In two moons."* Dull Knife continued *"Red Wolf and Sky will be joined, as will Running Elk and Clear Water."* A chorus of calls went up. Dancing and music started and the village came alive with wedding preparations. Elizabeth stood in silence. He'd lied to her and she'd given him everything. She knew only too well, Red Wolf could never, would never, confront his father in front of the tribe. The decision had been made for them. She'd been right all along. She had given everything and lost him after all. She wasn't sure how she'd done it, but she had stayed for what seemed an appropriate length of time and then made her way back to her tepee. White Dove wasn't long behind her. Carl had taken their ponies on arriving. And gone straight to the tepee. He was there when Elizabeth walked in. He'd heard the commotion but wasn't sure what it was all about.

She looked straight at him. *"I am sorry Carl, yesterday should never have happened, I have disgraced myself, it was my mistake and I'll have to live with it."*

As she finished White Dove walked in behind her, there was no mistaking her intent. *"Esa, you knew Dull Knife had intended this."* Elizabeth gave a waned smile. *"Yes, this is my doing White Dove and I accept it." "Will you be able to do this?"* White Dove asked her. *"I will have too, father would never understand if I left now."* Elizabeth answered her. White Dove hugged her, they both knew the next two days were not going to be easy. Carl looked confused at both women. White Dove took pity on him. *"Red Wolf is to have a tribal marriage to Sky in two days."* 'What' Carl thought. *"He can't."* Carl spoke angrily. *"What about Elizabeth and the two of them?"* White Dove took his meaning. *"This was a tribal decision Carl, Red Wolf will never be able to challenge it and Elizabeth understands that only too well." "So he would - just leave her?"* Carl asked incredulously, his voice rising. Elizabeth put her hand on his arm. *"He has no choice."* Was all she said, the sadness in her voice and her resigned manner told him the fight in her had gone. It was indeed over.

Red Wolf came to them later that night. He entered the tepee searching for Elizabeth but found all three of them waiting for him. Elizabeth spoke to him in that same resolved voice she had used earlier in pacifying Carl. She did not move to find some privacy for them, Elizabeth had set the stage for what she had to say and Red Wolf was expecting it. Elizabeth drew her eyes to his face and looked longingly at him. She managed to drag her eyes away and swallowed hard. In a voice that could barely be heard, she spoke to him. *"We had more in one moment than most ever have in a lifetime and now, we must do, what is expected of us."*

Red Wolf looked at her, he thought she'd never seemed so beautiful, not since the first time he'd seen her at 7 years old, running across the ranch yard, hair flying, to take her uncles hand. Or on the realisation, when she was leaving for back East. He had lost his heart that very moment, not even last night, when she had at last been his and given herself willingly to him came close to that moment. The strength she found now, gave her something that surpassed all that. Made him realise all the more, just what he was giving up. She was his life, she was the air he breathed, he couldn't remember a time, that didn't have her in it. Even the years she was away, he kept a part of her with him. He knew what those words had cost her and what they would cost him and he wanted her all the more for it.

Red Wolf acknowledged her words without speaking, he couldn't. He turned and looked directly at Carl. *"Look after her."* He asked him. Both men understanding what had transpired. *"If she'll let me."* Carl responded. Red Wolf nodded and walked out. Elizabeth never saw him again before his marriage. The next two days passed in a blur. Elizabeth and White Dove were expected to do many of the marriage things involved with the family. Elizabeth was torn, she wanted to help Running Elk, his marriage had been expected and she welcomed his happiness, only now her work also took the man she wanted from her. With each task she helped complete the further away he became. She thought she would die with the pain of it.

The morning of the wedding was beautiful. Elizabeth hadn't been able to sleep and had got up early. Needing some peace. Carl was also up and watched her leave the tepee. It was clear she was heading for her favourite place. He followed her at a discrete distance, watched her gaze out over the river and sit down. He eventually joined her. She was sitting cross legged and eyes closed. Without opening them, she spoke to him. *"I wish I were home."* Carl reached out and took her hand in his. *"You are home."* He told her kindly. They sat together like that until called. Elizabeth took her position behind Dull Knife and next to White Dove. The ceremony was quick and beautiful. Running Elk and Clear Water looked very happy. Unlike Red Wolf. It was clear to all those present that he was doing his duty. He ignored his 'wife'. He did not embrace her and held her hand for as short a time as possible. Elizabeth could not bring herself to look at him. But congratulated his new wife as was expected of the husband's family. She was after all, the Chief's daughter. What she did not expect, was Sky's response to her and what she said quietly to her. *"My husband will never love me because of you, you will not be welcome in my home."* And Sky walked away from her. Some lines were not to be crossed. It wouldn't be a difficult price to pay.

Elizabeth danced and sang as expected and joined in with Dull Knife and White Dove. The single women of the tribe started their traditional dance, of circling the fire in a clockwise direction facing outwards and Elizabeth was pulled in to join them, the single braves surrounded them, dancing in the opposite direction. When the music reached a joining point, you danced with the brave opposite you. It was a way of meeting for many of the young, expected or unexpected alike. Elizabeth found herself going through the motions, she wasn't looking for who might be her partner, it didn't matter. When the music beat stopped, Elizabeth looked up and there stood Carl and beyond him, stood Red Wolf. Carl wasn't there by chance and Elizabeth helped him complete the dance grateful to see him.

Great celebrations could go on for days, as the Harvest was due any day, the weddings and Harvest became entwined. It went on for a week. Red Wolf and Sky had left for the traditional wedding time alone, as had Running Elk and Clear Water. Elizabeth tried hard to enjoy the rest of her visit and not think. Everything was so painful. Elizabeth was emotionally drained and keeping up the pretence was killing her. The week soon ended and Elizabeth made ready to leave and return to the ranch. She would be gone before Red Wolf returned. On the eve of her leaving, Elizabeth had dinner with her father. White Dove and Carl joined them. After the preliminary greetings and the food, conversation was light and entertaining. Elizabeth left it for as long as she could, before bringing up the subject of Red Wolf and the Double T. She would have to word it carefully. *"Father, I feel that now, with Red Wolf being married his duty to the tribe must take precedence over the Double T. I understand should you now feel he should spend his time here."* Dull Knife was quiet for a time and considered what she had said. His daughter spoke the truth.

Feeling that time was running out for him, Dull Knife brought up a subject close to his heart. *"Daughter, you need a husband, it has been long enough."* He told her merrily. *"And you are passed marrying age, if you wait much longer, I fear you will only find old men like me"*. Laughingly he told her. *"Our land needs children, it needs a future, if you cannot find one daughter, I will be happy to find one for you from the tribe."* Dull Knife told her. Elizabeth didn't know what to say, it was clear the thought of Dull Knife finding her a husband was shocking after recent events. The atmosphere became very strained. It was equally clear to White Dove and Carl, that Elizabeth was close to tears. No one wanted to insult Dull Knife. Carl unsure looked at Elizabeth, she was unable to say anything and it would not have been right for White Dove to talk on her behalf. Dull Knife began to feel more was going on here, the atmosphere was becoming embarrassing. Carl cleared his throat. *"Sir, he told him, I have a great affection for your daughter and hope, in time, that she may have the same for me."* It was out of his mouth before he considered what he was saying. All three looked at him. Dull Knife broke into a wide smile and slapped him on the back satisfied that this was the reason for the strain. *"Good."* He stated loudly. *"You are a man. You understand our ways. Our tribe respects you, we would welcome you as part of our family."* And that was it, as far as Dull Knife was concerned the matter was settled. Unfortunately for Carl, as far as Elizabeth was concerned, it was far from settled.

"Are you completely mad." She asked him the moment they were outside and on their own. *"He was going to offer you a brave Elizabeth, the man's not well and he wants to see his daughter happy, married with a family of your own, if you had been listening to the tribe, you'd know the rush in Red Wolf marrying was for a reason. Would you prefer, that he found someone for you?"* He answered angrily back and continued " *You weren't in a position to answer him. He started to worry something was wrong and I didn't want to see you in a corner, this way, you have*

some choice, I'm not asking you to keep to it Elizabeth, I did this to help, not make things worse." It dawned on Elizabeth how singular she had been in her seclusion. She'd missed the bigger picture and it had taken an outsider to show her. *"How unwell is he?"* She asked them. *"I don't know but they are singing songs for him"*. Elizabeth turned to White Dove. *"Did you know this?"* *"Yes. He asked that I not tell you. He didn't want you to worry. But his time draws near. "*

"I'm sorry Carl, your right, thank you." Elizabeth spontaneously embraced him. Carl did not return her embraced. *"We have an early start tomorrow, we should go."* He told her. Elizabeth released him, smiled and nodded. They headed for the tepee. White Dove observed them from a distance. They may not know it, but she felt they belonged together. It would not be a 'love' match, Red Wolf held that ground, but still, it would work if they let it. The Double T party was up early, packed and ready to go. As expected, the

whole tribe came out to see them off. Many of the Double T staff were going back with them. There were a number of new braves joining them and some old ones staying behind for a while. All too soon, they were saying their goodbyes. For Elizabeth. For the first time ever, it couldn't come fast enough. Dull Knife embraced his daughter and wished her well. He also turned and offered a warm parting to Carl. White Dove as usual found it hard to say goodbye to friends and family.

It was then, that Elizabeth remembered that Red Wolf would not be leading them out. She mounted her pony and was suddenly unsure what to do. She looked to White Dove who nodded encouragement. Elizabeth called to her people. *"I thank you father, it is time to leave."* Dull Knife raised his hand in parting. Elizabeth acknowledged him and turned her pony and rode forward. The rest of her party followed after her. Carl found his place with Black Dog.

The ride to the Double T, followed the same route as before. Carl and Black Dog took it in turns to ride with Elizabeth. It was clear that now, she would have to lead her people and without Red Wolf. Elizabeth sent out scouting parties, several braves left and re-joined the convoy at intervals throughout the day. The first, being sent on to the Double T to warn of their arrival. Unlike on their outward journey, there were no unexpected visitors on her land and Elizabeth decided to make the push for home. They would not stop; they were not hampered by extra stock and goods. She asked Carl his opinion the last time he joined her. He agreed, there was no point in delaying their arrival. It was after nightfall when they entered the grounds of the Double T house. Elizabeth felt she had never seen anything more welcoming. She gave orders to see to the horses, store goods and equipment and gave her pony to Carl. Elizabeth looked at the house she loved so much and walked towards it. Anna and Kincade came out to welcome them home. Elizabeth was joined by Jake who gave her the biggest hug and started to catch up on the weeks she'd been away. White Dove joined them and they headed in to a late dinner. Elizabeth turned as she climbed the steps. *"Carl, join us for dinner." "Thank you mam."* Carl answered.

It was good to be back. The staff were happy at seeing them. The talk about the village, the weddings and the harvest. Elizabeth eventually asked if Ben had been heard from and Jake confirmed that yet they hadn't. They weren't expecting to hear from them for another couple of weeks, but somehow, Elizabeth needed to be comforted by Ben's imminent arrival. She realised that would have to wait.

As dinner finished Elizabeth made her excuses and headed outside with her coffee and sat on the porch. Carl came out, walked to the end and leaned on one of the posts.

They both kept their own council and looked out over the land. Eventually, Carl turned to say goodnight, sensing it, Elizabeth spoke to him *"I'd like to talk to you about the night in the caves."* Carl didn't know what to say, but came and sat on the steps beside her. He stared into his cup. *"You know, sometimes we can find ourselves in places that seem a step out of time, and, what happens there, should maybe, remain there."* He told her gently. Elizabeth smiled to herself. *"I'm not so sure, I'll be able to do that."* She spoke honestly and not naively. *"Such actions Carl, can have consequences."* She answered. *"Then you will face such challenges, as they come, maybe as your real father intended and if I can, I will help you do that."* *"I don't think even my father could have foreseen this Carl."* Elizabeth spoke wryly, leaning back and bracing her hands on the steps behind her. *"None of us knows the future Elizabeth, not even God."* With that, he rose and bid her goodnight.

Elizabeth watched him go. It was at that moment, that Elizabeth realised what a friend she had in him. She finished her coffee, rose and went into the house. She kissed White Dove goodnight and spoke to Jake about the coming day. They arranged to meet at breakfast. She bid them goodnight and went to her room. She found the confines of familiar surrounding comforting and got ready for bed. As she washed away the dirt of the day and got into bed, images of the last week came flooding back. Elizabeth was unable to hold back her tears. They flowed and did not stop until she fell into an exhausted sleep.

She rose early next morning. Went down to breakfast, ready to face her life without him. Elizabeth was already eating when Jake joined her. They talked about the ranch. The movements of cattle and horses and what needed to be done in preparation for Ben's return. Elizabeth was keen to lay plans for the days ahead in his absence. Jake had expected this. He talked Elizabeth through what he hoped would be acceptable. He outlined what he and the men had been doing over the past four weeks. Elizabeth realised that all seemed to be well and in fact, there was little for her to do. Jake had been doing this for many years. She decided then, to leave it all in Jake's capable hands until Ben's return. *"I intend to ride out each day and check a section at a time, I'll leave the rest to you, if that's ok Jake."* She told him. Jake's face split with a grin, he was more than happy with that and saw it as an affirmation of the work he had been doing. He happily agreed with her.

Elizabeth had to keep busy. If she were not exhausted her mind would betray her. Elizabeth worked herself hard. The next two weeks revolved around getting things back to normal. Elizabeth made her rounds accompanied by Black Dog and his braves. They headed out to check conditions of watering holes, the grasses, fences and stock and at the end of the second week, they made preparations for a trip into town.

Stores were running low and needed to be restocked. The night before, Elizabeth invited Jake and Carl to join her for dinner. They outlined what was needed in preparations for Autumn. They each turned in for an early night and rose before dawn.

Elizabeth was ready before White Dove came down. *"Are you alright Esa?"* She asked as she joined her. *"I am well White Dove, just excited about going to town that's all."* Elizabeth answered her. *"Well then, I guess we should get ready."* White Dove smiled and linked arms with Elizabeth as they went to prepare.

Breakfast was quick and efficient. Lunch was packed and the horses saddled. By the time Elizabeth walked out of the house, everything was ready. Carl was saddled and stood by her pony. *"Mam."* He called to her. *"Morning Carl, all ready?"* She asked him *"Yes mam."* He replied. They hadn't spent much time in each other's company since their return from the village. Carl felt that she could do with the space and it had given him a chance to catch up with Benny. He had been real happy to see him.

The journey to Brownsville was uneventful. The morning passed quickly and they rode in shortly after lunchtime. Their group consisted of 3 buckboards, Black Dog, 4 braves, 5 hands, White Dove, Carl and Elizabeth. Elizabeth had taken to wearing half buckskin, it was comfortable and the best clothes for riding. She wore her father's old Stetson and carried his bullwhip. She was an amazing sight riding into town. As on her first journey, the town came out to see them arrive. Elizabeth called out several greetings to old school friends and friends of the family. White Dove stopped at the General Store. Elizabeth made her pleasantries to Mr Jenkins and White Dove went in. The 3 hands from the buckboards would stay and help White Dove. Elizabeth rode down to the Bank. Mr Bell confirmed that Ben had deposited the money from the trail. He was happy to inform her that it looked like a good price. Elizabeth said her goodbyes and headed for the ladies store she liked so much. Vera was waiting for her.

"Elizabeth hello, it's been a while." She said coming forward and taking hold of her hand. *"I have lots of lovely new things for you."* She told her. Elizabeth grinned from ear to ear. *"Wonderful, just what I need some retail spending!"* She said laughingly. Black Dog waited outside with his braves. Carl had taken two men and headed for the post depot. Several parcels and packages had been delivered over the past few weeks. Carl checked them off and got them loaded. He then headed over to the grain store and got busy loading their order. By the time Elizabeth had finished at Vera's and was being escorted back to the general store, Carl was done too. The whole event had taken less than two hours. Elizabeth

relayed the information that Ben had completed the trail in good time and must be on his way back. White Dove had just come out of the store and seemed relieved, she had been worried for him. At that moment something exploded in the back of the Bank, a buggy bolted, Kate the younger sister of one of Elizabeth's school friends screamed. The horse out of control. Carl, Black Dog, several of the hands and towns people had already been rushing towards the Bank at the explosion and could only look as the buggy came flying past them. Blue, a brave and hand who had worked for them for several seasons, who had stayed with White Dove and was nearer, ran out in front of the buggy, as is raced past, he jumped and rode the lead horse, pulling it up just as it reached the school house. As he jumped down, Kate was trying to steady herself, she stood and fell, he caught her.

Blue held her for perhaps a moment too long. Kate didn't seem to mind. She was both scared and exhilarated at the same time and it wasn't all the buggy ride. Kate pulled

herself away a little and looked into the face of the man who

had saved her. He had bright blue eyes. That surprised her,

he was Indian. A smile broke out across her face and when

she caught her breath she spoke. *"Thank you. I'm Kate."* She

told him offering her hand. Blue stared at her. *"Blue."* He

said, turned and walked away. At the Bank, there had been a

hold up. It was foiled early, but the safe had exploded. To

Carls surprise, the men handcuffed were the same group of

men they had seen crossing Trelawney land before their

journey to the village. He checked that everything seemed in

order and headed back to Elizabeth. *"Everything ok she asked*

him?" "Fine now I'll tell you on the way home." Elizabeth

nodded. For a moment Elizabeth thought back to her father.

He had diversified their wealth when alive. He had bought

property back in Ireland. A lot of it and a grand house. It

employed many people and it was never to be sold he'd told

her. He'd also bought property around New York that was

now very important. And some in London. He believed in land. It was not a good idea to keep a lot of their money in one bank and she asked for pen and paper. She wrote to Mr Bell thanking him for all his assistance over the years and asking that two thirds of their ready cash be held at her New York Bank from now on. Most of their long-term investments were in London anyway.

Elizabeth gave the letter to one of the braves and asked him to hand it to the bank. As he ran, Kate, her parents and her older sister came to speak to Elizabeth. Caroline greeted her warmly and reintroduced her parents to Elizabeth. Elizabeth shook hands with them and asked after Kate. *"We'd like to thank you Ms Trelawney."* Said Kate's father. *"She could have been killed and the children at the school."* He continued. *"This is a dangerous world we live in Mr Cane."* Elizabeth responded. *"I fear though, your thanks is misguided Mr Cane, Blue saved her life and he did so seeing her in danger. It had nothing to do with my intervention."* She told him kindly. Mr Cane didn't know what to say, he looked at his wife who stared back at him.

Kate looked over at Blue who ignored her. Or the comments Elizabeth had just made. Caroline stood a little uneasy. Elizabeth felt she should break the ice and take the strain out of the situation, she bent and whispered. *"You know Mr and Mrs Cane, if an Indian saves your life, it belongs to him."* Elizabeth looked very sincere and to some extent spoke the truth, but, it had been a long time, since such events took such meaning. Blue smiled inwardly at the comment. Mrs Cane looked a little distressed and Mr Cane looked afraid his daughter was going to be picked up and taken from them. Elizabeth smiled, it was clear to all she was only joking. *"Blue."* She called. He walked over to her and stood next to her. *"You honour our family and yours, by saving her life at the risk of your own."* She told him proudly. Mr Cane came forward and stretched out his hand towards Blue. *"Thank you son."* Blue looked at him. Not sure of his sincerity but judging he was, took his hand and shook it. *"Your welcome sir."* Blue answered, much to everyone's, but Elizabeth's, surprise. Blue was a good man. Young. Strong and silent. His grandmother had been American. She'd been brutally raped and found half dead by the tribe. They had welcomed her and gave her a home. She'd healed and found love. Blue had found life not always kind to him. But he'd found his place in the tribe. He was a marvel with horses.

"I'm sorry but we have to leave." She told them apologetically. Elizabeth said her goodbyes to Caroline and invited her and her family out to the ranch. She gave her best wishes to Mr and Mrs Cane and turned to Kate. *"I'm glad you were not hurt."* She said to her. Kate smiled *"Thanks to Blue."* Kate turned to look up at him. It was clear she was more than a little smitten. She said and as an afterthought. *"Ms*

303

Trelawney?" "Yes Kate." Elizabeth answered. *"What's it like being an Indian princess?"* The group fell embarrassingly silent. This was not something that was spoken aloud. Elizabeth smiled *"I am honoured but there are easier choices Kate."* It was obvious to Elizabeth that Kate found it difficult to drag herself away from Blue. Elizabeth turned to White Dove. *"Ready?"* *"Yes let's go home."* She replied. Elizabeth signed for them to leave. Carl mounted and joined her. He told her that the brave was back from the Bank, Mr Bell seemed none too happy. Elizabeth smiled at him, she didn't expect he would be, but he'll do it. *"Let's go."* She told him. Turned and rode out. Carl rode beside her this time followed by White Dove, their goods and men. Caroline watched them leave. She thought Carl looked very handsome and set about making plans to visit Elizabeth after a suitable interval.

It was late when they got back. Everyone helped with the unloading. Dinner was served as soon as possible; the large tables were put together and everyone sat down to eat outside including Elizabeth. Tomorrow was Sunday. An easy day on the ranch. Most had the day off. Elizabeth decided she would spend the day over by Bend river. It was a lovely natural spring. Elizabeth rose from the table and spoke to Jake about her intensions for the next day. *"I'd rather not take Black Dog and his braves with me, Jake."* She told him *"Let them return home for a couple of days if they wish."* She continued. *"Like some company?"* Carl asked her knowing Jake would be unhappy at her riding alone. *"I'll be finished early?"* He told her. *"Sounds like a plan."* She smiled. Elizabeth turned and called out. *"Good night."* It suddenly hit her she was bone tired. It had been a tiring couple of days and she was grateful for it, at least, she wouldn't have to think.

Carl was waiting for her as Elizabeth came out of the house next morning. Both her pony and his horse saddled. *"I was beginning to think you'd changed your mind."* He teased.

"Sorry, I guess I was rather more tired than I expected." Elizabeth answered him as she mounted. *"Ready?"* He asked her. Elizabeth smiled and decided to use the one word that meant her life. *"Always."* She replied and she kicked her pony into action and rode off with Carl, following closely behind her. The spring was a couple of hours ride. It was a cool and inviting place. In the heat of the sun, it was a welcome sight. Both dismounted and unsaddled the horses to let them graze. Elizabeth picked her spot and laid the blankets Carl handed to her. A pic nic had been provided and Elizabeth found a copy of her favourite book. *"How did you know?"* She asked him. *"I asked White Dove what we should take and she told me how much you liked it but never seemed to get the time to read it."* He answered. Elizabeth smiled. *"I read it several times back East but she's right I love this book."*

Elizabeth settled herself under the shade of the tree and looked out over the river bed. 'It's lovely here' she thought.

The lands so welcoming. Carl got busy making a fire not that it was needed for the heat but he could do with some coffee and put it on to brew. Carl walked down to the river and decided to swim. *"I'm going in."* He called to her and without waiting for her response, took off his outer clothes and jumped in.

Elizabeth couldn't stop herself from laughing. He was like a child, splashing about and diving under. *"What's so funny?"* He asked her as he popped up out the water to her laughter. *"You are."* She responded. *"Your jumping about like a fish."* She shouted and continued to laugh. *"Maybe you should join me."* He asked her teasingly. *"Oh no, I like the view from here just as I am. Thank you."* She answered him. *"Well I'm not sure that's ok."* Carl teased and started to exit the water. Elizabeth realised he had very little on. As the water got to the point of below his waist, in desperation, she called out *"Alright, stop, I'll come in."* Carl had the biggest grin on his face. *"That's not funny."* She told him coming to the water's edge. *"Someone may have seen you."* Elizabeth took a look around. *"No one would have seen me Elizabeth apart from you."* He challenged. 'Yeah well.' Thought Elizabeth. 'That might not have been a good thing either.' Elizabeth had to admit. Carl was striking. The manual labour had given him a strong man's body. 'He would make someone very happy.'

Elizabeth pinned up her hair and took off her outer clothes and entered the water in her underwear. It was cool and refreshing. Carls noticed that she had not removed all her clothes. He swam beside her for a while. Kept his distance and came out to dry off. He banked up the fire for her and helped himself to coffee. It was hot and strong. He's senses came flooding back. From the bank he watched her. Her hair a cascade of colour. Elizabeth turned and realised Carl had left her. She waved to him and swam for the shore. The water had made her white shift pretty much see through. As Elizabeth walked towards him. Carl couldn't believe his eyes. He desperately wanted to tear his eyes away but could not, she was as beautiful as he remembered. It was only when Elizabeth saw his struggle that she looked down and realised that she was practically naked. She turned quickly and froze. Her shock, woke Carl from his dream. He picked up a spare blanket that he had warming by the fire and approached her from behind. He raised the corners of the blanket and surrounded her with it. Elizabeth caught hold of it and turned to face him. *"Umm I'm sorry."* He told her. *"I should have spoken earlier."* Elizabeth looked at him. *"It's not the first time you've seen me naked Carl."* She whispered. They locked eyes. Elizabeth searched his face and saw the hunger he had for her. She leaned forward to kiss him. At the same time, she opened the blanket and encircled him in it, drawing him to her.

The kiss was sweet and light. Her face cold against his. Carl had a choice. She had kissed him. He desperately wanted to kiss her back and touch her, but he didn't.

Elizabeth sensed his hesitation and withdrew. *"Did I make a mistake?"* She asked him. Part of Elizabeth needed to know, if the pleasure she had experienced with Red Wolf could be found with another man. She knew she wasn't being fair, but fair didn't come into it. Carl touched her face with his hand and stroked it. *"What are you asking me Elizabeth?"* Elizabeth ran her hand across his chest and down the curves of his body. There was no mistaking what she was asking.

Carl realised her need went further than wanting him. *"Any man would want you Elizabeth."* He told her honestly. *"But I don't want any man Carl."* She answered. He nodded at her. *"That's the point Elizabeth isn't it. You don't really want me."* He told her gently. Elizabeth wound her hands around his body and stood on her toes to kiss him. Carl moved out of her embrace and took hold of her hands. *"It would be very easy for me to take what your offering and in doing so, take advantage of you."* Carl told her. Elizabeth looked up into his face and shook her head in denial. Carl smiled at her kindly. *"The intimacy between men and women."* He continued as Elizabeth blushed. *"Is easily done, the passion, the emotion, the feelings."* Carl went on. *"These are all normal feelings between two people, the trick is."* Carl said as he lifted her chin to look in her eyes. *"Is that it should be with the right person, who fires those passions for the right reasons."*

Elizabeth had her answers. She squeezed his hands in her embrace and then covered herself with the blanket. *"Thank you, I'm sorry I don't know why I'm behaving in this way or what came over me, I did not mean to put you in a difficult position, apart from being an emotional wreck, it would seem that my judgement isn't too clever either."* Elizabeth said with a wry smile. *"There's nothing wrong with your judgement Elizabeth, your instincts told you right."* Carl said kindly if a little sadly. Elizabeth looked at him. *"For now. It's not the right reasons, that's all."* Elizabeth turned and went back to the fire.

As she bent down and warmed herself. Carl came up behind her and touched her shoulder and gave her a squeeze. *"Hungry?"* He asked her. Elizabeth looked up smiling. *"Yes – starving."* Elizabeth replied. It was a lovely day. Both settled themselves on blankets and ate, both felt revived by the coolness of the water, sunned themselves and talked easily of nothing. Later Carl slept and Elizabeth read her book. The meadow and the spring had a calming effect on both of them. Elizabeth recalled as she got into bed that night, that it had been a long time since she had felt so at ease.

CHAPTER NINE

Next morning Black Dog and his braves rode into the yard and set about their business. After breakfast unexpectedly, Elizabeth had visitors, a lot of them, the Sheriff, Mr Bell, the Preacher Mr Jones and Town Mayor Mr Green, along with Mr Jenkins ride into the yard. Followed closely by Jeff Brennan the new owner of the Saloon and pleasure house. Elizabeth was surprise. She'd never heard of him going to visit anyone. And certainly, had not come out to the Double T before. They were escorted by several of Black Dogs men. Elizabeth always found it annoying that after all this time, the men looked very comfortable except that is for Mr Brennan. Elizabeth had been discussing feed and stock with Jake and Carl when they rode in. Elizabeth walked over to greet her visitors at the same time signalling to the braves to withdraw. *"Morning gentleman, can we offer you refreshments? What brings you out here so early?"* She asked them.

"Morning Elizabeth." The Sheriff answered her. *"We had a break out of the jail yesterday. They took the Bank as well."* He told her. Elizabeth looked at Mr Bell, he was looking decidedly ill. Elizabeth knew the news was not going to be good. *"You had better come in gentleman and take that refreshment."* Elizabeth indicated the main house to them. As they moved off, Elizabeth gave silent instructions to Black Dog regarding her guests. For those fascinated by it, you could not miss, the command she held. White Dove alerted to the guests, greeted them as they entered the house. Elizabeth made introductions to her aunt and asked her to arrange for drinks, food and coffee and to join them in the dinning room. Elizabeth on instinct, turned in the doorway. *"Can you join us Carl, Jake you to."*

"Gentleman please take a seat and make yourselves at home." Once everyone was settled. Elizabeth turned to the Sheriff as

he thanked Anna for his breakfast. *"So. How bad is it."* She asked. The Sheriff told her everything of the breakout and the bank heist. *"How much is gone?"* Elizabeth asked, Mr Bell cleared his throat. He continued to look ill. *"All of it apart from change."* He told her wiping his face. Mayor Green cut in. *"Apart from what you have lost Ms Trelawney, the town is bankrupt."* He told her. Elizabeth looked around the table and turned back to Mr Bell. *"Did the transfer go through?"* She asked him. *"Yes."* He nodded. *"Insurance?"* She asked him. Mr Bell shock his head. *"We cannot get it out here."* *"So what did we lose?"* *"Do you want me to discuss it here Ms Trelawney?"* He asked her looking around the table, registering who was present, it was hardly private. *"Mr Bell if the town is bankrupt then I feel it right to discuss our loses right here with everyone else."* She told him. *"I transferred the entire deposit account and two thirds of your cash account as you asked and that left about $50,000."* He told her, Elizabeth nodded *"And the town?"* Elizabeth asked *"About $240,000."* He told her.

Elizabeth was surprised. *"I wasn't aware the town was so well healed Mr Bell."* Elizabeth countered. *"That would be because of me."* Jeff Brenner cut in. Elizabeth turned to look at him for the first time. He was a handsome man. Tough. Hardened. He continued. *"As you may or may not know, I recently took over the Jade and brought finances to cover it and invest, I had visions of expanding."* He told her wirily. *"Do you have insurance Mr Brenner?"* Elizabeth asked him. *"Please call me Jeff, all my friends do."* He told her using a considerable amount of charm. Carl disliked him intensely. Elizabeth smiled *"You can save the charm Mr Brenner. Do you have insurance Mr Brenner?"* She asked again. *"I had the same problems Mr Bell had."* He told her digging into his breakfast.

The Mayor felt it time he explained what they were doing here. Putting his knife and fork down. *"I will get straight to the point Ms Trelawney. The reason the Town Council is*

316

here. *We were hoping that the Double T could see its way clear to covering some of the towns losses and keep town going. Otherwise. Its dead."* There was an embarrassed silence. Carl couldn't believe what he was hearing. The Double T had just lost $50,000 and they wanted her to cover their loses too? It was unbelievable. Elizabeth took a long swallow of her cooling drink.

Elizabeth turned to Preacher Jones. *"Pastor, how much did the church loose?" "Everything we had child and I cannot cover the loan from the bank that was used to fix the heating." "Mr Bell, did you bring the towns accounts with you." "Yes Ms Trelawney." "And the business accounts?"* She asked. *"We have each brought our own and the other businesses."* The Mayor told her. *"Well gentleman, this will take some time, make yourselves comfortable, I will go over the books with Mr Bell and give my decision. Pastor Jones I will cover the churches loses immediately and the loan. It is my gift to the town. Anna please offer the gentlemen brandy if they wish it."* Elizabeth went to rise from the table as Mr Brenner

spoke. *"Urr Ms Trelawney. I've no wish to offend you but do you*

have any experience with handling accounts." She heard him ask

her. Elizabeth continued to rise, and Carl thought he would

thump him. *"Rest assured Mr Brenner, I did not spend 6 years of*

my life East, with the family I have, doing nothing but sitting down

at dinner and being fixated with the latest fashion. My Aunt would

never have allowed such a stupid child." She told him. *"I meant no*

offence as I said, but the town is depending on this, I'm sure you

understand my concern." He told her. Elizabeth did not

acknowledge his last statement, she turned to Mr Bell. *"If you*

would." And herded him towards Ben's study, without

hesitation Mr Bell followed her.

Elizabeth took her time, she went over each of the

banks accounts twice and verified their loses, then checked the

business accounts, checked the figures, the loans taken and

conferred with Mr Bell when something seemed unclear and

she made a number of notes. After several pots of coffee and a break for a sandwich. She turned to Mr Bell. Elizabeth was tired, mentally it was very draining. *"How much did the towns folk lose?"* She asked him. *"In total about $40,000 in all the personal accounts."* He told her. *"And the other ranches and farms?"* Mr Bell looked uncomfortable. *"About $200,000 in total."* Elizabeth sat for a moment and looked out of the window. *"I will want to see those accounts Mr Bell."* Mr Bell was most impressed. For such a young woman, she was prepared, business like, asked the right questions and knew what she needed to know.

"Did you bring any transfer cheques with you?" Elizabeth asked him. *"Yes."* He replied, Elizabeth nodded. *"Did it ever cross your mind that I might say no Mr Bell?"* She asked him. *"From what my predecessor told me. No. Not if your your fathers daughter."* He told her kindly. Elizabeth nodded and pointed in the direction of the dinning room. *"Did they know that?"*

"No." She sighed. *"There was never a question of us not helping Mr Bell. I will need simple contracts drawn up. Come, let us join the others then."* Elizabeth rose from her chair. Opened the door and walked to the dining table. Elizabeth asked Anna to let the gentlemen know she was back. The men were scattered about the dining room, parlour and outside. *"Gentleman if your ready."* She called to them as she took her seat back at the table. They joined her. *"So let me be clear, the town is bankrupt, every business, every family is finished, unless we can cover the loses somehow, is that right?"* She asked them. *"Yes."* Both Mr Bell and Mayor Green replied.

Elizabeth looked around the table at each man in turn and finally coming to rest with White Dove. Elizabeth realised she had several choices here. She could make or break this town. She took a deep breath. *"A dead town is no good to any of us."* She told them. *"Our family has a long tradition with Brownsville and I personally have many friends there.*

So, I will cover the town losses." She told them, there were some relieved men around the table. The was an expectant silence. *"Which ones Elizabeth?"* Mr Bell asked her. Elizabeth looked directly at him. *"I will cover them all Mr Bell."* She told him. *"I want the Doctors loss covered immediately. And the personal accounts of the towns people. They will be interest free loans that the bank will cover in time Mr Bell. But with the businesses there will be conditions to the loans gentleman."* Elizabeth opened her note book. *"Mr Bell, from this point forward, the bank here will align with our bank in New York. It will be the banks policy to hold an account at our New York Bank and transfer all private holdings immediately. A float will only be carried directly by the bank here, all deposits and withdrawals will be covered by the businesses of the town in the first instance, no deposit money will be held here in future. Second, the church is also covered in such a fashion if the preacher agrees. Third, for the term of the loans, no person or business will be able to borrow against their holdings without my consent. Fourth, personal loan periods will be at a rate that can be actually repaid, not set by the bank, and Mr Bell, the bank will not make a profit on these loans, business loans will be paid in accordance to their previous business accounts. The outlining ranches and farms will be covered for both their personal accounts and their loans. No child, man or woman goes hungry here. Mr Brenner, should you wish me to cover your losses, I will cover your business loses on one condition and you may not like it."* She continued. *"You will release your indentured women. Only those who choose to work for you freely, for an agreed price will do so. You will have the Doctor visit your ladies regularly. Your house will be clean. Your personal loses I am happy to discuss and as you are new to our town, the Bank will set a rate in line with everyone else."*

There was shocked silence around the table. *"Well gentleman, do you each agree and Mayor Green do you agree on behalf of the town?"* She asked them. Each man round the table, in turn, gave their agreement. All that is. Until it was Mr

Brenner's turn. *"Ms Trelawney you drive a hard bargain, I stand to lose a great deal of money on my ladies if I do as you ask."* Elizabeth nodded. *"Possibly. You could always invest in men?"* There was a shocked silence around the room. Mr Brenner however, came from New Orleans. Men in that trade often did very well she had heard. And wondered, how well Mr Brenner knew that. Elizabeth smiled. *"Maybe not then. But Mr Brenner, you will lose a lot more if I do not cover your losses."* Elizabeth responded. There was an embarrassed silence around the table. Suddenly Mr Brenner had the feeling that he had a very bad hand at a poker table. He laughed out loud and banged the table. *"How right you are mam. I will take a personal loan on one condition, you are a partner and it's not just a financial loan. It would only be fair."* Elizabeth looked at him. *"I will not gain from another's pain Mr Brenner, should you agreed and before you do."* Elizabeth lent forward and placed both arms on the table in front of her. *"Know this. I will break you, if*

I find otherwise." She told him calmly. Mr Brenner returned her gaze. *"Yes I believe you would."*

"Well then, we are agreed, Mayor Green you are our legal man, draw up the papers with Mr Bell. Mr Bell write me a credit cheque for $500,000 and request the financial value to be made available from my New York business account. That should be enough to settle everyone's account. Sheriff I would like you the Mayor and Preacher to oversee the money transfers to each person at the Bank. And explain that cash will no longer be a big deposit at the towns bank and time needed for large withdrawals." Carl choked on his lemonade and Jake slapped his back. The Sheriff took a huge sigh of relief and Mr Bell and Mayor Green couldn't stop thanking her. Jeff Brenner sat in silence. Elizabeth turned to White Dove. *"Are you ok with this?"* Jeff Brenner watched the exchange with fascination. White Dove smiled. *"It's your money."* Mr Bell wrote the Cheque and passed it to her. Elizabeth signed it and gave it back to him.

"And the interest Ms Trelawney for the towns people's money?" He asked her. Elizabeth looked at him. *"None, we are all victims here Mr Bell, Oh and gentleman, I do not want the town folks knowing it was the Double T who helped them."* Elizabeth's dignity shamed them all.

She shook hands with each of the men in turn. As she came to Mayor Green he told her. *"You could have owned the town you know."* Elizabeth smiled, *"I don't need to own it Mayor Green."* Jeff Brenner stood behind him. He came forward and took her hand and held it. *"I came from nothing and worked every day I can remember. Doing somethings I'd sooner forget. But it got me my own life and what I have here. Not many would have done what you have today, Ms Trelawney, I am very grateful and will not forget your kindness."* He told her. *"Mr Brenner, I may not like the business' you're in but that, is your concern not mine. The Double T needs the town, as much as the town needs us. It was not a hard decision to make. Good day and safe journey."* Carl followed her to the door and watched them leave. *"That was a lot of money Elizabeth."* He said to her, still shocked. *"Yes, but it's a loan and we'll get it back many times over, unlike our own loses. It's just as well I transferred what I did, but we'll get that back too with interest in time."* She told him. *"Can you cover such a sum."* Carl looked worried and embarrassed. She turned to look at him and smiled. Clearly Carl had no idea and she smiled at him. *"You really don't know us at all, do you Carl?"* She said laughing and walked out into the sunshine. He was truly her friend. Carl turned back to Jake. *"What did I say?"*

"Don't you know lad?" Jake asked him putting his hand on his shoulder. *"The Double T, is not the only thing the Trelawney's own, they also have a lot of investments back East."* *"I knew the family had money."* Carl answered. *"Money?"* Jake laughed and slapped him on the back, and started to walk away. *"Carl, Esa's worth millions, many of millions, the protection*

she has from Black Dog and the braves, it's not just for Dull Knifes benefit." Carl stared after him in disbelief, he was staggered. What had he been thinking. This woman was way out of his league. A week later, Pastor Jones and Mayor Green came out to see Elizabeth. They confirmed that all the accounts had been settled and her plans put in place. They thanked her again, stayed for lunch and then left. Mayor Green offered her a seat on the Town Council. Elizabeth declined. Thanking him. She told him the Towns affairs were their own.

It had been a busy week, the usual round of pasture, stock movement and feeding Elizabeth realised that she had not seen much of Carl since her visitors last visit. Elizabeth went looking for Jake. *"Jake have you seen Carl lately."* She asked. *"I thought you knew. He asked to take a look at the high pasture ready for the new stock, he's been gone for some time, I don't expect he'll be back for several more days, anything wrong?".* "No, *just wondered thanks."* Elizabeth told him and went back to work.

Ben came home three days later. He was carried across his saddle. He'd died on the trip home. They had picked up the new stock and were on their way home. A snake had spooked his horse and he'd fallen. As he landed he had hit his head on a rock. He never regained consciousness. White Dove was destroyed on seeing him. Elizabeth went to her and they cried and hugged each other. Elizabeth sent three riders from the Double T, one to the village, one to get Carl and one for the preacher. Bens funeral took place two days later. It was a large affair. Food and drink laid on. The preacher led the ceremony. The prominent members of the tribe came out in force as tradition expected. Dull Knife, both Red Wolf and Running Elk came with their wives. The funeral took on an Indian theme. The traditional death songs were sung by the women. White Dove cut her hair and bordered on hysteria.

As much as Elizabeth tried to comfort her. It was not enough, in her distress White Dove had chosen to return to the village with Dull Knife and be with her family. Elizabeth felt betrayed and alone in so many ways.

The Town also came out in force. All the prominent members arrived one after the other along with several of Elizabeth's school friends including Caroline and her family. Every member of the town council paid homage to Ben and gave their condolences to both White Dove and Elizabeth. Uncomfortably for Carl he heard several discussing Elizabeth's financial position now that she was on her own, this worried him.

Elizabeth had made a point of avoiding as much contact with Red Wolf and his wife as possible, but before they were due to leave, Dull Knife and his sons came to her, as expected. *"Daughter, this is a sad time for all of us, I am unhappy* to see you in this way, you will need help and your brothers are here for you." Dull Knife looked around him and continued. "There is much here, and some, may try to take it from you." Dull Knife looked hard at her and moved to hold her shoulders, tears came to Elizabeth's eyes. "And you need a husband child." He told her.

Elizabeth felt like screaming, the last thing she could cope with was Red Wolf at the ranch day after day, having just lost Ben, she was too vulnerable. Carl who had been observing from a short distance. Approached her and put a hand on her arm, she turned towards him. The tears in her eyes broke free and she fell into his arms. "I see my daughter has made a choice, she is in good hands." Dull Knife told him kindly and griped his arm man to man. Dull Knife then turned and walked away followed by Running Elk and his wife. Red Wolf stared at them, torn, Elizabeth was crying uncontrollably now, she should have been in his arms.

Unable to avoid the atmosphere. Carl looked at Red Wolf, there was nothing for either of them to say. Red Wolf's wife Sky. Walked forward from behind her husband and embraced them both. Silently she turned to face her husband and waited for him to recognise her presence, it took several minutes for Red Wolf to draw his eyes away from Elizabeth. He turned and followed his father. Sky walked after him.

White Dove left that day with the tribe and Elizabeth saw them off. There was no will to read, no goods to distribute. Ben had never been materialistic and it wasn't the Indian way. To ensure White Dove would be seen in the status she deserved. Elizabeth had put together horses, cattle and packed all her personal items. Elizabeth knew she was doing something unusual for White Dove and not sure how it would be taken by the other widows of the tribe since tradition expected a widow with no sons to be adrift of the tribe unless someone took them in. In White Doves case,

Elizabeth had talked with Running Elk and they had agreed that the cattle and horses would go into the tribal stock but they would be hers. And White Dove would have her tepee. Money would never be a problem for her. Elizabeth had told her that and hoped, she could return soon.

Elizabeth soon found herself alone in the house. Not since her parents had died had she felt so alone. Elizabeth made herself a drink and sat in Ben's favourite chair by the fireplace she rubbed her hands up and down the leather arms. It was getting cooler in the evenings now and a fire had been lit. Elizabeth welcomed the warmth both inside her and out. She was desperately trying to hold back yet more tears. Carl had been talking to Jake, discussing his fears about the towns folk and their knowledge of Elizabeth's worth. *"You're the head man here Jake, I don't what to step on your toes, but I think we need to start upping security around the spread. I know there was an incident some time back. I don't want anyone pulling anything and she goes nowhere alone from now on."* Jake nodded in agreement. *"Your right, I'll say my goodnights and get the hands sorted we'll start tonight."* Carl and Jake came in from the yard.

"Everything's alright girl." Jake told her as he walked towards her. *"If you need me, you know where to find me."* He bent to kiss her on the cheek and gave her a hug. *"Night Carl."* He called as he turned and headed back to the door. *"Yeah, night Jake see you tomorrow."* She called after him. Watching him leave. Not wanting to intrude Carl remained where he was, waiting for a response from her.

"Come sit by me and have a drink?" She asked him. *"Tough day."* He said as he poured himself a drink and refilled hers, Carl sat down opposite her. Elizabeth smiled sadly. They were both lost in thought for a long time gazing into the fire. Elizabeth sighed deeply. *"This house, it's too big, just for me, maybe I should go back East for a while."* She said eventually

gazing around the room. Too many memories. Carl was devastated hearing she may leave. Quietly, in a voice he hardly recognised as his own he answered her. *"In time, you will have family of your own and then this house will not feel small at all."* He told her knowingly. *"But, they will not be Red Wolfs, of that, I am now certain."* She answered him. Red Wolf stood in the doorway. Neither had heard him walk in. The pain Elizabeth was suffering that day became too much for him and at the displeasure of his wife, he left the tribe and rode back to her. Part of him had hoped he had given Elizabeth a child on their one night together. Now it seemed, she was confirming that had not happened and again he felt like something had been taken from him. Seeing she did not need him, as silently as he came. He left.

"Nothing is ever certain Elizabeth." Carl responded. *"Everything in life has a cycle. Even you. Only if that cycle*

remains unbroken, can you be sure and even then. This life throws things at us that we are not prepared for. Are you sure, Elizabeth." He asked her. She looked at him resignedly and rubbed her eyes. "No, I'm not." Carl nodded. "You will soon enough. Nature finds a way." He told her. "And if it is broken?" She asked. "Then this house will welcome new life." He answered her. Elizabeth was overcome with emotion. "Thank you." She told him. They remained in silence until Elizabeth fell asleep. Carl picked her up and carried her to her room. As he laid her on her bed Elizabeth stirred. "I could not do this without you." She told him. Carl tucked her in and walked to the door. As he put his hand on the latch he turned to look at her. He would be her friend, he'd decided. She was beyond him, but he could be the friend she needed. He turned and closed the door quietly behind him.

Over the next few weeks, life came back to the ranch. Jake came to Elizabeth accompanied by Carl every evening after dinner and they decided the best action for the coming day. Plans were put in motion to keep the new stock moved to pastures that could feed them. The usual round of fences were mended and the watering holes kept clean and clear. Carl took control of the hiring of new hands with Jake and only took those who were known or had references that could be checked. Black Dog followed Carls instructions to the letter. Elizabeth went nowhere alone.

Sometimes Carl was asked to stay to dinner other times, Elizabeth preferred to be alone. The option was left open to them both, if needed, Carl sort her out and had drinks with her late into the night. Often, not talking about much or making decisions, just company for the both of them. Just over a week from Bens funeral, they were sitting in front of the fire, the nights had been drawing in, Elizabeth broke the silence between them. *"It would seem, my cycle isn't broken after all."* She said. Carl looked up. *"Are you sorry?"* He asked her. Elizabeth sighed. *"Yes and no."* She answered honesty. *"I would have liked to have had a child. Especially now Ben's gone, but Red Wolf's child now, would have been a joy as well as a burden. He would never have left us and the tribe would not forgive the betrayal of this to his wife. So I expect it was for the best."* Carl finished his drink and bent down in front of her. He touched her hand lightly and they locked eyes, in that moment, an unspoken truth passed between them. There would be other children.

CHAPTER NINE

Autumn 1879

Elizabeth had been home for eight months, sometimes it felt like eight years. She had thrown herself into the running of the ranch. Red Wolf and Running Elk took turns to come and stay and help run the place. Each had taken it in turns in running the horses. This now became their lead and they worked it out between them and Blue. Sometimes they joined Carl and Elizabeth and Jake for dinner other times they choose not to and Elizabeth was grateful for that. The freedom of choice made things easier for them all.

Tradition still held sway, and all those in the yard were welcomed for dinner no matter who they were. Business was conducted after it when coffee and drinks were served. Life took on a sense of its own and found its own rhythm.

Caroline and her sister Kate came out to see Elizabeth often. Since Bens burial, the girls had come on a Sunday nearly each week. It was a long and tiring journey to be made in one day, but they didn't seem to mind. Elizabeth was glad to see them.

Caroline's initial infatuation of Carl had lost some of its appeal having seen him with Elizabeth. She knew from the first Sunday she saw them together, that there was an unspoken bond between them, she would not and could not break it. Caroline settled for being a dear friend to them both and grieved for another lost chance. Kate used her time to make herself useful round the house and yard on these occasions and spent as much time as she could in search of Blue. It had not gone unnoticed. Blue chose to ignore her as much as possible. Going out of his way to work in the pasture. It was after such a visit that Elizabeth found Blue standing quietly in her hall. It was passed dinner and her guests had long gone. Elizabeth was sitting by the fire alone, reading, something stirred her from her peace and he was standing there. Elizabeth put her book down. *"Blue, how nice, please come and join me, could I get you something."* She asked smiling and beckoning him forward, indicating a chair opposite her and walking to the drinks table she poured two.

Blue took the chair she had indicated and waited for her to return. Elizabeth handed him his glass and returned to her chair. Elizabeth looked up at him and raised her glass. *"May mother earth be kind."* She told him lifting her glass to her lips. She took a swallow. The liquid was cool, in the mouth, and hot in her body. The explosion in her chest reminded her of the good times with Ben. Blue nodded at her toast and joined her. Elizabeth watched him and said nothing more, letting the drink warm and relax them both. Blue sat in the chair and looked into the fire. Elizabeth kept her peace and waited for him to gather the courage to speak. It was awhile coming. Their drinks were nearly done, when at last he spoke. *"Esa, I have a problem with Miss Kate. I have no wish to offend you or her family. She does not know what she is asking."* Blue looked at her with a desperation in his eyes. Elizabeth rolled the drink around her glass. *"Is she asking for something you cannot give?"* Blue drank the last of his drink. *"She follows me when she visits here. Is around while I do my work. Gets food for me. Asks if she can get me anything. Is always there. Talking and pointing things out. It is becoming harder to be here on a Sunday and harder still to work, the rest of the week till Sunday comes around again. She does not know what she is saying or asking. She says she loves me and wants to be with me. But she cannot live at the village. She is not like you and I could not live in town."* Elizabeth smiled kindly at him. *"Do you love her Blue?"* She asked him. It was Blues turn to smile. *"Since the first day I held her."* He spoke sadly. *"You are an only child with no parents Blue, you are a man who can make his own choices, if your*

341

problem here is solely that you have nowhere to live, then I gladly, *give that to you both on your marriage."* She told him. Blue dropped his head and sighed like a huge weight had been lifted from him. When he looked up, tears were in his eyes. *"What about her family?"* He asked. *"I don't know Blue, it is something you must ask them."* She told him. *"If you wish, I could invite the family for a gathering next Sunday, it would give you the chance to talk to her parents."* Blue rose from his chair and Elizabeth joined him, Blue came forward and outstretched both hands. Elizabeth took them. *"Thank you."* He told her and left.

Elizabeth sat back down and smiled. Kate got her man after all.

Elizabeth must have fallen asleep, she was roused from her sleep as she was lifted and carried from the chair. She felt the body familiar and instinctively nestled into it. Her body climbed the stairs and was carried into her room and she welcomed the bed beneath her as she was laid upon it. Elizabeth felt the comfort of a blanket as it was tucked in. She drifted once again into sleep and heard a voice whisper to her. *"I wish you could have solved our problems as easily as you did Blues."* Elizabeth smiled, and in her dreamy state she answered him. *"It was never mine to solve."* And she went back to sleep.

Elizabeth woke next morning knowing Red Wolf had spent most of the night with her. It both excited and worried her. She had thought that they were passed such things, clearly Red Wolf thought differently. It would have to stop. Elizabeth got dressed and entered the dining room to find both Red Wolf and Carl at the table deep in conversation. As she crossed the floor, the conversation died. A frown crossed her face as she joined them at the table. *"What is it?"* She asked them. *"Some men that work for Brennen, were overheard* talking about their boss's benefactor and how the town survived after the bank heist after a visit to you." Carl told her. "And?" She asked. Red Wolf swallowed and looked at her. "They were saying how they could do with some of that, especially as it came in such a nice package." He told her reluctantly, their meaning was very clear.

Elizabeth took a deep breath, sighed and sat down. "I can't control what other people think and nor can either of you." She told them. "But." She continued. "I can go and see Brennen, I'm his partner after all and have a little chat about that." "If you go into town, you'll be walking right into them." Carl told her. "Maybe." She answered him "But it might just bring them out." And with that she smiled. Carl didn't like it and thought she was crazy. Red Wolf nodded. "I don't like the idea of them coming for you in their time, Elizabeth." Red Wolf eventually told her. "Nor do I and I don't want to be looking over my shoulder, so let's deal with it now." "Then we go in force and make *sure the entire town knows just how protected you and the Double T are."* He told her. *"Agreed."* Carl looked from one to the other and thought they were both mad, but the decision had been made.

They made ready for the following day. Riders were sent out to bring in the far herds and horses. Men came into the ranch all day long. Jake had never seen so many hands at once at the big house. The bunk houses were full and never had there been so many braves at once at the Double T. There was a huge effort in feeding and housing everyone. Those braves not normally working for them at that time, took up residence in the barns. Elizabeth went out to greet them all. Some of the old timers that had been offered housing on their land greeted her warmly. Although not really working for them since shortly after her father died, they were paid a retainer. Many she remembered fondly. They had all come at her call and she was both honoured and grateful.

They breakfasted early the next day, in all, it was an army. Elizabeth came down and skipped breakfast. She settled for coffee and took it out on the porch and watched the party get ready to depart. Both Carl and Red Wolf came to her. *"We're ready."* Carl told her as he stared at her. Every hand and brave carried a rifle. Elizabeth turned to them both. *"Then we should go."* Putting her cup down and walking to the edge of the porch, Elizabeth put on her riding gloves and strode to her pony. As she walked proudly past them Carl turned to Red Wolf. *"I'll kill any man that hurts her."* He told him. *"In that, we are agreed."* Red Wolf responded. And there. In love. Both men were bonded.

The braves took up their place at the front of the line. Several of the younger braves took up point. Six rode before her one of them Blue. Elizabeth was flanked by Carl on one side and Red Wolf on the other. Behind them came the rest of the braves headed by Black Dog and his men, followed by the hands and finally the wagons, the trip had other uses besides reinforcing Elizabeth status. Each man rode with one thought, her.

Elizabeth rode with over one hundred men. She had chosen to wear traditional Indian buckskin leggings, with an over tunic, her hair was half braded and it was covered by her Stetson. She was an exotic mix of Indian and western. The ride was uneventful and shortly before noon, they rode in. On Red Wolfs signal. Just outside of town, every man in the troop, released his rifle, held it high and rested the butt on their thighs. It was a magnificent sight and in amongst them all, rode Elizabeth with her strawberry blond hair blowing in the wind.

Brownsville, came alive. Every man woman and child came out to see what was happening. People stared in ore, several were nervous at seeing so many Indians. Elizabeth gave the signal for the wagons to go to the store and get provisions as she continued on to the Brenner place. Those riding point took up their positions forward of the pleasure house, the rest of the braves led by Black Dog surrounded them at the rear, the hands took up positions along main street down to the mail depot.

Mr Brenner came out to meet her and looked around nervously. *"Ms Trelawney, how lovely to see you, please come in, I have looked forward to having you visit."* He told her. Elizabeth dismounted, carrying her whip and Carl and Red Wolf came with her. Both still carrying their rifles. As Elizabeth walked through the pleasure house, several men and women made way for her. Mr Brenner showed them into his office at the rear of the premises.

"Please sit down." He told them, but only Elizabeth took a seat. Carl and Red Wolf stood behind her. Mr Brenner looked decidedly worried. *"Thank you Mr Brenner, but, I'm afraid this is not a social call."* She told him. *"It would seem we have a small problem, one, I'm afraid that cannot be ignored."* She continued. *"I'm sorry Ms Trelawney, I don't understand."* He told her talking his own seat. Elizabeth removed her gloves and placed them on his desk. *"Several of your men were overheard talking about your good fortune with Ms Trelawney as your banker and how they would like to have such a lovely package for themselves."* Carl told him. Mr Brenner was visually shocked. *"My men?"* He questioned. There was silence in the room. Mr Brenner opened the draw of his desk and took out his gun. He checked it was loaded and got up from his chair. Elizabeth, picked up her gloves and followed him with Carl and Red Wolf. Mr Brenner came into the bar, and called to his men. *"Steve, I want to see every man we employ now."*

Elizabeth stood flanked by Carl and Red Wolf by the bar. Mr Brenner stood in the centre of the room with his back to Elizabeth and faced the men coming in and down from the rooms. Several of them looked surely and uneasy. Steve nodded to Mr Brenner to indicate that all were present. *"I understand that some of you."* Mr Brenner stated as he started pacing up and down and waving his arm to indicate each and everyone of them. *"Think, that I've been luckier than I should have been in my business dealings with Ms Trelawney here and in fact, that they think they deserve a bit of it."* Mr Brenner continued, clearly very pissed. *"Now, not only do I feel that I have been betrayed, I feel sure Ms Trelawney here has been insulted. We can all clearly see from outside, the length, reach and strength, of Ms Trelawney and her family."* Mr Brenner indicated Carl and Red Wolf. *"And what they intend to do, to rectify this situation. So, I want to know, who made the mistake of involving themselves in my business."* He bellowed.

The silence was deafening. Mr Brenner raised his gun. *"I'm not a patient man. I will shoot each and every man here unless I get some answers."* He told them. No one moved. *"You have 5 seconds and then I'm going to shoot Danny here, when I'm finished with him, I'm going to shoot the man next to him, then the next, and the next, until I get either an answer or I get the men I want."* Mr Brenner started counting *"1,2,3,4,5"* He raised and cocked his gun and was about to pull the trigger when Danny cried out. *"It wasn't me Mr Brenner it was Bert, Jean and Cole."* As the last name came out of his mouth, a shot was fired. Cole had shot him to keep him quiet, all hell broke loose. Both Bert and Jean went for their guns. Carl and Red Wolf discharged their rifles and Elizabeth caught Jean around the body with the whip. Distracting him as Mr Brenner shot him. It was over in less than 2 minutes.

All three men were dead, as was Danny. The Sheriff came running in as the firing stopped. *"Any man involving* themselves in my business and that includes ideas about Ms Trelawney here, will answer to me, her men and her family and should any man still feel the need to try, let me spell it out for you, you're a dead man." Mr Brenner told them. He turned to Elizabeth. "Ms Trelawney, my apologies, it will not happen again." He told her. Elizabeth recoiled her whip and approached him. As she did Carl and Red Wolf followed her. Elizabeth extended her hand and shook his. "Thank you Mr Brenner, I welcome your partnership in business. My compliments, good day." She told him and left the saloon. "Sheriff, my apologies for the disturbance, I would have come to see you first but our numbers here made that hard to do, I feel my point has been made. Please apologise to the towns folk for any disturbance, as soon as our goods are ready, we will be leaving." She told him. "Is everything ok Elizabeth?" He asked her. "Everything's fine now Sheriff, just some gentleman who I understand felt I was easy pickings, something they could own, I'm sure Mr Brenner can fill you in."

Elizabeth walked outside and signed to the men to disperse. Several took up posts along the main street. Black Dog and his men, including Blue, stayed with her. Elizabeth turned and spoke to Red Wolf. *"I'm going to the bank to see Mr Bell, could you check to see if there is any new stock or mail from back East."* Red Wolf nodded and headed off. *"Carl, could you go see Caroline and her family, extend my apologies for the disturbance today and ask them if they would come join us on Sunday?"* She asked him. *"You going to be ok on your own?"* He asked her. *"Carl, when am I ever alone?"* She answered and indicated Black Dog. *"Fair enough."* He told her and walked down street towards the home of Caroline and her family.

Elizabeth crossed the street and walked into the bank. As she did, Elizabeth noticed two things. Mr Bell was rushing back inside and there was the most handsome oriental gentleman not much older than herself sitting in the reception area. Mr Bell appeared to have left his office mid-way in conference with another oriental looking gentleman who was in his late 50's she guessed, wearing silk robes. Elizabeth thought how wonderful the fabric looked, a far better quality than she had seen before. She walked in and settled herself in the outer office with the younger man and offered. *"Good morning."* To him. Rather surprised he looked at Elizabeth. *"Good morning."* He replied and both of them could overhear the conversation going on in the main office. It wasn't particularly private and Mr Bell was using his position to full effect. *"I'm sorry, Mr Chan, I cannot lend you money without collateral, and we don't lend money to foreigners around here."* Elizabeth got angry, Mr Bell was a snob and she hated that. That man would have to go, she thought. Her companion became embarrassed. Mr Chan tried again and put his proposal again to Mr Bell stressing the business opportunities and the profit to be made for the town and for his family. Elizabeth listened with interest. Before Mr Chan came out she'd made up her mind. Mr Bell was puffing and blowing and trying to get rid of Mr Chan. As he practically forcedly removed him to the outer office, Elizabeth stood. *"Ms Trelawney, sorry to have kept you waiting."* Mr Bell fell over himself in greeting her, Elizabeth felt compete distaste. Elizabeth cut him off. *"Ah, Mr Bell, I see you have already met Mr Chan, we're business partners you know."* Both Mr Bell and Mr Chan looked shocked. Elizabeth extended her hand to Mr Chan. *"I'm so sorry Mr Chan for keeping you waiting, shall we all go back into Mr Bells office and secure your loan."* She told him. Mr Chan, not quite sure what was going on, but hearing the words loan, followed Elizabeth back in.

As Elizabeth took a seat. She addressed Mr Bell. *"Mr Chan has a number of business interests that I'm keen to invest in."* She told him. *"As the Double T stands collateral for the bank, I wish the bank to back Mr Chan. Half what he is looking for and the Double T will take the other half."* Mr Chan suddenly understood. Elizabeth turned to Mr Chan. *"I am sure Mr*

Chan, you would prefer me to be a silent partner?" She asked him and Mr Chan nodded in gratitude. *"And."* She said turning back to Mr Bell. *"Mr Chan will need premises, buy it under the Double T, with the option of Mr Chan buying it from me at an appropriate rate."* She told him. Both men were again showing surprise. *"There is Mr Chan, one condition."* She told him. Mr Chan looked at her with an expression of 'here it comes'. Elizabeth smiled. *"There are to be no opiates Mr Chan, unless it's for proven medical reasons and only dispensed if the Doctor approves it."* She told him. Elizabeth had seen its effects first hand back East. She didn't want it here.

Mr Chan, looked shame faced and spoke to her for the first time. *"Madam, I have never traded in opiates, I have no intension of doing so now."* He told her. *"Then we are agreed."* She told him smiling and extended her hand. *"The interest Ms Trelawney?"* Mr Chan asked before taking her hand. *"The bank will charge the standard rate the other business are getting and I am sure you will arrange a rate for my part that is reasonable."* She told him. *"Please keep me informed of your progress."* Elizabeth stood. *"Oh and Mr Bell, I wanted an update on the other business' we are doing, perhaps you could arrange to come out and see me next week."* She told him. *"Mr Chan."* Elizabeth extended her hand again. *"It's been a pleasure, should you wish to see me, you will find me at the Double T. Please feel free to call any time."* Mr Chan took her hand. *"I cannot thank you enough."* He told her emotionally. *"Yes you can, thrive and do well for both our families."*

As she walked passed his companion he stood. Elizabeth looked at him and he stared back. Elizabeth thought he had lovely eyes, she inclined her head as if to say your welcome, turned and left. As she did so, Black Dog walked up to her followed by Blue. He spoke quickly to her. Elizabeth signed the order to leave and mounted her pony. They rode for the store, from the window of the bank, one oriental young man, took in every movement. Women here, hold a different place he thought.

There had been a problem at the store. Elizabeth dismounted and went in. Carl had walked in behind her. Elizabeth walked up to the counter. *"Is there a problem here."* She asked. *"Oh Ms Trelawney, I'm sorry they have disturbed you, one of the settlers got a bit loud with the hands loading your wagons, thought they were being short changed, they did." "Why would they think that?"* She asked. *"They wanted to get moving. We were holding them up. Thought we were taking some of their goods."* Kincade told her. Elizabeth looked around her. *"Give them what they need and apologies for the inconvenience."* She told Mr Jenkins. Elizabeth looked at Carl. *"I think I've had enough of town for the time being."* She told him leaving the store and stood outside. Red Wolf approached from the mail post. His men carried several packages. *"I see we have mail."* She told him smiling. *"Umm, your Aunt."* He grumbled. Elizabeth smiled, it was welcome news indeed, she would look forward to hearing all the news from Boston. For the first time that day, Elizabeth felt like a young girl. She looked at both her men. Carl and Red Wolf and felt fortunate. *"Let's go home."* Red Wolf signed and the entire party mounted and they started to ride for home.

Elizabeth was glad to be back at the Double T. She felt uneasy about all the attention she'd had today. As she dismounted and stood on the porch she addressed her men. *"Thank you, all of you, the Double T, has never been in better hands. I know my father, honorary father and Ben, would thank you, each of you, as I do."* She told them. Smiled and went inside. Carl and Red Wolf saw to the animals and men. Both men in their own time, came in to join her. Elizabeth was sitting by the fire, she had refused dinner. Red Wolf came in first, carrying the parcels from her aunt. *"Is it a special occasion?"* He grumbled, lifting the packages and putting them on the side table. Elizabeth frowned then smiled. *"It's my birthday in two weeks."* She told him. *"21."* He sat in the chair opposite her. Without speaking Elizabeth got up and made him a drink, and passed it to him, he took it without looking up at her. As he took the first sip, Carl came in to join them. Carl stood to one side feeling he had interrupted them. Elizabeth again got up and made him a drink, she held it out to him and indicated the chair between her and Red Wolf. Carl took it.

All three sat in silence sipping their brandy. *"Long day."* She said eventually. *"I'm going up, thank you, both of you."* She said and rose from her chair, crossed the room and ascended the stairs to her room.

Both men stayed in their chairs. Eventually a member of staff brought some food and they ate. Not a word was spoken. Once Carl had finished his food, and the last of his brandy he rose from his chair. *"Red."* He spoke and left the house.

Red Wolf sat there wishing Elizabeth was with him. He did not wish to leave. What was the point of going back to the village, to his, he could hardly think the word, 'wife'.

He was still sitting there when Elizabeth came down early next morning. The house staff had not yet arrived to start breakfast. The fire in the hearth was still going. Elizabeth descended the stairs, headed to the bathroom and then the kitchen in need of coffee. Her sleep had been broken. She wasn't surprised to see him still here. Put on the coffee pot and walked back in to him. *"Been here all night?"* She asked him quietly. She stood in front of the fire and added more wood to it. Red Wolf just stared into it. *"Coffee?"* She asked him, he nodded in a resounded way and she headed back into the kitchen. Elizabeth came back with the coffee and handed one to him. She sat in the chair she'd used last night. Eventually she asked. *"How did you know about Blue?"* He looked at her. *"He came to me first, I told him to see you and he came back with your answer, you made him very happy." "Did I?"* She responded knowingly. *"I think only time will tell that."* Taking a mouthful of coffee Red Wolf leaned back in his chair. *"You can't keep doing this."* She said gently. The silence was deafening. *"It's the only place I want to be."* He told her. Red Wolf rose. Put is mug down he walked to her chair. Putting both hands on her face and looked into her eyes. *"This is all I see, awake or asleep and the only place I want to be."* He told her quietly, lovingly caressed her face with his fingers, taking in every small detail and left her.

The house came alive shortly after. Carl and Jake came in for the usual breakfast meeting. Elizabeth had decided while waiting for them, that it was time to move on. The Doubly T needed to be more. Time, to put plans into action that would take the Double T, into the next century. Elizabeth outlined her ideas to them both. Neither seemed much surprised. Elizabeth wanted to expand the horse and herd bloodlines. She wanted breeding programmes that took the best of the Indian horse mustangs, mixed with the very best Europe and the Arabs had to offer. She wanted to bring the best Beef stock from Scotland and build a new breed of cow, that would feed a nation. Both Jake and Carl told her, it would not be easy. *"We don't do easy."* She told them. They both smiled. She was right.

Sunday, Caroline, Kate and their parents came to dinner. Blue was also invited. He'd dressed western style for this meeting and pulled his hair back. Elizabeth spent most of the day showing Kate's parents just how well established both the Double T and Blue's involvement was. As the tour finished she stopped by a building going up in the rear pasture. Mr Cane asked after its purpose and commented on its wonderful view. Elizabeth took the opportunity to inform them of Blues new home. *"Actually, Mr Cane this is to be the*

new home of the man who is to head our horse bloodline programme.
We are expanding in to specialities. We will be bringing in new
bloodlines from Europe. Blue is heading this project up." Elizabeth
turned and looked at Blue. *"Well, congratulations Blue."* Mr
Cane held out his hand to him. *"Thank you Mr Cane."* Blue
responded. Kate beamed. Elizabeth continued the tour and
after dinner. Blue asked Mr Cane to join him and the men left
the ladies in the parlour. They were gone for nearly an hour.
Kate was becoming more agitated as the time moved on.
When they came back, both men were very serious.

"May I speak with you and Kate Elizabeth in private?"
Elizabeth took them into her office. Mr Cane lost no time is
putting his concerns to them. *"Well Kate, Blue has asked me for*
your hand." Kate looked both elated and concerned. *"Elizabeth,*
do you support this." He asked her. Elizabeth did not hesitate.
"Mr Cane, Blue is a good man, he came to me seeking my advice on
this matter and he tried very hard to persuade Kate that her

affections were misplaced. Kate would not have it. She was very sure and he loves her very much." She told him. *"But do you support it."* He asked her. Elizabeth took a moment. *"I support him Mr Cane. He's my man and will never be anything else and if Kate marries him, her life may have some complications, they will have to overcome, but one of them, will never be, somewhere they belong."* She told him. Mr Cane thought for a moment. *"And financially?"* He asked her. *"Blue will be paid for what he does here and it will represent he's worth to us and as the business grows and profits do so will he."* She told him. *"Do you want to marry him Kate?"* Her father asked her. *"More than anything father."* Mr Cane nodded his head and suggested it was time they join the others.

On entering the parlour Elizabeth offered a smile of encouragement to Blue and took her seat. As Mr Cane came in Blue stepped forward. Kate came to him and Mr Cane went to his wife and took her hand. *"It seems that we have lost a daughter and gained a son Mrs Cane."* He told her smiling. Mrs

Cane initially shocked saw the delight on her daughters face

and stepped forward towards Blue. *"Welcome to the family."*

She told him and hugged him. Caroline started clapping and

Kate and Elizabeth joined in. Their excitement drew the staff

and Elizabeth informed them of the good news. Elizabeth

asked them to break open several bottles of champagne and

ask the hands that were at home to come in and join the

celebration. The party, for that is what it turned into, went

well into the night.

Elizabeth took all of the next week to outline her ideas

for the Double T in more detail. She sent cables to the best

blood stock leaders of Europe. Made enquiries and spent a lot

of Trelawney money. Elizabeth talked over her plans for the

horses with both Red Wolf and Running Elk. The Mustang

would be essential to the blood line and Elizabeth wanted the

Indians to have ownership of it. The three of them decided

what breeds to bring out and try. Elizabeth remembered seeing Spanish and Arabian horses do some marvellous things back East and had talked extensively with their owners after seeing several shows. Elizabeth cabled her Aunt and asked her to contact them for her. It was decided to have both stallions and mares. The mix of both sexes improved the breeding possibilities, it was a programme that would take years, the benefits spoke for themselves. Not only would it establish the Double T as a leader in providing good breeding stock, it strengthened the bond with the land and its people for years to come.

On the last of the horse breeding programme meetings, Elizabeth had requested the Mayor to join them. Both Red Wolf and Running Elk were surprised to see him sitting at the table when they came in. Both acknowledged him and sat down. Elizabeth got straight to the point. *"Mayor, you're our legal man and I need you to draw something up for me."* She told him. *"Of course Elizabeth, how can I be of help."* He asked her.

Elizabeth took a deep breath. *"The Double T are starting a breeding programme of horses based on the Indian Mustang. Both Red Wolf and Running Elk will oversee this programme with mainly Indian manpower and Blue will run it. I want to legalise the partnership."* She told him.

Mayor Green paled. *"Err Elizabeth you know Indians cannot own land, or property."* *"Yes Mayor Green I know that so I am proposing we do this…"* She told them taking a deep breath. *"I want Red Wolf, Running Elk and Dull Knife legally adopted by the Trelawney name."* Elizabeth waited for objections from both Red Wolf and Running Elk. She looked at them both, saw no objection so carried on. *"Then, I want the Indian Nation on Trelawney Land established as a company in its own right under the Trelawney Corporation. Then I want a shell company from that set up to own the land on which they live and lastly, I want a second shell company listed from the land ownership corp, to own the horse bloodline and breeding programme on the Double T. The Partners will be myself, Red Trelawney, RE Trelawney and DK Trelawney."*

The Mayor saw the reasoning and thought it might work. He leaned forward. *"Ok Elizabeth, it might not stand up in court now but who knows what the future holds. I'll try it."* He told her. Elizabeth handed over her notes and wishes that she had painstakingly put together the night before. She turned to both Red Wolf and Running Elk. *"Is this ok with you both?"* She asked them. Running Elk looked at his brother who was looking at her. He turned back to Elizabeth. *"Will this mean, we, the tribe will legally in the white man's world, own the land we live on?"* He asked her. *"That is my hope yes."* She told him. *"And if not now, then in years to come when the world changes it will."* Running Elk came close to tears. *"Father will want to see you."* He whispered. Elizabeth nodded. *"Well if that is all?"* Mayor Green questioned. *"Yes thank you."* Elizabeth responded and held out her hand to him. *"I'll bring the papers over next week. All of you will need to sign them."* He put his hand out for Red Wolf to take. He did. Followed by Running Elk. Elizabeth saw Mayor Green to the door. He took with him a hamper of goods as well as Elizabeth's gratitude.

Elizabeth came back to the table and asked Anna to serve dinner. Both men were very quiet. When finished she thanked the staff and withdrew back to the parlour. Running Elk followed her in and said his goodbyes. *"I will need to let father know, he will want to see you."* He reminded her. *"I know but when it's done would be better."* She told him. Running Elk nodded and headed for the door, he paused at the entrance and looked at his brother who returned his stare. Running Elk nodded at an unspoken statement and left.

Elizabeth was standing by the picture window when Red Wolf came in from the dining room. *"I never get tired of looking at it."* She told him. He came and stood next to her.

"It would seem to be your week for miracles." He told her.

Elizabeth turned to him. *"You know better than that."* And

walked to the fireplace and sat down. *"I can never offer you so*

much in return." He told her. *"I'm not asking you to."* She told

him. *"No. And that's the problem. You don't ask anything of me."*

Elizabeth turned in her chair to face him. *"Please don't do this."*

He approached her and knelt before her. From his waistcoat

pocket he pulled a small parcel. Elizabeth took it and opened

it. Inside were two things. A nugget of raw gold and an

uncut diamond. Elizabeth was speechless. She looked at him.

"I would have had it made into a ring or something but.." He told

her apologetically, it was Elizabeth's turn to now be close to

tears. *"It's your birthday tomorrow. I have not forgotten."* *"Both*

came from our land."

"They're beautiful, thank you." She told him. Elizabeth's

emotions were raging. She found it hard to look at him and

he knew it. He withdrew and sat opposite her. Elizabeth wanted to thank him properly but feared the consequences. He knew that too. *"You did a wonderful thing today Esa, father will inform the tribe and they will want to give thanks to his daughter. You give him much to be proud of. I wish I could do as much."* He told her. *"You have done everything he's asked of you."* She told him. Red Wolf smiled. *"Then why, do I not feel like it."* *"We do what we have to.* She reminded him. Red Wolf fell back in his chair. *"Dam it Elizabeth. I'm not sure how long I can keep this up. I've had enough of what we have to do."* Elizabeth was visibly shocked. *"You do not mean that. Father loves you very much, he wants you to lead the tribe well."* *"I know. I know."* He told her irritated. *"I'm just not sure I want to."* Elizabeth got up and called to Anna for some coffee. Although she had the feeling that she could do with something stronger. She didn't trust herself. Elizabeth returned to her seat and Anna followed her in with the coffee. *"Thank you Anna."* *"Do you want some?"* She asked him. *"I should leave."* He told her. Elizabeth refused to be pulled into his emotional turmoil, hers was bad enough. *"I'll say goodnight then."* Red Wolf got up to leave. She called to him as he reached the door. *"Thank you again for my gift."* He nodded. *"I wish I could give you more."* He told her opening the door he walked through it.

Elizabeth held on to her gift and stared after him.

On the day of her birthday the Double T put on a party for Elizabeth. People came from all over. The town came out as well. A steer had been butchered and a massive BBQ set up on the yard. Table and chairs were put up as well as bunting and lights. There was music in the evening. And an area had been cleared for dancing. Anna and the kitchen staff had worked magic and the food was wholesome and lovely. Her cake beautiful. Mr Bell tried to talk business and Elizabeth had to remind him it was a party. Vera brought her something feminine and personal and told her to open it when alone which made them both laugh. Kate, Caroline and Mr and Mrs Cane brought her a lovely set of novels by her favourite author. Jed came with his sisters. Elizabeth was reminded to visit. The hands and the house staff had clubbed together and purchased a new saddle for her and one of them had engraved her and the Double T's crest on it. Elizabeth was very humbled. Running Elk, Black Dog and the braves, brought gifts from her father and White Dove and The tribe. Running Elk reminded her that Dull Knife wanted to see her. Elizabeth promised she would once the papers had been signed and reminded him that the Mayor had promised to bring them back in a couple of days.

Carl managed to find her on her own to give her his gift. Elizabeth had popped back into the house. Carl was a little unsure giving her something personal. *"Elizabeth."* he called to her, as she turned she realised he had something in his hand. Elizabeth smiled as Carl walked towards her. *"I err, hope you like it."* He told her nervously. Elizabeth took to box from him. It was wonderfully ornate. Inside was a silver plaque. Engraved across it, was the Trelawney crest, entwined with it, was the tribe's emblem. It was beautiful. Elizabeth looked up. *"Carl its lovely, but it's too much, it must have cost the earth." "Well actually, once the Chan family found out it was for you, I had trouble paying anything towards it. The only way I could get it was to agree that it was from both of us."* He told her. *"Thank you."* Elizabeth frowned. *"Why are the Chan's not here."* She asked. *"I understand that the town organiser Mr Bell, didn't invite them."* He told her. *"That man is a bigot and I am coming to the conclusion that he will never change. I will have to thank them and apologise and we will put this at the entrance of the house grounds." "You like it then."* He asked her not sure *"I love it."* She answered. *"It's amazing and very thoughtful."* Elizabeth leaned forward and kissed him. It was the first time she had. Elizabeth linked his arm and they both went back to the party.

Elizabeth formally introduced Carl to Mr and Mrs Cane and as she left them, asked him to look after Caroline. It was clear that Mr and Mrs Cane liked him very much. Elizabeth already guessed Caroline did. Elizabeth asked Caroline if she could do something for her and told her what she needed. Caroline was happy to obliged. Everyone stayed longer than they intended and the braves gave them an escort home.

Mayor Green came out the following week as promised. He brought the papers with him. Elizabeth, Red Wolf, Running Elk each signed where needed. Elizabeth would sign on Dull Knifes behalf. Carl and Jake had been asked to counter sign as witnesses. They were registered if not quite legal but they were according to the legal requirements of the land and had been registered at her New York office. Elizabeth had effectively given up several thousand acres, should the tribe ever be able to claim it. Elizabeth thanked Mayor Green for his help and escorted him to the door. It was then he remembered the item Caroline had given him. Elizabeth thanked him again and headed up to pack for a trip to see her father. Running Elk would be staying to keep the place going along with Carl and Jake.

When she came down her horse was waiting for her. Along with Red Wolf. *"Is not Black Dog taking me?"* She asked him. *"No, father asked me to do it."* He told her. Elizabeth was dressed for the journey, there was a chill in the air, she mounted. Carl and Jake and the house staff said their goodbyes. Elizabeth had confirmed her instructions for the next week and rode out.

Elizabeth set the pace. She was in no urgent rush to get there and wanted to enjoy the journey. The horses were paced from running to walking to save them and allow her to enjoy the change of season. Winter was coming. You could smell it in the air. They rode in silence for several hours. At last,

Elizabeth indicated that she would like to stop, rest the horses and take in the breath-taking view. Elizabeth stood and stretched. Red Wolf passed her the water bottle and some dried food. Elizabeth took both and for a time, lost herself. When she eventually turned, Red Wolf told her. *"Welcome back."* Elizabeth smiled. *"It's lovely here."* She told him and bent to give him the water bottle back, as she did so, a chain came loose of her neck line and dangled in the light. Red Wolf caught it and looked it over, there was his gift. The gold nugget had been made into a mount. Oriental in design but still rough in shape as the earth had released it. And in its clasp, the uncut and unpolished diamond. *"You had it made up, you did not want it cut and polished?"* He asked her turning it over and looking at it. *"No."* She smiled. *"I wanted it just how you gave it to me, they did a good job don't you think?"* *"I asked Caroline to take it into town for me and have it made up. They did a good job don't you think?"* *"It's as beautiful as its owner."* Elizabeth turned from him. She couldn't let him see how much his words affected her. She gazed at the dying sun and recognised the lateness of the hour. *"We should go."* She told him, they mounted and rode on.

Dull Knife knew they were coming before they got within half a mile of the village. He had been asked by Elizabeth not to celebrate something that had always belonged to them. Dull Knife had respected her wishes. The tribe had been asked to greet a returning daughter on a visit to her family. They all knew what she had done for them and respected her reasons for it. The elders came out to meet her at her father's residence. Each greeted her and offered their thanks. Elizabeth asked to speak to them all in pow wow. Elizabeth was only too aware of the great honour she had done Dull Knife and was concerned that his own sons could not do as much. Dull Knife ushered them all in. Pleasantries were offered and the men smoked the pipe of peace. It was not offered to Elizabeth and she did not expect it to be, only the men of the tribe smoked in this way. The elders talked of

things past, of things present and then of the future.

It was then that Dull Knife told them that his daughter

had something to tell them. Most of the elders understood the

white man's language but out of respect for them Elizabeth

asked Dull Knife to translate. Elizabeth explained about the

White man's law. She was asked to explain how they could

not own what was always theirs's. Elizabeth told it as it was.

That whether they had fought the white man or choose to live

with them, the white man had taken what he wanted and

decided without consulting those who had always been here,

what they wanted or what they would do,. They just did it.

They made a new country, a new world and new laws to

govern it. They were silent and she continued. She explained

that with the help of Red Wolf and Running Elk and her

Father Dull Knife she had found a way to get around this.

She told them, they had to used the law as it stands in the

white man's world and protect their way of life. Elizabeth explained about her legally adopting Dull Knife and his family as they had her in the White man's way. That a paper had been made and signed that would not only be legal within an American law system but may never come to light that it is actually an Indian Nation who owned the corporation. They were protected for infinity. Elizabeth outlined the one condition in the contract, that both, the Trelawney family and the Indian tribe were bonded in blood and land and neither could relinquish it. The elders nodded quietly. Told her they needed to talk on the matter some more and would talk with her later. Elizabeth thanked them and withdrew.

Elizabeth walked through the doorway and into fresh air. She felt she needed it. She hoped they understood. Red Wolf was waiting for her. She walked up to him and just stood there. He instinctively put his arms around her and held her close to him. His lips in her hair. Her face on his chest. They were both unaware of the people around them. Red Wolf eventually let her go, took hold of her hand and led her away to her favourite place. With a squeeze of her hand he left her. White Dove found her there some time later.

"Elizabeth is it wonderful to see you." Elizabeth looked up and smiled at her Aunt. How she had missed her. *"White Dove."* She called as she got up and walked to hug her. *"I have missed you Aunt."* She told her. White Dove hugged her back. *"Come I have dinner waiting and much to tell you. What you have done for the tribe is a wonderful thing Esa".* White Dove told her linking arms and walking back to her Tepee. Elizabeth frowned. *"I hope they accept it."* They talked about what she had done since Ben's burial and White Dove told her how much she had missed her too.

Dull Knife sent for her next morning.

The tribal elders were waiting for her. She entered alone and sat where they told her. The eldest of them spoke. Dull Knife translated for her. He told her, that mother earth gave the land they live on to them and no man, White or Indian, can take what is given freely but, the White man, had more power than the Indian and the Indian ways were no longer respected by them and war, lost many braves on all sides. Elizabeth nodded. He went on, if what she had done, may help protect them from the advances of the White man, she had done well and would take their thanks with her. What came next was unexpected. *"Child."* He told her. *"If we are to be bonded in blood on this land. As your paper demands. Bound together. ..."* Dull Knife was not happy at translating the next statement and hesitated in doing so. Elizabeth became to fear what he was going to say. *"We wish."* The old man told her. *"To honour you in the same way you have honoured us. You are to be more than an daughter adopted to us.*

We would wish you to be our daughter and the mix of our blood lines will preserve us all for many generations to come." They got up and left.

Elizabeth turned to Dull Knife and quietly asked her. *"Do you understand their wishes."* Elizabeth nodded. *"Yes father, they wish me to marry and are instructing me who it should be."* *"You could tell them you wish to choose otherwise."* He told her. Elizabeth smiled at him. *"No I could not. It is the words on the paper and it would dishonour you and undo everything I have tried to do."* Dull Knife sat tall. She knew her duty too well. He put his seal on the papers she gave him. Elizabeth continued. *"Father, I must tell you, had I been given this choice shortly after my return from back East, I would have taken it gladly."* She informed him sadly. It was at that moment that Dull Knife came to realise why he's eldest son's affections were not with his wife. *"You should return to the Double T."* He told her. *"This does not have to be decided now."* *"Thank you."* She told him and went to pack. White Dove was waiting for her. *"Your leaving, going back to the Double T?"* *"Yes father felt it best for me to go."* Elizabeth explained what had happened. White Dove saw the irony of it all. She leaned over and hugged her. No words could compensate for that knowledge. *"Come with me?"* Elizabeth asked her. White Dove looked at the only daughter she was ever likely to have. *"I was there for you as a child but my life there was Ben, without him my life is here."* She told her. Elizabeth smiled. *"I will miss you."* White Dove hugged her. *"Let me help you pack."*

Elizabeth said her goodbyes and rode home the way she came. Red Wolf did not go with her, or say goodbye. Her escort saw her safely to the house, Carl and Jake welcomed her home. Elizabeth went to bed she'd had two very difficult days.

CHAPTER TEN

Winter 1879

Elizabeth's plans for the ranch started early the next day. Jake told her some of the new stock would be arriving into Brownsville. Over breakfast, they discussed the details. Elizabeth decided she'd take a trip into town and make all the necessary arrangements. Black Dog and his men were back on duty and followed her in.

Elizabeth made her way to see Mr Bell. They discussed the financial arrangements with the towns folk first, then went onto the arrangements needed for the new stock. Elizabeth was well pleased. Everything appeared to be in order. For all Mr Bells, questionable attitude. He did know banking. Elizabeth was still torn with the events of her party and the lack of an invite to the Chan family. *"Mr Bell, before we* conclude our business, I would like to thank you for arranging for the towns folk to attend my party." She told him, Mr Bell visibly primed. "However," she continued. "I was surprised that not all my business partners were present." Mr Bell now looked visibly confused. Elizabeth felt the need to explain. "The Chan's family, Mr Bell, they were not invited I understand." She told him. "Well yes, Elizabeth, they are – Chinese." He told her. "Yes Mr Bell, in the same way I am Indian." Elizabeth took a deep breath. "Let me be very clear Mr Bell." She continued. "The Chan family and I are in business, I expect them to make me a great deal of money and in doing so, this town. If I were a wise man, I would be falling over myself to ensure my good favour with them. Good day Mr Bell, always a pleasure." Elizabeth rose from her chair and held out her hand. Mr Bell was clearly not sure if he should take offence or thank her. He decided it would be good business, to do the latter and shock hands seeing her to the door.

Elizabeth made her way across town to the new buildings, followed by Black Dog. The Chan family owned three with Elizabeth. The centre one, doubled as their home. Elizabeth walked into the shop as it was opened for her. Elizabeth recognised the younger man who had been in the bank that day. *"Good morning, I'm Elizabeth Trelawney."* She told him holding out her hand. The young man instinctively took it and held on to it. Elizabeth smiled at him and shock it for him. This woke the young man and he quickly responded. *"My lady, my father would be honoured to see you. Please wait here and I will get him."* Elizabeth took the seat offered to her. Both Mr Chan senior and his son came back quickly. Elizabeth rose form her chair and outstretched her hand to Mr Chan Sr. *"Mr Chan."* She said and they exchanged pleasantries. *"I have come to offer my apologies and thanks."* She told him. Both Mr Chan senior and Jr, looked at each other. Elizabeth clarified. *"I understand Mr Bell organised for the towns folks to attend my home for my 21st birthday and he did not*

extend the invitation as he should have done, to all my partners."
She told them. *"And I particularly wanted to thank you for doing this."* Elizabeth took out the chain they had made for her.
"And the plaque, it was beautifully done." "You have nothing to be apologising for my lady." He told her. *"Please join me in my office, I would like to show you how we are doing." "I would like that very much."* She told him. *"Do you require your protection."* He asked her indicating Black Dog outside the shop. *"No Mr Chan, his place is outside."* And followed him through to the back.

Elizabeth was offered the bosses chair at his desk and offered tea and some delicious food. Elizabeth accepted and commented on just how lovely it was and she meant it. Mr Chan Sr, showed her all the business accounts. Elizabeth asked about products, supply and delivery. Elizabeth was keen on knowing about the silks and jewellery. She felt this was something they could expand on. Elizabeth mentioned

Vera's shop and that it might be good to talk to her. Mr Chan agreed and answered her questions eagerly. She was particularly interested in the jewellery. She asked about re-investment and they talked for several hours. When they were done, Mr Chan offered to show her around the other two shops and the stock. Elizabeth was very happy to do both. Mr Chan asked his son to accompany her. Mr Chan Sr, bowed to her and she went with Mr Chan Jr. Elizabeth looked at the stock and wondered at the quality of the silk, she enquired on its manufacture and the quality of the stitch designs. She was most impressed and could not remember seeing such quality back East. Elizabeth felt it would be much prized and said so to Mr Chan Jr. *"Mr Chan, may I ask you, do you have a first name?"* *"Why yes my lady, I am called Jin Tao Chan."* *"Well, Jin will do nicely."* Jin, she told him. *"I am Elizabeth".* Jin not too sure if that would be appropriate seemed to hesitate. Elizabeth smiled. *"I guess that is something we need to work on."* And continued to look over the jewellery. Making suggestions that they might like to look into buying gold. That the shop may need some security and she'd be happy to supply it. She found the laundry very efficient, as were the restaurant and the store. It was all most impressive and she told Mr Chan Sr when she came back. He seemed most pleased and extended an invitation to join them at dinner. Elizabeth thanked him for his hospitality and stated that at any other time she would be most happy to accept but she had business still to do. Mr Chan accepted this and she held out her hand for him, Mr Chan took it and he bowed over it. *"My lady."* And bowed to her again. *"Mr Chan, you do not have to call me lady."* She told him. Mr Chan Sr., was thoughtful for a moment. *"You are royalty here are you not?"* He asked her. Elizabeth smiled. *"Mr Chan, that is complicated question."* *"Just so."* He told her. *"But none the less, you are and our family will honour our partnership and you in such a manner that befits it. Good day my lady."* Elizabeth smiled kindly, and thanked him for his hospitality and hoped to see him again soon. As Jin opened the door for her. Elizabeth thanked him and held out her hand. *"Jin, it was nice seeing you again, both you and your father are most welcome at the Double T and should you have need of us, send one of the boys."* She told him. *"Thank you – Elizabeth."* Mr Chan Sr on hearing the exchanged corrected his son in Chinese. *"My father does not approve of me using your first name." "I see."* She told him. *"May I still use yours?" "I would like that very much."* He told her. Elizabeth thanked them again and went in search of Vera.

Elizabeth spent the remaining day between business and pleasure while in town. She saw all her business partners. Returned the papers to Mayor Green to be notarised and sent to land and company registry. It was dark when she left having spent a very pleasant evening with Mr and Mrs Cane, Kate and Caroline.

It was after midnight when she got back. There were lights on in the house, Black Dog took her horse and the other braves dispersed with her thanks. As she stepped onto the porch the door flew open and there stood Carl, Jake and Red Wolf, they all looked like they were about to kill someone. *"What's happened?"* She asked, they each looked at each other registered her concern and Jake started laughing. *"Night boys."* He called out. *"Glad your back safe Elizabeth."* He told her giving her a hug as he went by. Elizabeth started to look confused. *"What's going on?"* She asked. Red Wolf turned and went back inside the house. Carl still at the door was left to explain. *"Well you see Elizabeth, I came back and Jake said you'd gone to town this morning early with Black Dog and he was kinda expecting you to be back a couple of hours ago and then Red Wolf turned up and we realised you weren't with him and it was getting later by the minute and..."* Elizabeth cut in. *"You all panicked."* She told him. Carl looked somewhat embarrassed. *"Yeah I guess we did."* Elizabeth tried not to smile. This was serious.

They had to stop treating her like a child that needed looking after. She couldn't run this place and not go anywhere. This was ridiculous. *"Carl, I'll discuss this in the morning with you and Jake, I'm too tired now, good night."* She told him sternly and walked passed him. *"Good night."* He called after her, knowing tomorrow wouldn't be pleasant and closed the door behind him.

Elizabeth slumped in her favourite chair, the fire was still going. She was pissed. Black Dog was with her and his braves. *"Did I not say, this has to stop."* She told him. He ignored her. *"You know what. Ok, I'm done here. Fine, good night."* Elizabeth got up and went to her room. She threw her hat and gloves on the chair and pulled her riding jacket off and flung it over the back of it. She went to the window and pulled back the curtains. There was a chill in the air and she decided not to open it. Elizabeth pulled her shirt from her trousers and sat drained on her bed facing the window. She instinctively started to un braid her hair and stopped. She was exhausted. She had not heard the door opening but was not surprised to feel his presence or the bed sink behind her and hands taking the braids from her and start where she had left off. Elizabeth sighed. Neither of them said anything, it was not needed. Red Wolf ran his hands through her hair. It felt wondering. Elizabeth leaned back against him, it was all too comfortable. A task a warrior did for his wife. *"You should go."* She told him. He did not move just let her lean on him as he stroked her hair. *"Father spoke to me after you left, I think he waited till you went."* He told her gently. Elizabeth did not want to hear what was coming. *"I'm tired this can wait."* She told him and got up.

"Tired?" He challenged. *"Tired? Shall I tell you about being tired Elizabeth."* He told her biting off the words and rising from the bed and coming round to face her. *"I'm tired of having to do what I'm told. I'm tired of having to share a home*

with a woman I don't care for and dishonourably ignore her. I'm tired of seeing you with Carl." Red Wolf felt his temper rising. "I'm tired of being miserable. I'm tired of not being able to make my own choices, but mostly. I'm tired of not being. Not laying. With the woman, I love." They both were a little surprised by his outburst. He had not meant to say so much, the air around them was electric. "Then stay." She told him honestly too tired to argue knowing her heart would not be in it. "Stay with me tonight. If not as my husband, then as my brother I would welcome the company." She told him quietly. "Esa, you ask the impossible." He told her turning away. Elizabeth raised her hand and touched his arm. "Stay." She said again. "Lay with me. Just being with you will be enough." She told him earnestly. Elizabeth needed him. If she could not have him physically she would take what she could get. Elizabeth undid her trousers and pulled them over her boots. Her boots followed with a clank on the floor and she pulled back the covers of her bed and slipped in. She turned on her side and nestled against the pillows and closed her eyes. She was aware of movement around the room and the lights going out. What she welcomed was feeling his body laying next to hers and his arms reaching around her and holding her tight. Red Wolf pulled back her hair and whispered to her in the darkness. He sighed. *"You are my love. My life. Without you it means nothing."* Elizabeth smiled and sleepily replied *"Always."*

She woke in the morning alone. She had expected it. But still, her heart hurt knowing he had gone. Elizabeth bathed and came down to breakfast. He was sitting at the table with Jake and Carl. They were talking about the new stock. Elizabeth went to the kitchen, called to Anna *"Good morning."* Grabbing some coffee and joined them.

Elizabeth listened for a while until they sort her views. It was decided to do a roundup of the horses and start on weeding out the lesser stock and working with the best they had. As they went to break up, Elizabeth told them she had something to say and did not mince words. *"Each of you. All of you."* She told them looking from one to the other. *"Need to let me go. I am not a child any longer. I cannot run this ranch, the business, the larger corporation, if right here, I cannot go into town and stay for dinner without you calling out the hands to find me. You need to know and trust, I have my protection and that I will use them. That I will be safe and should I not be, my men."* She stressed. *"Will protect me against all. I, need to know, I have your support and your confidence and that you know I can do this. Otherwise, I may have well have stayed East and run the business from there."* She concluded. Each man was quiet. Jake cleared his throat. *"Ok girl, we never thought otherwise. Just got over worried is all."* He told her touching her arm and left. Elizabeth looked at the other two. Both nodded. *"Right then, let's go to work."* She told them.

The weeks that followed were hard on them all. It took everyone at their best to get the jobs done. Elizabeth laid out how she wanted the new horse pens. New paddocks went up in front of the house, new stables and barns further out. Elizabeth remembered seeing the riding homes she visited when East and tried to combine their practicality with what she wanted. Several miles of new fencing went up and Elizabeth hired more men from the town whose job it would be to paint it white. The boys tried to tell her painting it was not practical but it looked good. When the new stock arrived, the men were busy. Real busy and more came from the tribe to help. Elizabeth loved it all. The hard work, the sweat, the dust, the comradery and the animals. Elizabeth fell in love all over again. She was torn between the beauty of the Arabians, the elegance of the Spanish blacks and the magnificence of the Mustang.

Red Wolf tried to keep his distance and let her go.

When the new beef stock arrived in Phoenix, the men led by Carl were waiting for them. They came with their handler as had the horses. The cows were different from the steers they were used to. No horns, they were fat, red and white. They were drawing a lot of attention. Jake saw them off the train and introduced himself to their handler. The handler was very explicit these cows had to be looked after carefully. Walked not run and slowly or they could lose too much body fat and not too far. Carl explained that it was several days' ride to the Double T. In that case, he told him, it will take several weeks. Carl was not a happy man. He sent riders back to the Double T to let them know.

When Elizabeth received the news, she was far from concerned. She took it in her stride and felt it gave her more time with the horses before they arrived. This pick up had turned into a major trail. She could imagine Carls face.

Elizabeth understood how important it was that they were established on the land before winter fully set in. If they were to have any chance of a good start to the breeding programme come Spring.

She turned her attention to the stallions and mares. They were well housed. Each had their own space and shared one of the new paddocks. Elizabeth took to watching them from the gates. The way in which the Indians worked with them continued to amaze her. Even the handlers that had been paid to escort their charges and to pass on specialised training tools for these breeds were impressed. Within a very short space of time, it was clear that a mutual respect existed on all sides.

The horses had to be kept separately and it was a full-time job. Several hands led by Red Wolf were having difficulty keeping them under control. More than one male nearly got stepped on. Red Wolf got swiped sideways and landed on his rear. Elizabeth could not help but laugh. He was not impressed. His hurt pride was soon mended. Elizabeth spent much of her time back in the kitchens helping Anna and the other new kitchen staff putting food stock away for the winter and serving food to keep the troops going. It did feel like they were feeding an army. The days were very long. It was soon clear to Elizabeth that they were going to have to secure additional grazing, straw and feed. Over the next few days, she invited the local farmers to dinner. She expressed an interest in converting some of the existing acres out to the West to farm land. They listened with interest and offered help and support if she wished to try it. Elizabeth also gained an understanding from them, that she could buy their excess produce should she need it. It was a good deal for all.

At the end of the week Red Wolf came to dinner. He came in late, did not contribute to the conversation and moved off early to the parlour. Mainly hands were with them and were use to his silence. No one really paid much attention, everyone was tired and left them early. Anna served coffee to them and Elizabeth said good night to her and thanked her for all her and her families hard work. Elizabeth looked at him. He gazed into the roaring fire in the chair opposite her. She poured coffee for them both and handed one to him. He took it. *"I must go back."* He told her. *"I have not been home since…"* Elizabeth had not realised this; he had not always been around as was his way. He had not stayed with her other than that one night. She took it for granted, that from time to time, he had returned home, clearly, that had not happened.

"You should have gone sooner." She told him honestly. He looked at her. She was punishing them both. They both knew why he had not. *"I am unsure when I will be back."* He told her. Elizabeth understood. He had left it too long, now

he was being ordered home. *"Running Elk will be here tomorrow to take over the horses."* Reluctantly, reverently, he brought up the subject that had been on his mind for the last few weeks. *"Esa, I'm sorry but I have to ask. Do you have an answer for the council of elders?"* Elizabeth sat perfectly still. *"No."* She told him. Red Wolf nodded. *"Then you run the risk of them making one for you."* He told her. *"Maybe, maybe not, tell father, I am working hard to secure our future and once that is done, I will make a decision I can take to the elders."* *"That will not hold them long."* He told her. *"And you will not be short of suiters."* He told her seriously. *"It seems I have made matters worse instead of better."* She replied. *"Not for the tribe."* He had spoken the sad truth; Elizabeth had given much and it will cost her dear. Neither wanted to think about it.

Elizabeth after a time put down her coffee and stood before him and held out her hand. He took it, rose with her and ascended the stairs. They entered her room together and he closed the door behind them. Elizabeth ran her hand across his chest and under his waistcoat, and slipped it off his shoulders. The shirt under it pulled free of his trousers easily. As Elizabeth went to slip the buttons free, he stopped her and held her hands. He looked at her and remembered their time together. His senses came on fire. *"I will not do this a second time to you."* He told her. *"I will not dishonour you, knowing that I cannot be a husband to you."* Elizabeth leaned into him and his arms went round her. *"Then stay with me till the sun rises."* She asked him. Elizabeth moved out of his embrace, removed her outer clothing and got into bed. He came to her quickly and Elizabeth gave up to his embrace. She was soon asleep.

Elizabeth was dreaming. Her body was on fire. Her emotions running high. He was arousing her to great heights. Elizabeth felt his body, running her hands down his back and across his buttocks. He instinctively reflexed and became hard. Elizabeth moaned, she felt his rough hands run across her breast, felt his breath on her skin and moaned aloud. Red Wolf woke her and for a moment she was unsure where she was and why he was not touching her. Red Wolf took in her flushed face, the heat of her body and the need in her eyes. Her moan, told him what she had been dreaming and Elizabeth realised this and looked away. *"Don't."* He told her and lifted her chin to look back at him, her mouth felt dry and she ran her tongue over her lips to try and moisten them. It failed. He kissed her. Elizabeth opened her mouth and greedily kissed him back. There was no restraint. She needed him. She wanted him. Any good intensions he had were lost. He removed the bed clothes from her body and quickly undressed her. Elizabeth felt him loosen his trousers as she pulled the shirt from his back, she was desperate to feel him naked against her and ran her hands up and down his back from his head to his thigh, it was Red Wolfs time to moan as she cupped him against her and opened her legs for him. Neither could wait, he touched her as she guided him, he hesitated above her for an instance, Elizabeth moved her hands and hips and joined with him. It was shallow but he was inside her. Red Wolf placed his forehead on hers and looked at her. Elizabeth groaned. *"Don't stop."* She told him breathlessly. He responded by lifting her hips from the bed and thrusting in deeply. She clung to him and held him to her. It was Elizabeth that started to move under him. He joined her thrust for thrust, pace for pace, Elizabeth was insatiable she drove him on. Taking everything he had to give her, she wanted him, had to have him, Red Wolf suddenly stopped and started to withdraw. *"We can't, you could have a child."* He told her desperately. *"I want it. I want you."* She told him. *"Please, I need you."* She begged him. She reached out and caressed him. He became harder, under her hands. Harder than he thought possible. A child, he repeated, his child, her child, he wanted that as much as he wanted her. He pushed into her again, finding greater depth. He looked in her eyes, there would be no going back, he thrust hard into her and she gasped and called out his name and he rode her whispering hers, for the release they both so desperately needed. Elizabeth fell asleep in his arms Red Wolf kissing her shoulder, whispering his love. He left her before sunrise.

Red Wolf rode into the village and went to his lodge and his wife. He entered quietly, she was a kind women, it was not her fault that he did not love her. He could not bring himself to touch her. She was frustrated with him, angry. He could not blame her. He slept on the other side of the room and woke to her cooking. His father sent for him soon after. As he got up to leave, Sky spoke to him. *"I need a husband who is here, who needs me, who will love me and give me children."* She told him. He hesitated by the doorway and turned back to her. *"This was not my choice."* He told her. *"Or mine."* And for the first time, he understood her, she had accepted her fate and honoured it, she had done better than him. He came back to her and took her hand. *"Forgive me."* He told her. *"I do not know if I could ever be the person you deserve."* He told her honestly. Sky nodded. *"Then I will talk with my father."* She told him. *"You know what that means?"* He asked her. *"Yes, it will not be easy."* Red Wolf looked at her bravery and smiled, any warrior would be proud to have her as his mate. Part of him wished things could have been different. He went in search of his father.

Red Wolf entered his father's lodge. Dull Knife was clearly unwell. Concerned Red Wolf went to him. Dull Knife told the others to leave them. When they were alone he spoke. *"My son, I am an old man, your brother has found happiness in this life, a wife who loves him, who is to give him a child in the spring, he knows he's place is here. You are my first born and I see you unhappy. I see you torn between two worlds and I am to blame for some of that."* He told him. *"If."* He continued. *"You cannot make your peace with who you are and what is expected of you, you will not be the leader our tribe needs."* Red Wolf swallowed hard. *"I have tried father."* He told him. Dull Knife nodded and touched his arm. *"I know son, but it is not enough, it is time you made a choice."* He told him. *"Father, the council of elders made it clear what they want from Esa." "Yes, my son, but that cannot be you, you are already married and you cannot break that without bringing shame on us and you will never be able to lead."* Red Wolf hung his head, his father was right. He had failed his father. Elizabeth had asked him to let her go and he had not. He had failed her too. Sky had asked him to be her husband and he had not. He'd failed her as well. His father was now asking him to be the warrior he should be and lead his people, it was time he did what was expected of him. *"I understand father."* He told him and went in search of his wife.

He found her sitting beside the stream. He sat down with her. *"Do you want me Sky?"* He asked her honestly. *"After everything, do you still want to be my wife?"* Sky looked at him, he was a true warrior and she had loved him, but since their marriage, she no longer knew. *"I do not know."* She answered truthfully. Red Wolf was silent. Sky had to make this choice he had done enough. *"Do you want me as a wife?"* She asked him. Red Wolf knew he could have lied, but there had been enough deception. *"I have only ever loved one women, I cannot get her out of my blood, I have tried."* He said turning to look at her. *"I did try."* He told her earnestly. *"I know."* she told him. *"I knew before I married you, seeing you together, it never felt like a brother loving his sister, we make excuses, say it is the difference in blood that bonds you closer and the way she came into our tribe, but a woman who shares that affection knows."* She told him. *"And you still married me?"* He asked her. She smiled at him sadly. *"Duty and honour."* She told him. And there is was, duty and honour. Then, so be it.

They agreed, the would both try, start again. He would stay away from the ranch. Start to lead the people and in time, they both hoped, he would learn to love her. White Dove brought the news to Elizabeth. She arrived at the Double T and asked to stay a while. Elizabeth happily agreed. They sat on the terrace swing and White Dove held her hand. She explained that Red Wolf had sort her out and explained it all to her. In doing so, he asked that she go to Elizabeth and tell her what he had done. That he would do what she and their father had wished, he'd let her go. Elizabeth closed her eyes on hearing it. She had been expecting it. It hurt no less for hearing it now. White Dove held her and let her cry. Elizabeth again found herself grieving for what she had lost. This time, it was easier. It had come as no big surprise to her that in the end, Red Wolf chose duty.

Elizabeth got up the next day and went back to work and White Dove was there waiting for her each time she returned. Caroline and Kate came to visit on their usual day as did Vera on occasion. Vera had struck up a business relationship with Mr Chan and it was proving to be beneficial all round. Caroline had talked about how close Mr Chan Jr seemed to be with Vera. Elizabeth was happy for them. She now went to town each week and met with what was now The Brownsville Town Board. She'd been voted in in her absence as Chair and this time had accepted it. They discussed the Trelawney loans, the towns businesses and new opportunities. Elizabeth voted Mr Chan Sr onto the board, some of the others were not happy about the nomination. Elizabeth explained that all and any business in the town needed to be present. Only then would they all benefit. She got her way without declaring her interest and an invitation was sent out and accepted. And wherever she went, Black Dog and his braves followed. She was never alone.

Carl came home along with the new beef stock. He was tired and glad to be back. Elizabeth watched them ride into the yard. She had been waiting for them having been alerted of their arrival. *"Welcome home stranger."* She told him with a

big grin as he came up to the house. Elizabeth walked

towards him and hugged him. *"It's good to see you."* She told

him. *"Thanks, what'd I miss?"* He asked her. Elizabeth smiled.

"Not much, come on, I'll get you a drink." And she led him in.

The nights were drawing in and it was getting colder. Over

the next month, Elizabeth helped in getting the new beef stock

out into pasture land across the spread. Winter Shelters were

put up and stocked with feed and water to last a good month

should the snow be heavy. Feed was stored ready for the

winter freeze. Carl came to dinner most nights. The free and

easy routine back in place. They would talk about their day,

the work, hands and stock. Whenever something particularly

bothered him, he would contemplate it before discussion it

with her. This night he had some concerns the hands had

raised with him over the new beef stock Some felt they

would not last out the winter, they were not tough enough.

Elizabeth believed it would work and the mix of both breeds

would make a more marketable product come next season. If this came off, the Double T stood to make a lot of money. Elizabeth felt sure, this was the future of the beef industry.

Running Elk with Blue, kept her informed of the horses, they were doing well. They had several breeding possibilities. Elizabeth was keen to see how the mix of the Arabians and Spanish Blacks came out. She thought they would be wonderful animals. If highly strung.

When Kate and Caroline came next, it was to welcome news, Kate and Blues house was ready. Kate had spent much time working with how she wanted it. She was very proud of it. Kate announced that they would be married in a month. There was only one problem, her parents wanted a church wedding but Blue being more Indian than white did not and Kate just wanted him. Elizabeth offered a compromise, her gift to them, to hold the wedding at the Double T. The

Preacher, would come out and do it she told them. Kate could not believe it, she thanked her. Holding the wedding at the Double T meant that it could take any form they wished and it would be the compromise to suite all. It was a marvellous idea and made everyone happy.

As Elizabeth said her goodbyes to her friends, White Dove came to say goodnight. *"I wish you could make yourself as happy as you make others." She told her hugging her.* Elizabeth just smiled. *"Sleep well."*

The month passed quickly. The house was taken over by the bride and her family. The preparations took over ranching and the house. It was gradually converted in wedding fever. With a couple of weeks to Christmas. The house took on a magical element. The day of the wedding arrived soon enough. The guests arrived by carriage and horse. There were plenty of them. Dull Knife, Red Wolf,

Running Elk and their wives led the Indian wedding party. White Dove welcomed them. Elizabeth kept herself busy. When alone, she welcomed her father and spoke of things still to be resolved. She assured him she had not forgotten and wished that he was feeling better. Dull Knife embraced his daughter. Thanked her and told her how happy she had made Blue. Elizabeth felt numb, she sat with him for a while until Red Wolf and Running Elk were heading over. She left him then and told him she would see him again soon. White Dove was speaking with Clear Water she was very pregnant and a pang hit Elizabeth. She desperately tried to ignore it. Next to her was Sky. Elizabeth offered them the welcome of family but did not stay. It was far too painful for her.

Carl found her in the stables stroking Patches. She was not hard to find. Black Dog was outside. *"Everything ok?"* He asked her. Elizabeth ignored the question, it was easier. *"I just wanted to check on the horses."* She told him. Both knew it was not entirely the truth but let it go. After a while he told

her. *"You can't hide here for long. Guests will be asking for you."*

"I was hoping to avoid today as much as possible." She told him.

"I can understand that." "You know Carl, I sometimes think you

understand too much." She told him smiling. He smiled back at

her. *"Just as well one of us does."*

They went back and party went on for hours.

Elizabeth danced with many of the guests. Nearly everyone

from town seemed to be there. Vera had enjoyed herself

greatly. Carl too asked for a dance but she declined. She

was feeling very tired and Caroline was standing with her.

Elizabeth asked him to do her the honour of dancing with one

of her best friends and held out Caroline's hand. Carl took it,

he liked Caroline and led her to the dance floor. Elizabeth

could hear him telling her, as they walked away, how badly

he did this and hoped that he would not break any of her toes.

The Indians continued to celebrate well into the next day.

Kate and Blue left in the early hours and retired to their new home. Once Elizabeth had joined with the others to wish the newlyweds well, she too gave her goodbyes. Wishing them all to stay as long as they wanted she went up. Elizabeth stopped at her door and listened. The house was still full, lively. There were some very happy people here this night. Elizabeth smiled, she had done a good thing and instinctively knew Black Dog was behind her. He had been hovering all night and none too happy with some of her dance partners. She recalled. He would not normally come into the house but strangers were still here. His job was not done. Elizabeth suddenly felt exhausted, drained and her eyes showed the strain. Black Dog held out his arm to her. She took it and looked at him. He missed nothing and understood too much she thought. *"I do not wish to see anyone."* She told him, he nodded understanding her clearly and sat down outside her door. This day had affected her greatly.

Elizabeth woke sometime later to voices, Indian voices, they were both quiet, both insistent. It did not last long and seemed to be over as quickly as it started. She had not been disturbed and drifted back to sleep. Elizabeth slept for 12 hours. When she came down. Black Dog had gone as had her guests. The house was quiet. It was Sunday. There would be no visitors today. And she was glad of it. She found White Dove out by the horses. *"Good morning."* She called to her. White Dove turned to her. *"Esa, are you ill?"* She asked her with concern. *"No, I'm fine."* She told her. *"I was getting worried but Black Dog said you were fine. You slept long." "I was tired that's all."* She told her. *"Our guests have left?"* She asked. *"Yes."* Elizabeth brightened. *"I'm starving let's go in, its cold and have lunch."* Elizabeth linked arms with White Dove and led her in.

They got their own meal and took it to the table. Elizabeth went back to the kitchen and poured milk for them both. Elizabeth ate well, she did feel very hungry. White

Dove was first to break the silence. *"Black Dog tells me you had a visitor last night."* Elizabeth was confused for a moment, they had had, lots of visitors last night, then realised her mistake. *"I had already told him I did not wish to see anyone."* White Dove nodded. Elizabeth did not need to know who the visitor was.

Elizabeth put her food down, suddenly no longer hungry and pushed her plate away. She took a deep breath. To speak the words only brought them to life and made it harder but she did so anyway. *"I wake, every morning waiting for the pain, the realisation, that my life is not what it should be. Some days I get as far as coming down for breakfast, other times it hits me before I'm fully awake, those are the bad days, the days it's hard to get up and get out of bed but I do, I keep getting up and carrying on as normal, like, I'm normal, but inside."* She looked at her with tears in her eyes. *"Part of me is dying."* White Dove reached across and took her hand.

If anyone knew how she felt it was her. *"You love him."* White Dove said to her. Elizabeth closed her eyes. *"Always."* Carl popped his head in at that moment. *"Sorry ladies. I need you Elizabeth, do you have a moment."* He asked her. Elizabeth returned White Dove's caress and went after him. *"Problem?"* She asked him. *"No, not really, I'd like some time off, can you do without me for a few days?"* He asked her. *"Sure, anything I can help with?"* She asked him. *"Thanks but no, I just need to do something, its personal."* *"When do you want to go?"* *"Tomorrow if that's ok I'll ask Buddy to double up and some of the boys will be happy to help."* *"Have a safe trip."* She told him and held out her hand. He took it and held it. *"I'll see you when you get back."* She told him more calmly than she thought and watched him leave.

Christmas was a week away and Elizabeth was beginning to think that she might be ill after all. She was sleeping longer, tired earlier, she felt really hungry and then not hungry at all. She felt strange and not herself. Elizabeth tried very hard to keep this to herself. There was no point in worrying anyone un-necessarily. She was sure it was nothing serious. There were plans to make. It was traditionally a time of great celebration at the ranch. Her parents had started it. Bringing all the staff together for a party on Christmas Eve and she would continue it. She had a large shopping list. There would be plenty to eat and drink and a present for every person who worked for them. There would also be gifts for the tribe. Elizabeth spent a lot of time making arrangements for these things to be delivered or picked up. It was only once they started to arrive, she knew Christmas was here. Two of the men had been out and found her a tree. She had sent several men to town to secure the supplies and items on her list, she did not feel up to going herself and to invite Vera to join her.

Vera shut up shop and came back with them and declared that if she wanted her, she could stay till after New Year. Elizabeth felt overjoyed. It was a lovely surprise and there would be plenty to do. The day before Christmas Eve, Carl came home. He came in at dinner and was asked to join them. They spoke of the coming festival and of the party tomorrow. Dinner was light and entertaining. Vera was full of stories. Elizabeth left the table feeling better than she and for some time.

Carl joined them for a drink after dinner. White Dove declined the drink as was her way. *"You had a good trip?"* Elizabeth asked him passing his drink. *"Yes and no."* He told her. Elizabeth turned in surprise, she waiting for him to continue. He swallowed his drink, *"My father was ill."* He told them, Elizabeth sat down. *"A letter was brought out by Mr Jenkins at the wedding. He, died shortly after I arrived home."* Each of them offered their condolences. *"I've brought my brother with me."* He told them and turning to Elizabeth. *"I hope that's ok." "Of course he can stay or leave as he wishes."* She told him. *"We always need good hands." "Ty, had looked after our father, I feel I owe him. I didn't know he'd been ill for so long, they went through a lot."* He told them. *"Carl, go get him, I'd like to meet him."* Elizabeth told him. Carl came back with a tall man. He was blonder than Carl. Heavier built, he seemed a little younger and held his hat in his hand, unsure of his place in this world. Elizabeth warmed to him. *"Elizabeth, White Dove, Vera, this is Ty, my brother."* Carl told them placing his hand on his back. Elizabeth came to him and held out her hand. *"I'm so sorry for your loss, your brother is like family to us and you are welcome to stay as long as you wish."* She told him. *"If you have any problems finding anything, you can ask me, I'm new here too."* Vera told him, holding out her hand, for him to take, clearly she was smitten. *"I'm Vera."* She told him. Ty barely acknowledged her. He was looking at White Dove, she had not spoken. Elizabeth looked from one to the other.

"Your Indian?" He asked her directly. "White Dove is a member of my family." Elizabeth cut in. "I meant no disrespect mam." He said turning to her. "You will find here." Elizabeth told him kindly "Many, that are from the Indian nation, they are my family." "Carl did tell me mam, I apologise, I was surprised is all. The lady is beautiful." He said turning back towards White Dove, he spoke directly to her. "Forgive me mam. That was rude of me and not intentional." White Dove inclined her head and looked away. "We will see you tomorrow then Elizabeth, ladies." Carl told them. "Good night Carl, Ty." Elizabeth told them. "And Ty welcome to the family." Vera called good night after them as Elizabeth saw them to the door. "I will also say good night." White Dove told her on her return and kissed them both and retired upstairs. Vera was quite excited, she chatted on throughout the night, leaving Elizabeth little room to join in. Next morning was Christmas Eve and a very long day began.

When Elizabeth came down the next morning it was to find White Dove, Carl and Ty arranging the Christmas Tree in a corner of the room. Decorations from previous years lay out on several chairs. Elizabeth wished them good morning and each in their turn returned it to her. Elizabeth went up to White Dove and kissed her. *"It looks lovely."* She told them. *"I thought we'd bring it in now."* Carl told her. *"It will give you ladies plenty of time to decorate it."* Elizabeth smiled, indeed it would take hours. *"I would be happy to help."* Offered Ty. *"That's just what we need."* Elizabeth told him. *"A man to do the higher bits. Thank you."* She told him. Ty visibly reddened. She left the two of them and walked with Carl to the door. *"Everything ready out there?"* She asked him, *"Jakes and his men will be seeing to carriage housing for those coming from town, the boys will take it in turns to drive them into the barns, keeping the front clear, horses will be doubled up in the new stables, there's plenty of feed were ready."* He told her. Elizabeth was grateful to him.

Elizabeth went into the kitchens and talked with Anna. There were food preparations everywhere and plenty of help. She was assured all was well. Elizabeth helped herself to coffee and food and retired to the dining table. The dinning doors were open and she observed the dressing of the tree. She sat there remembering other times the tree had been dressed, with her parents, then with Ben and White Dove. It brought back a mixture of love and sadness. She went and replenished both her coffee and her plate. *"Hungry?"* Anna had mocked her. *"Yes very, these are just too good Anna."* Elizabeth had replied taking a small cake with her. Anna had laughed. *"You'll get fat."* She told her kind heartedly and for a split-second Elizabeth thought she was right and took it anyway with a smile.

Elizabeth continued to watch White Dove and Ty at work. What surprised her, was their warm manner towards each other. Ty was careful and considerate. He asked White

Dove her thoughts. Asked for direction in where things

should go and looked to her for advice. White Dove

responded openly and seemed almost eager to help him.

Elizabeth wondered if their bereavements drew them to each

other and if so, she was very happy for them. Vera came

down after lunch. She apologised for the tardiness of her start

to the day and could only think that it was a combination of

the excitement of the moment and her visit. Elizabeth

laughed. *"Or too much chat and one or two too many glasses."* She

told her warmly. Vera burst out laughing. *"Maybe so."* She

told her.

They spent the afternoon in decorating the house. Time

was soon gone and Anna reminded them that guests were due

in an hour. Vera had brought dresses for them both. White

Dove chose to wear ceremonial dress as was her custom on

this occasion. Vera helped Elizabeth. Strangely, her dress was a little snug in the bust and waist, she had put on weight. Vera tried to tighten the corsetry but Elizabeth complained it hurt her stomach. Vera commented on it and was able to let out the sides a little, it helped. Vera told her to stay away from the cakes. Elizabeth had laughed remembering Anna's comments from this morning.

They came down as the first of the guests arrived. Music was provided from town. Dancing and celebration was the order of the day. Furniture had been moved out to make room. Elizabeth stood at the door with White Dove and Vera to greet her guests. Several mentioned how well Elizabeth looked and indeed, her gown fitted in all the right places and she had a bloom to her cheeks that was most becoming. There was gayety and laughter throughout the house. Kate and Blue, Caroline and her family joined them. The party was in full swing when Running Elk arrived with Clear Water who was very pregnant. Red Wolf with Sky. They came with apologises from her father. He did not feel up to the journey. She enquired after his health, is was not good. White Dove welcomed her blood family and Elizabeth moved off unable to avoid Red Wolfs eye contact any longer, to welcome other guests.

The Indian's only partly celebrated Christmas. Their Indian beliefs mixed with the Christian teaching of the missionaries. Vera was thoroughly enjoying herself. She danced with every available man and some that were previously occupied. Elizabeth smiled, she envied her. Elizabeth handed out drinks, brought out food and mixed with as many guests as possible. She kept herself busy and away from Red Wolf. Carl and Ty were standing with the other hands. Elizabeth made her way over to them. *"Not much dancing going on gentleman?"* She enquired. There were several embarrassed looks. *"I'd like to dance mam."* Ty told her. *"Do you think White Dove would dance with me?"* He asked her.

"I don't know Ty. You'd best ask her." She told him. *"But, would her family object?"* He asked. *"If they do, I'm sure they will tell you, but I have a feeling that if White Dove wishes to do so, they will not complain."* Ty made his way over to White Dove. He asked and was accepted, much to everyone's surprise. White Dove had not shown any favour to a man since Ben. Elizabeth thought it a good sign, she sometimes forgot that White Dove was only five years older than her.

Vera came over, not too happy. *"Guess I missed out."* She told her pointing in Ty's direction. Elizabeth smiled. *"I'm sure that one of the boys here can help you out."* She told her and sure enough she had several offers to keep her happy. *"Can I interest you in a dance?"* Carl asked her. *"Thank you yes."* She told him and they joined the others. The dancing was vigorous and fast and Elizabeth soon found herself out of breath. One spin too many and her dress gave way down one seam. Carl apologised thinking it was him. *"Don't, for some* reason the dress was too tight." She told him, "Vera loosened it for me but it was still too tight, I'll go and change." Elizabeth called to Caroline. "This man needs a dance partner; would you help him out?" She asked her. Caroline was only too happy to oblige. As she left the dance area, Black Dog met her having noticed the dress. "Nothing to worry about." She told him "I just need to change." Black Dog escorted her to her room.

Elizabeth was back down in less than 10 minutes and headed back to the kitchens. She wanted to make sure that the kitchen staff got a chance to enjoy themselves and not just work. As she was leaving Red Wolf blocked her way. "Everything ok, you changed?" He asked her. "Yes fine, my dress split, guess I've been eating too much." "You? I find that hard to believe." He told her. There was an awkward silence. "I need to go." She told him and went to move past him, as she did so, he grazed his arm across her breast. Elizabeth cried out. "I'm sorry, I did not mean to catch you." He told her, a little embarrassed. *"You didn't."* She told him surprised at her body's sensitivity. *"Guess I'm a bit too sensitive as well as putting on weight."* She told him bitingly. *"I need to go."* *"Wait, father has asked me to remind you."* He stopped. *"The council of elders are getting anxious."* It was just one more thing she did not need to deal with.

She looked at him. *"Did you really have to remind me of that?"* *"Do you think I want to?"* He told angrily, dragging her to her office closing the door behind them. Elizabeth sat down. *"I can't do this."* She almost shouted at him. *"It's just too hard."* She said more quietly. For a moment, he did not speak. *"I- also wanted to give you this."* He told her. Red Wolf placed a box on her desk, in front of her. Elizabeth sighed. *"Thank you. I'm sorry I don't have anything personal to give to you."* She told him. *"It seemed best to keep it to the ranch gifts."* Red Wolf stood there looking at her. She had put on weight. Was eating more. Her flushed face, her body swollen more sensitive in places, the bloom in her eyes, the glow of her skin. He took everything in and worked it back in his head. *"O but you do."* He told her intensely, walking towards her. Grasping her face tenderly with his hands and lightly kissing her cheeks. Before opening her office door and walking back to the party. Elizabeth felt confused. She had no idea what he meant.

Her Indian family left shortly after, the gifts for the tribe loaded in wagons to take with them and the rest of the guests, left as expected around midnight, wishing in the day. Carl escorted Caroline and her family back to Blues. Vera was having a very difficult time saying goodbyes to Buddy and White Dove walked Ty to the door. Strangely and more surprisingly, he'd stood by her all night. Elizabeth watched as Ty leant towards White Dove, hat in hand and spoke quietly to her then kissed her on the cheek and left. Elizabeth took herself off to help with the clearing up. Black Dog came up behind her and waited for her to acknowledge him as was his way. Elizabeth turned expecting him to wish her good night. *"I sleep in the house now."* He told her and headed for the office. It was the first time he had ever done so. Elizabeth had no time to consider the change, she was far too busy.

The ladies sat down around 1 am. Tired feet and heavy arms. Traditionally Elizabeth's family exchanged personal gifts after the last of the guests had left. Elizabeth removed both Vera and White Dove's gifts from under the tree and gave them to them. They were small personal gifts. Both were silver pins with their initials on them, entwined with the Double T

They both loved them and chatted well into the night. Eventually Vera made her excuses and left the two of them alone. Elizabeth wanted bed but felt restless. They both sat for a time and somewhat reluctantly White Dove eventually spoke. *"Red Wolf told you?"* She asked her. *"Yes, time I fear is running out."* Elizabeth acknowledged what she was saying. *"He spoke to me before leaving."* *"Please, not another lecture, I already told him I can't keep doing this."* White Dove nodded. *"He seems to feel, there is something your not saying."* Now Elizabeth was both annoyed and confused. *"That man is going to kill me. I have no idea what he's talking about."* She told her. Elizabeth changed the subject. *"So Ty?"* White Dove found this harder to talk about. *"He seems a nice man."* Elizabeth offered. White Dove nodded her head. *"Yes he does. You know Ben was my life?"* Elizabeth smiled sadly at her. *"Yes, I know that and so did he. But your still here, he would want you to go on living."* Elizabeth got up and hugged her. *"Time for bed."* Elizabeth told her and up they went.

Elizabeth pulled off her clothes and fell into bed. She fell asleep as soon as her head hit the pillow. She was so tired, her body ached in places, that did not seem possible.

437

Elizabeth stirred restlessly in her sleep, something stroked her face. *"Thank you for my gift."* A calming, familiar voice told her. *"Sleep now, you will both need it."* Elizabeth smiled. The touch and voice familiar, soothing her, she turned over and slept soundly.

Elizabeth woke around 9, refreshed and to excited voices and much joy. She dressed quickly and joined the fun. Eating as she went. Elizabeth exchanged gifts. Several hands came and went as the morning progressed. Elizabeth had drinks made for them and wished them joy. Some stayed to sing carols. The kitchen staff having the day off, lunch was a buffet affair, plenty laid out for those who wanted it. People came and went and by mid-afternoon, all the ladies of the house were alone and asleep in chairs. Fairly exhausted with recent events. They were woken by fire crackers. Carl, Buddy and Ty announced their arrival in style, they were followed by

Kate, Blue and her family. They all exchanged gifts and played party games well into the night.

The morning brought more bad weather, Mr and Mrs Cane were escorted back to town. Vera wanted to stay, but was afraid of being snowed in. She had a store to run. Elizabeth said she understood and wished her well. As a parting gift, Elizabeth ask Buddy to see Vera safely back. He seemed very happy with the task. Christmas was over. The tree remained up till after New Year.

New Year's Eve, was celebrated quietly with a visit to a friend or two or it was in the East and her parents had done so here too. But, since their death, New Year's Eve, had been a time of contemplation, thoughts of the past as well as the future. Elizabeth saw in the New Year with White Dove. Both happy in their own company. Next day, was New Year's Day and a day of reflection. After that it was back to work. The New Year started early at the Double T. As the snows hit.

The breakfast meeting took place as normal. Elizabeth listened to what Jake and Carl had to say, they made the decisions on the weeks work and the men went out. Elizabeth would not be riding out for the time being, or anyone else, there was too much snow and Black Dog had advised Carl against it. For once Elizabeth listened.

The men kept the yards clear as much as possible and Elizabeth worked on seeing to the horses, mucking out and feeding. It kept her busy and more hands than usual came to dinner and that made more work and everyone mucked in.

By the end of the week, the snows stopped falling and the frosts came. This was worse than the snow, frost was a killer. Fires were lit in all rooms. The winds dropped the temperature even more. It was biting cold outside and it was going to be a tough few weeks. Elizabeth had no choice but to change her routine. They concentrated on cleaning house, mending and feeding the troops and she had to content herself with the occasional trip out to the horses.

In the village, the winter was made easier by the contribution given by the Double T, the braves still hunted, but they would not starve, if they failed to find any prey. Red Wolf had been asked to address the council of elders on the topic of his sister and her blood bond with the tribe. He had been waiting for this. It had given him many sleepless nights, Red Wolf felt for the first time in a long time very happy. He solemnly came to the council and joined them. When asked, he responded honestly. *"Has your sister made her choice?"* The elder asked him. *"It is done uncle, Esa, has made a blood bond with the tribe."* He told them. They each looked as surprised as Dull Knife felt. *"Then the tribe's future is secure?"* The most respected elder asked him. *"It is uncle."* Red Wolf assured him. It satisfied them. He knew he would have questions from his father but he could do that later. For now, they had the answer they needed.

News soon got around the village. Many were surprised that no celebrations had been held, it was a cause for celebration, a blood bond was highly regarded. Most put it down to Elizabeth being white and traditions being different. Sky waited for Red Wolf to come back from hunting. She had heard the news that morning from an aunt of the council of elders. When he entered his lodge, it was clear she was waiting for him. *"Esa?* She questioned and waited for his answer. He had put this off and it was poorly done, not honourable to her. She shamed him. He went to her, sat with her and took her hand.

"I have a great affection for you, and we have tried to make this work." He told her. *"But."* She cut in. *"You do not love me, any more than I love you. And you could not bring myself to lay with me."* She finished for him. *"I am sorry and do wish things were different."* He told her. *"Don't it does not help. Yes we did try, you and I, we did what was asked of us."* She told him. *"I will go to my father and ask for a divorce, I will say that I cannot live with a childless union."* She told him. *"They will think it is my fault?"* He told her. *"Yes they will, you will have to live with the shame of not giving me a child and I will have to live with the shame of a failed marriage. I expect, my shame will last longer than yours."* She told him sadly.

Red Wolf left her and went to his father. He entered and sat with him. *"Father, Sky is to divorce me."* He told him quietly. Suddenly many things came clear. Dull Knife was torn between anger and happiness. Joy that his son had a chance of happiness, shame at the dishonour of having his eldest son, cast off by his wife, a man, a warrior who is to lead their tribe. *"You will be dishonoured."* He told him. *"Yes, and I may not be the man to lead this tribe."* Red Wolf finished. Red Wolf got up to leave. *"Is it worth it."* His father asked him. *"I'm sorry father, she's worth everything."* His father knew he spoke the truth.

Sky moved back in with her father. It was not done easily. Dull Knife had to make amends on behalf of his son. Red Wolf became segregated from some of the tribe. Others treated him with disrespect. The weeks that followed were not easy. It was soon clear, that Dull Knife had no choice but to speak to both his sons. They came when called. *"I am not well my sons."* He told them. *"I have no choice, I must leave the tribe with strong leadership that will not be questioned."* He continued. *"This give me no pleasure; I must ask you my son."* He said turning to Red Wolf. *"If your life were your own, would you choose to lead this tribe or live with Esa?"* He asked him. *"I fear it cannot be both."* Without hesitation, Red Wolf answered him, *"I would choose her father, I am sorry."* Dull Knife expressed understanding sadness. *"My son."* He said turning to Running Elk. *"If your life were your own, would you choose to lead this tribe or live quietly with your wife?"* He asked him. *"I would welcome leading the tribe father with my brother's support."* He told him. *"Then it is done, I will speak to the council of elders and ask them to support a change in leadership."* All three men stood, Dull Knife embraced both sons one after the other. *"I hope the gods and mother earth are kind to us."* He told them sadly. The council agreed. Red Wolf would be free to pursue his choice in life, it was hoped that he would strengthened the ties with his family. It was done. Red Wolf stayed with his father for another week. He wanted to make sure that the village understood there were no disagreements, no resentment, no grievance, no dispute. Then he left for the Double T. The weather was not improving.

CHAPTER ELEVEN

Red Wolf had gone prepared. His horse had protected leather foot wear, several blankets and enough food, a shelter and fire makings should he be kept outdoors longer than expected. He was not unduly worried; he had travelled many times in such weather. It had stopped snowing. The going would be easier. He travelled with two braves. Even a Chiefs disowned son still got protection After a couple of miles, it was clear it was going to be harder than he first thought. The terrain was deceptive, frozen hollows that looked solid ground and then gave way. Several times the horses lost their balance. They changed direction more than once and doubled back to go to higher harder ground. But that was colder. They had not gone five miles all day. They decided to find shelter within some trees and camp, hoping tomorrow brought better news. It was a long cold night. The following day was not much better.

They rode steadily throughout the day. The snow was very deep in places. As the sun went down, it was clear they had not gone far. They camped and hoped for better weather. The sun came out next day and with it the terrain became slippery and loose. They tried to stay to the lower ground this time. Snow is deceptive. It looked solid but wasn't. The snow slippery and ice deadly. They ploughed on. They lost one of the horses just before mid-day, it lost its footing and went down taking one of Red Wolfs braves with him. The horse broke his leg and had to be put down. They were now one horse short and one man heavy. They doubled up and took turns in running and riding. By the end of day three, they were less than half way there.

Day four, was not much better. It was slow and tough going. Both the men and horses were suffering from cold exposure it was hampering their progress. They knew the signs. They needed to make it tomorrow or they would be in serious trouble.

Carl set out next morning to check on the higher range stock. They had some serious concerns over the condition of beef herd. He took a dozen men with him. It had started to snow again, lightly but it was laying. Carl was worried. If the herd were not hardy enough, they may not survive, Elizabeth stood to lose the lot. They headed for the low-lying pasture. The men spread out but kept within eyesight of each other. He had decided to ride out for 4 hours try to check as much as possible and then make their way back. It would be a long day but might give them some positive results. It was seriously hard work, the horses struggled with the demands of the elements. They spotted several dead cows. Half buried in snow. It did not look good. They were on the point of turning back when Black Dog spotted something on the horizon. Carl let him check it out and they followed. There fairly frozen, were Red Wolf and his men. Between them, they brought them safely home.

Elizabeth stood in the door way shocked, she ordered hot baths for everyone. Red Wolf was brought into the house and taken straight to the bathroom, Anna had run the bath having been forewarned of their coming. Fully clothed, Red Wolf was placed in it, heaters were placed in the room with him. Elizabeth provided warm drinks and towels. She left him, only when she was sure, he was ok, warming up and went out to the bunk house to check on the others, the men were getting similar treatment. Elizabeth called for more blankets and towels, heaters and for fires to be lit, the Indians were submerged in hot water tubs. The hands in make shift baths. The horses hot rub downs and warm blankets. Their feet frozen. Lotions and leather wraps were put on them. Heaters placed in the barns. It was dangerous as fire was a real possibility but if they were to survive it had to be done.

The hands and braves took turns rubbing the horses and checking the heaters. Never leaving either alone. Elizabeth and White Dove carried over drinks to them, they entered and it felt like a bath house. Carl and Buddy were also partially frozen; they were covered in Blankets near one of the fires. Buddy did not look too good. Elizabeth was very concerned. She ordered several of the feed barrels that were sealed to be emptied and filled with more hot water, she ordered them both in them. White Dove put in herbs she knew would help them. It was a very long night. Elizabeth went back into the house only when she was sure they were all going to be ok. White Dove stayed with them.

Elizabeth went in to check on Red Wolf. She entered the bathroom to find him fast asleep. She changed some of the water, topped it up, and banked up the fire in the house and heater in the bathroom. She opened the connecting door to the office and went to lay down. It was nearing sun rise.

Elizabeth kept re-filling the bath for the next 5 hours while he slept and kept the rooms very warm. He woke with her sitting opposite him. She looked exhausted but smiled at him none the less. *"Welcome back."* She told him. *"Hungry?"* Red Wolf smiled at her *"Yes."* He crocked. Elizabeth squeezed his arm and left to go to the kitchens. She bumped into several kitchen staff doing the same as her. Running around feeding the men. She took hot soup, bread, cheese and meat to him and she kept feeding him. *"The men and horses?"* He asked her. *"They all made it"*. Red Wolf visibly relaxed. All the while, not allowing him to get out of the bath. White Dove came by with Ty with medicine to fight the effects of the cold. After another hour, he begged her to let him get out of the bath and sleep in a bed. She did on the condition that the fire was kept going and that he covered up with several blankets. They were using every bed pan in the house to warm beds. She tucked him in like a baby. *"Are you staying?"* He asked her. She shook her head. *"I have to check on the others, I'll be* back soon." She told him. *"Good, I need to tell you something."* He told her sleepily. Elizabeth nodded and went in search of her staff.

She found them all very busy. Elizabeth crossed the yard and entered the bunk house. The men were out of the tubs and in warm blankets. *"How's it going?"* She asked White Dove. *"Everyone's ok, they will be fine. They were lucky."* Elizabeth offered up a silent prayer. She went to see Carl. *"How are you feeling?"* *"Cold and tired. Hungry"* He smiled at her. *"Good, then your still with us then."* She told him patting his arm. Elizabeth called to the staff, plenty of food and drink, plenty of warmth and no one goes outside for anything, the animals were housed and would be ok for a day.

Elizabeth went back to the house and checked on Red Wolf, he was already asleep. She left him and fell asleep in her own room. When she woke, sometime later, she was not alone. Red Wolf lay beside her, his arms wound tightly around her. She would not question it now, she had nearly lost him, that in itself, was too much to think about. She went back to sleep. Morning came early and Elizabeth unwound herself from his embrace. She left her room and went to her toilette. She washed and cleaned herself up. Elizabeth realised she had been in the same clothes for two days, they were not clean and everything seemed to be too small. Elizabeth quietly came back to her room and went through her wardrobe pulling out trousers that would not do up. She was getting more and more frustrated. *"Try the buckskins."* Red Wolf told her rising from the bed. Elizabeth turned to him. *"Good morning."* Red Wolf pulled open a draw and handed her the buckskins. *"They will fit and move with you."* He told her going back and checking the others in her wardrobe. *"How many do you have?"* He asked her *"Three."* She told him amused. *"I'll speak to White Dove about getting some more."* He told her and left the room. Elizabeth sat there, not sure what that was all about, he was right, the buckskins fitted better and did move with her, Elizabeth went to look in on White Dove.

She was asleep. Something caught her eye in the corner, Ty was asleep in the chair. subconsciously he must have known she was there, he stirred and looked first at White Dove then the door. When he saw Elizabeth, he got up and came to her. They closed the door behind him. Elizabeth waiting for an explanation. Ty stood before her not sure how to explain it. He spoke honestly. *"Mam, I can assure you, nothing improper happened in there."* He told her indicating the bedroom. Elizabeth remained silent. *"She would not rest, I asked her too several times but she would not leave, I practically had to drag her up here and the only way to keep her in there was to stay."* He told her. Elizabeth smiled. *"Ty, White Dove is my cousin, she was married young, to my Uncle. It was a love match and she has been a widow for six months. If your intentions are not for life, you should stay away from her."* She told him equally honestly. Ty nodded. *"I'm not sure I can."* he replied. *"Then, be sure, as her family, would be unforgiving."* She warned him as they both descended the stairs.

Red Wolf was checking on his men. No one injured, no one dead. That was good. Carl caught his eye and he went over. *"Not a good time to come visiting?"* Carl told him good naturedly. Red Wolf gave a resigned look. *"No choice."* He simply told him. The call to breakfast sounded out. Both men headed into the house. Elizabeth was already at the table tucking in. *"Everything ok?"* She asked them as Jake came in behind them. *"Just fine."* Jake told her and kissed her on the cheek. *"We were lucky."* It had stopped snowing in the night, when the sun came up, it seemed the worse was over.

Elizabeth asked about the trip out and the stock. Carl repeated what he had seen. It was not good. Elizabeth looked worried. Carl offered to go out scouting again. Elizabeth rejected it. *"I want feed put out in all the pastures."* She told him. *"Let's keep feeding them, even if we can't see them."* They had nothing to lose. Elizabeth did not offer to go out with them, she stayed around the house. The winds had dropped and the sun stayed out. The snow melted. Each day the men came back late and they fed them. Sometimes with a sighting of the stock but mostly not. The animal shelters had been stocked before the worse weather hit and were still under snow. The weather was defiantly improving. They'd have to start digging out soon.

Elizabeth had taken to wearing the buckskins, they were the only thing that fitted her. *"Feeling alright?"* White Dove asked her late one evening sitting in front of the fire. *"Yes, I'm fine, I feel a little tired, but I guess it's been tougher than I expected."* She told *"When did you last have your woman's time Elizabeth?"* White Dove asked her. Elizabeth thought for a moment and then it hit her. She could not remember. *"Dear* god." Elizabeth spat out and put her hand to her mouth. It started to shake. She could not remember. *"You are having a child Esa."* She told her kindly. *"No."* Elizabeth told her, that cannot be possible. *"I can't."* She told her. "Can't?" White Dove repeated, understanding Elizabeth's shock. *"I think, mother earth has other ideas."* Elizabeth closed her eyes and leant back in her chair. Of course, it was possible, had she not begged him for just that, she remembered. *"Does he know?"* Elizabeth asked her. Already having her answer. *"Do you want the child Esa?"* White Dove asked her. *"I – need time and what choice do I have?"* She told her. Rose and went to her room.

She couldn't sleep. She was restless. Dear god, a child. How had she ignored the signs? She was not a stupid woman. She knew about life and creating it. Yet, she had begged him for this. Why had she not considered it possible. It kept going over and over in her mind. She paced the room.

Elizabeth sat for a while and paced again. She tried to sleep but to no avail. The knock at the door, did not come unexpected. She knew he would hear her awake. She chose to ignore him. Elizabeth heard him call her name, ask her to let him in, told her they needed to talk. She said nothing and eventually he went away. What was there to say, she thought, he had a wife and now, she thought again, he, they, would have a child or even worse, if that were possible, he may think it to be someone else's. That thought stayed with her. Someone else's child, if he thought that, maybe it would settle the problem she reasoned. If it were not his, he would not be torn between her and the tribe. It might work and he would have to let her go after all. Could she do it? She wondered. Could she tell him she had been with another man? What man would make him believe her. Elizabeth ran her hand protectively across her stomach. A child. The thought filled her with as much joy as it did sadness. How did it come to this, she thought? What had she done.

Elizabeth eventually found sleep. It had not come easily. She had woken late and the house was empty. She was glad of it. Elizabeth headed into the Kitchen and found a tray had been left for her. She took it into her office and went over the books. Anna came in with coffee sometime later and Elizabeth worked through the day. She did not want company and was grateful to be left alone. Red Wolf was not happy. He wanted to go to her and talk about it. Let her know that Sky had divorced him. That he was free to be with her. White Dove tried to calm him, she tried to sooth him with words of understanding, but he couldn't hear her. She told him that Elizabeth needed time. Time to get use to the idea. Time to realise what she wanted, with or without him and without his persuasion or influence. That it needed to be her decision to accept this child and come to terms with what that means to her. Not because of him alone. Red Wolf found it hard to accept it and left the house. Would nothing be simple he asked himself.

Elizabeth isolated herself for the next few days. She could not face seeing Red Wolf each day and know that she carried his child. She felt lost. Unsure of what her future held. Not even sure, after wishing for it, that she wanted a child, his child. That was such a terrible thought it scared her. Having a child scared her. Giving birth scared her. Being responsible for a child scared her. Raising a child seemed unimaginable to her. She did not feel ready for this. And yet, she had to accept she had begged him for it. Elizabeth came to seek out White Dove. She asked her to sit with her she needed to talk to someone. Elizabeth was struggling to speak. She eventually felt calm enough. *"Having this child scares me, but I do want it more than anything, it scares me to be responsible for another being, it scares me to be on my own doing this and it scares me more, that it will tear open the relationship between Red*

Wolf and the tribe. I know he will never leave me and his child. I can only think that I must tell him, this child belongs to another."

White Dove looked shocked. *"That would not be wise."* She told her. Red Wolf stood in the doorway. He had heard her say the child was not his. Red Wolf looked like he would explode. *"I'll kill him."* He told them and ran for the bunkhouse. Elizabeth and White Dove followed him but they were not so fast. By the time they arrived, several men were holding him back and Carl was on the floor bleeding. Elizabeth came to realise her mistake. Red Wolf would never accept another man. She came and stood between them and turned to Carl. *"Are you alright?"* She asked him. This upset Red Wolf more. Carl looked at her. *"I'm as confused as hell but I'm ok".* She turned to Red Wolf and looked at her brave warrior. He would never be any more magnificent than he was right now.

"You are mistaken here." She told him evenly. *"You have wronged him and me."* It was Red Wolfs turn to look confused. *"But I heard you."* He told her. *"You heard the end of a conversation that was not complete, come back to the house."* She told him. She turned to Carl. *"I'm sorry that happened. I will explain later."* Red Wolf felt like a fool, he had acted like a fool. This was not honourable. He left and rode out.

He came back next day. Calmer and in need of answers. He found her in her office. The door was slightly open and she was on her own. She was turning over the gift he had left her. *"Why don't you open it?"* He asked from the doorway. He pushed the door wider and looked at her. *"Can I come in?"* He asked. Elizabeth looked up. *"That depends, are you going to listen or jump to conclusions."* Red Wolf cringed. He deserved that. They looked at each other for a while. Elizabeth sighed and opened his gift. It was a piece of ivory, carved on it, was one Indian symbol. She looked back at him.

"It's beautiful. What does it say?" She asked him. "Always." He told her.

He looked away first and walked in. "Truce?" He smiled. "Agreed." She returned his smile. Red Wolf sat down. For a time neither spoke. Each not sure who should tell the other their news first. Both started to speak at the same time. Stopped and laughed. "Ok, I think I should go first." She told him. "I am, expecting a child and the child is yours." Red Wolf broke out in a huge smile. He wanted to hug her, kiss her, make love to her. Elizabeth held up her hand. She wasn't finished. "I wanted this." She continued. "This is my doing and it seems that I got exactly what I asked for." She smiled resolvedly. "I will not let this be something that breaks apart everything my father and ours, has worked so hard for all these years." Elizabeth was on a roll; it all came out. "I will not share you and offer a child a part time parent, and you cannot change what is expected of you. The elders need a blood bond and I can now give it to them. I will tell them it is a child of the tribe, that will be obvious to everyone in time. The only problem will be having a brave to acknowledge it. I hope our father can help with that." She finished.

Elizabeth was amazingly calm. "Are you done?" He asked her. Elizabeth got cross all over again. "Done?" She asked pissed. She had just unburdened her soul and he asks if she is 'Done?' Red Wolf indicated she should calm down again. "Getting up set is not good for the baby. I came from the village with one purpose." He told her quietly. "If it had not meant my life to me. I would not have put mine or others at risk." He told her honestly. It was Elizabeth's turn to look concerned. "Is father alright?" She asked him. "Yes he is fine, that is not what I am talking about." He continued. "Sky." Elizabeth shrunk visibly in her chair. "Has divorced me." He told her. "Divorced you? How?" She asked. Red Wolf explained the circumstances and events to her. "Err she made *them believe you couldn't give her a child? Don't you think that's going to be an issue soon?"* Red Wolf looked at her and grinned widely. *"It will tell them she was wrong." "And your leadership of the tribe?"* She asked him. *"That will pass to Running Elk."* Elizabeth sat shocked. *"Red Wolf I am so sorry; I feel I am much to blame for this." "We are neither to blame, it was just the way it was going to be."* He told her. So much wasted time. So much confused. Traditions and expectations. Elizabeth wasn't sure she wanted to bring a life into the world in the middle of all this. She wasn't sure she could do it. *"The tribe has what it needs to carry on. My father is comforted that his son and grandson will lead them onwards. The elders are happy that there is a blood bond with them. It is settled."*

Elizabeth frowned. Red Wolf eventually spoke. *"Esa, I need to ask you again, do you want me as a father to our child. Do you want me as your husband, your mate?"* Elizabeth thought how strange that sounded. After everything that had happened since she'd returned from back East. From her arrival at the stage post and Red Wolf riding proudly in on his horse to get her. To him first asking her that question. 'She did' she thought. More than anything she wanted this male and a life with him. She knew it had drawn her home. She knew it would not be easy. He was demanding and dominant. She was stubborn and wilful. But he understood her. Would worship her. Would fight and die for her if he had to. And he would cherish their children to the ends of their days.

The silence was killing him. Eventually Elizabeth looked up from the gift he had given her and looked into his eyes. He was an amazing example of man she thought. The only man she had ever really wanted. She had come back for him she realised. He had known all these years and had waited for her. There was only ever really one answer. *"Always."*